DA[W]

HOPE

Joni,
Thanks for the interest. :)
hope to see you again.

[signature]

PETER PRICHARD

outskirtspress
DENVER, COLORADO

Outskirts Press, Inc.
http://www.outskirtspress.com

Paperback ISBN: 978-1-4787-4694-2
Hardback ISBN: 978-1-4787-4907-3

Outskirts Press and the "OP" logo are trademarks belonging to Outskirts Press, Inc.

PRINTED IN THE UNITED STATES OF AMERICA

Acknowledgements

To Barbara: "Nothing else matters in the whole wide world when you're in love with a Jersey girl." —Tom Waits

To my mother, Lucy Todd, who insisted on fighting for what is right; my stepmother, Elena Townsend, who taught me that "can't never did a thing"; my mother-in-law Esther Smith, who was one of the strongest people I have ever met; and to all the other strong women who have helped me along the path.

To my father, for the intuition.

To my sons, for being caring, decent young men who are positively impacting our world.

To all the activists, singers, writers, teachers, and creatives who have worked to lessen abuses of power, increase respect for personal freedom and human dignity, and educate individuals so they can reach their goals.

PART ONE

—⁓⁓⁓—

"Life shrinks or expands according to one's courage."
Anais Nin

"I must uphold my ideals, for perhaps the time will come
when I shall be able to carry them out."
Anne Frank

One

RICHARD PHILLIPS DESCENDED the six steps from the stage at the Adams Amphitheater, feeling good about the speech he had just given to the students, their families, and the townspeople of Fair Shore, Connecticut. He was met at the bottom by an enraged Dawn Mortenson, a student in his Senior Honors Symposium at the high school.

"Nice job, professor," she sneered sarcastically, moving to within six inches of his face as he completed the last step. "I thought you supported what we are doing here. I thought you wanted to help challenge people to make some changes in this town, not put them to sleep."

She finished with a growl, "Why don't you go have a few shots and beers, and relive the glory days? Because *these aren't them.*"

Pushing past him, she vaulted up the steps and ran onto the stage, grabbing the microphone from the stand, looking intently at the audience, and saying, "Thanks for coming. We have the chance today to celebrate inclusion and equality here on the shore of an Atlantic Ocean that has brought millions of individuals toward an expectation of fairness and respect for human dignity."

Richard stood stunned, only partially hearing the words of the high school senior who had entered his life only eight weeks before.

Richard had always enjoyed watching his Senior Honors Symposium students filter into the first class of the new high school year. It signaled the end of a summer when he had too much time to remember, and the beginning of a new attempt to recreate his life separate from the agony and glory of his past.

He usually knew almost all of the students, having had them in various classes in their first three years at Fair Shore High. The only exceptions had been the transfer students, of which there had been few, since most families did not move to a new town with a senior in tow.

There was only one new student this year, one whom he and everyone else noticed the moment she walked into the class. Dawn Mortenson, tall and thin with long legs and straight red hair down to the middle of her back, stood in the doorway, her pale green eyes taking in the whole room.

Drew Winston was the first to move toward her, turning from his friends to stand in front of her, looking down into her gold-flecked eyes. "Hello there, good looking; I am sure glad to see you," he remarked. Staring up at the 6'5" All-American quarterback, Dawn smiled and walked toward the middle of the room without acknowledging his greeting.

Moving quickly, followed by two friends, Drew again positioned himself in front of her, blocking her way. "You must not know who I am, or else you would have let me ask you out tonight to show you the sights."

Dawn looked him up and down, continuing to smile. All conversation had stopped in the class; all eyes focused on the center of the room, Richard Phillips as interested as his students.

She stepped back to take a longer, more deliberate look at her adversary, which caused him to smile as well, preening for what he thought would be an appreciative response. Moving closer to him, she murmured, loud enough for all to hear, "Yes, I have heard of you. Everyone in this state has heard of you." Drew smiled broadly, looking smugly at his two friends.

Pausing for effect, she concluded, "You're the big guy with the little brain who's blocking my path."

Drew Winston didn't respond; he just stood still while staring intently at his new classmate. Nobody else in the class moved.

"You have no idea of the trouble you have caused for yourself, Number 37. You and I are going to get to know each other," he replied pointedly, the whole class listening, "very, very intimately." Not waiting for a reply, Winston sauntered to the far side of the room, followed by his entourage.

Dawn quickly scanned the room, noticing disbelief on most of the faces of her new classmates. Suddenly tired of being the center of attention, she moved toward the nearest chair and sat down, putting her backpack on the floor and looking toward the teacher. He returned her look momentarily, and then said, "Let's get to our seats, students; the bell is about to ring."

Richard was in his 36th year of teaching in the English Department and working in the Guidance office at Fair Shore High School. He had caught people's attention with his ponytail, his light-brown beard with shades of gray, and his pale blue eyes. Solidly built, he had added thirty pounds to his six-foot frame in the past few years. Those who had known him were beginning to notice less energy at the

Monday morning teachers' meetings, where he would always start the week with a review of the prior seven days—short and humorous comments on the local, national, and international scene.

He had created the Senior Honors Symposium five years before. The symposium focused on helping students to understand their place in the world through discussion and analysis of books and music that he had hand-picked. The symposium was offered to all seniors who had been on the honor roll for at least one semester during their high school career. It attracted the elite of Fair Shore's students and generated projects that had gained national attention for the school.

Dawn Mortenson had been excited about being in the class, thinking that it would be a good way to connect with bright seniors at her new school. The incident with Drew Winston, however, had left her preoccupied.

Dawn was jolted from her reverie by a booming voice. "Good morning. I am Richard Phillips and we will be gathering in this room at this time for the next eighteen weeks." Looking around the room at the thirty students who had settled into their seats, he smiled. "I have known most of you for what seems like decades. I guess that's what three years at Fair Shore High might seem like for some of you." As the class laughed, he looked at a short, pudgy student in the back row. "Ed Pearson, I in fact have known your family for over two decades. Either one or another of your brothers has been in my classes for the last twenty years."

Ed smiled, responding, "You're right. I am the last of a large and unique group of scholars that has graced Fair Shore High with our wit and intelligence for exactly twenty-three years."

The class groaned and Richard continued, "As I look around, I see only one new student in our midst. Dawn Mortenson joins us from the Boston area, where she was an honors student each semester and a three-sport athlete. She will have a chance to tell you a little more about herself when we go through introductions in a few minutes.

"My goal in this class is to take you on an emotional roller coaster as you find out about yourself, music, literature, history, change, and the relationships that are most important to you. This course is not for the faint of heart. If you don't keep up with all the reading you will do poorly. But I think most of you know that, because of the controversy last year when I gave Bernard Sikes his first grade ever that was not an "A" and his parents sued the school. Your first assignment is to have read *One Flew Over the Cuckoo's Nest* for our next class, which you have already known about, since it had been on your summer reading list. Any questions?

"No? Then let's get into introductions. I want you to give your name and your answers to these two questions."

Turning to the blackboard, he wrote the following questions in large, bold letters:

WHO HAS BEEN THE MOST INSPIRATIONAL PERSON IN YOUR LIFE AND WHY?
WHAT IS SOMETHING ABOUT YOU THAT NOBODY ELSE IN THIS CLASS KNOWS?

The introductions, interspersed with laughter and commentary, had taken the remainder of the class time. As class ended, Dawn decided to stay seated to avoid eye contact with Drew Winston, not wanting to end the intriguing class on the negative note on which it had begun. Nobody approached her as she continued to sit, until three girls walked over— right after Drew and his buddies had walked out the door.

The most assertive of the three extended her hand. "Hi," she said, "I'm Jan Ostraczyk and this is Missy and Lois." Missy awkwardly shook Dawn's hand while Lois smiled shyly and remained behind her two friends.

"That was gutsy, what you said to Drew. I bet no girl has ever talked that way to him."

With other students coming into the classroom, the four moved slowly toward the door. Dawn happened to look back over her shoulder and noticed Richard Phillips staring at them. Catching up with Jan and her friends, Dawn replied, "Well maybe that's why he acted like such a jerk." She continued, "Is there some way we could finish this conversation later today? I'd like to find out more about this place, and I think it's cool that you all came over and said hello."

Jan glanced at her two friends, lowered her voice, and replied, "It might be hard to talk in school. Give me a call tonight and I'll fill you in." She handed Dawn a note on which she had scribbled her name and number, turning down the hall as Missy and Lois walked together in the opposite direction. Dawn didn't have far to go, having checked that her next class was only three doors down. She thought to herself that she would ask Jan, when they talked that evening, about the "Number 37" that Drew had called her. The bell rang as she entered her second-period class. The teacher closed the door and she sat down quickly at the first free desk.

"Hi Jan. It's Dawn from Honors Symposium." The grandfather clock in the Mortenson living room had just announced nine o'clock when Dawn made her call.

"Hi Dawn. Good to hear from you. I was excited to talk to you, because your little conversation with Drew sure got a lot of attention at school."

Dawn, surprised by Jan's comment, waited for her new friend to continue, which she did without taking a breath.

"As I said after class, nobody talks to Drew Winston and his group like that; it is always the other way around. They can say and do anything, and they aren't used to having it given back to them."

Jan inhaled and quickly proceeded.

"And that's from everyone: teachers, parents, coaches, graduates, and students for sure, especially girls. They rule the roost and can do anything they want. So when you said what you said, it got around fast."

Dawn listened intently, and then interrupted.

"But who spread it around? I wouldn't think that's something they would have wanted to pass around, and it sounds like other people might not want to spread it."

"You're wrong on both counts. Drew and his crew were bragging about what they were..." Jan suddenly stopped. Dawn waited a few moments before saying, "Jan, is something wrong?"

Still not hearing anything, Dawn asked, "Jan, are you all right?"

After a few more moments, Jan got back on the phone and slowly said, "You know, it's probably not a good idea for me to be telling you all of this. I'll see you in class tomorrow."

Before Dawn could respond, Jan hung up. Dawn sat for a while, thinking about the strange first day of her senior year.

Two

"HERE SHE IS guys. Here comes my new best buddy." Drew Winston smiled at his friends as they waited in the hall outside the Honors Symposium. As Dawn approached, twenty guys wearing varsity-letter jackets in the 90-degree heat stared at her as she attempted to enter the classroom.

"Nice looking package, wouldn't you say?"

Dawn stood still in the middle of the crowd. Calmly, she looked slowly at each of the looming athletes.

"I don't know, Drew, her boobs aren't much. I'd say she's average at best." Brent Wood, All-Conference tackle on the football team, stared at Dawn's body after making his statement, one that received a murmur of agreement from the crowd.

"Ya know, Brent, I like long-legged girls. She just might suit me fine." Jeremy Foxwood, a forward on the basketball team, edged closer to Dawn.

"What do you think, Legs? Want to wrap them around a real man?"

Drew Winston pushed the forward aside, planting himself in front of Dawn. Looking her in the eyes, he then turned to Jeremy. "I wouldn't get near this one if I were you, Jeremy. She's mine. I'll fill you all in on everything about her body when I do her good. Until then, she's off limits."

A larger crowd had gathered in the hall to see what was happening. Richard Phillips pushed through it toward his classroom, hearing the end of the All American's comment.

"Slow down there, stud. You are going to have your hands full in my class—you'd best not be thinking of your next conquest on my time." Richard stood next to Dawn, looking up at Drew Winston. "Get on into class, Drew; you all are blocking traffic here." To the rest of the crowd he remarked, "You all have had your fun. Move it on out; wouldn't want you to exert yourselves too much this early in the morning."

The group members looked to their leader, who nodded briefly and turned to enter the class. Dawn, who had stayed still during the encounter, called softly, "Hey

Drew, don't leave yet."

He turned back toward her. Richard Phillips, already in the doorway, stopped and watched. The rest of the crowd followed suit.

Continuing to talk softly, Dawn said, "I want to tell you something private. Come here."

Drew leaned over to hear what she had to say, and as he put his ear to her lips she pushed him away while extending her leg to trip him. He tried to twist himself to keep from landing on the floor, while Dawn attempted to grab him when she realized he was falling toward a marble water-fountain. Neither one had succeeded in slowing his fall, as his forehead hit the corner of the fountain. Before he crumbled to the ground, his head began bleeding. As he lay unconscious, his whole body began to convulse, causing a number of neighboring students to scream involuntarily.

Half of the group stood rooted in place; the other half moved toward the bleeding football hero. Dawn grabbed her backpack from the floor, walked past a stunned Richard Phillips, and strode down the hall.

Pushing through the double glass-doors and into the main high-school office, Dawn shoved through a crowd of students and announced to the staff behind the counter, "There is a student, Drew Winston, who is seriously hurt and bleeding on the ground outside of room 114. You had better call an ambulance and get him some medical attention as quickly as possible."

Students and staff began leaving the office and running toward room 114. Dawn stayed by the counter. She noticed a large man in a tailored suit leaning against the doorframe of an office with a sign that said "Principal" overhead. He stared at Dawn. Their eyes locked and held until Rebecca Saunders, the chief administrative clerk, pressed Dawn for an answer. "Excuse me, young lady, we have the ambulance on their way, and they want to know what happened to Drew Winston."

Continuing to look at the man in the doorway, Dawn replied purposefully, "He said he was going to rape me. I pushed him away and tripped him, and as he fell he hit his head on the corner of a water fountain. He's bleeding from his head and is in convulsions."

Gasping, Rebecca Saunders hurried back to the phone, turned her back, and whispered what she'd just heard from the student whom she didn't know.

Dawn turned, and as she reached the door, she felt a large hand on her shoulder. Spinning, she dropped her bag and looked into the deep-set black eyes of Brian McMullen, the Principal of Fair Shore High for the last twelve years. A graduate of the school, he had played professional football as an offensive lineman for three different teams. His muscular body carried no extra weight. He stayed in shape playing sports year-round and coaching the offensive linemen at Fair Shore High.

"You can relax now, young lady. Nobody's going to hassle you here. I am Brian McMullen, the principal here at Fair Shore, and I know we haven't met."

He offered his huge right hand to her, which Dawn ignored.

"And I'd like to hear about what happened. Preferably now, rather than later when this place loads up with interested parties. Would you come into my office, where we can have some privacy?"

Dawn stepped through the doorway and looked around, noticing that she and the two school employees were the only people in the office. The corridor outside had filled with running students and adults. "I'll follow you."

The principal walked across his large office, and stood in front of a stuffed chair that faced a couch and a chair similar to his. He motioned to Dawn to select either the couch or the chair.

Dawn sat in the chair placed in front of the principal's large mahogany desk and looked around the well-appointed office filled with trophies. Principal McMullen asked if she wanted a glass of water.

"No, I'm fine. And the sooner this is over, the better. I need to call my mother and tell her what happened."

"I understand. You will be able to do that very shortly. You also understand that it is important for me, as the principal, to know all that I can about what happened. Drew is a very important person here at Fair Shore High, and I am sure I'll be getting a lot of questions from concerned staff, parents, students, and members of the community. The more I know, the better it is for everybody."

"Then our conversation will be a short one. Yesterday when I walked into Senior Honors Symposium, your guy accosted me. I moved away and he came back saying I must not know who he was or I would let him take me out that night. I told him I *did* know who he was, that he was the big guy with the small brain who was blocking my path. He got pissed and threatened me, saying I had no idea of the trouble I was in and that I was going to get to know him intimately.

"Today, as I tried to get into class, he was blocking my way again, with about twenty of his jock friends. He introduced me as a nice-looking package, or some garbage like that. Two of his friends proceeded to comment on the size of my breasts and how they would like my long legs wrapped around them. Drew then said that I was off limits to them, that I was his and that he would let them know about my body when he did me good."

Dawn's face flushed as she told the story, her voice getting more accelerated and higher pitched. "It was then that I told him that I wanted to tell him something privately, and when he leaned over I pushed him away and tripped him, as I told the secretary. As he fell, I tried to catch him as I saw him falling toward the water fountain, but I wasn't fast enough. I left him lying there while I came to tell you all what happened and get him some help."

Brian McMullen was listening intently, leaning forward in his chair, elbows on his knees, and chin in his hands. When she completed her short recounting of the events, he unclenched his hands and leaned back in his chair. Dawn did the same, resting her hands on her lap, while taking a deep breath.

Once again they looked at each other, with the principal quickly breaking eye contact. "So you're telling me that you fought Drew Winston in front of twenty of his friends, leaving him bleeding on the ground, before you walked over to this office to admit what you had done?"

"Yes, that is exactly what happened, although I wouldn't use the word 'fought.' I tripped him."

Incredulous, he responded, "You have created one major problem for yourself, young lady."

Dawn rose quickly. "We'll see about that. The facts are that I was confronted by a mob, threatened by the mob leader, and that I chose to defend myself. The fact that you don't take my story seriously probably shouldn't surprise me, considering the way my first twenty-four hours have gone in this school. If you need to know anything else, you can reach me at home or on my cell. I'm getting out of here."

Dawn wheeled, grabbed her backpack, and walked quickly out of the office, leaving Principal McMullen sitting in his chair, staring at the door.

Erica Mortenson opened the door to her New York City office, looked out, and saw her seventeen-year-old daughter sitting quietly in a chair by the desk of her executive assistant, John Osgood.

Looking into Dawn's eyes, Erica told her assistant, "Push back my meeting with the operations folks to later this afternoon, John, and hold my calls except for Jennings."

Putting her arm around Dawn, she led her into her office. Sitting by Dawn's side on the couch that faced her desk, Erica said, "So give me the full story about this incident with the football player. Right after you called to tell me that you were getting a train into New York City because of what happened, a Mr. McMullen called, saying that we needed to have a meeting tomorrow about what had happened between you and an All-American quarterback who is in the hospital."

"I didn't give you the whole story on the phone, Mom, because I had interrupted your meeting and didn't think they would get to you so quickly."

As Dawn related the story for the second time that day, her mother took notes on a yellow pad. When her daughter finished, she put the pad down, inched closer to Dawn on the couch, took her right hand in hers and asked, "Are you all right? Did anybody touch you? Are you hurt?"

Dawn looked at her mother. "No, Mom, I'm physically all right. But those idiots have done a number on my head. Am I going to have to confront those morons every day that I'm there? If that's the case, I don't know if I want to play that game. Senior year has enough going on with my applying to colleges."

Pausing, Erica agreed, "Yes it does, and we'll find out quickly what is in fact going on, and we'll make the decision that's right for you."

Relieved that her daughter seemed to be all right, Erica got up and went over to the crystal water pitcher on the stand by her desk.

"Want a drink of water?"

"That would be great."

Dawn, relaxing, took a moment to look around her mother's new office. "Nice digs, Mom. This is even nicer than your last office in Boston with that awesome view of the harbor."

"This company has treated me well. They really wanted me, which was a nice way to move from Boston and Beckman Consulting, who had also treated me well, as you know. We shall see, but so far, so good. So let's talk about how we're going to handle this situation."

One decision that was made during their conversation was to call the psychologist who had been seeing Dawn since she was 12, in Boston and during the last year in New York City, and see if she was able to fit Dawn into a meeting in her Greenwich Village office that afternoon. They were both very glad that she was able to get a six o'clock appointment.

After leaving her mother's office, Dawn caught the Lexington Avenue subway to Washington Square and walked around Greenwich Village until it was time to meet with her therapist.

Dawn sat alone in the flower-rich waiting room of her therapist, flipping through the *New York Times*. She turned in her seat when she heard the door open and smiled at the person who had so positively changed her life. As she stood, Dr. Francis walked quickly over and gave Dawn a big hug, stepping back and looking at her, saying, "You look great. I was surprised by your call since we were going to meet in two weeks. Come on into my office and let's talk about what's going on."

"Thanks so much for fitting me in at the end of your day."

"Are you kidding? You said it was important and I know you well enough from our five years together to know you don't cry wolf. I'm really interested to know what's happening."

As Dawn and the high-energy, gray-haired woman in her sixties settled into their respective chairs, Dr. Francis said, "I have a number of questions, but please, tell me what is going on."

Dawn recounted in specific detail the events that led to Drew Winston's hospitalization. Dr. Francis listened carefully, taking a few notes in the leather-bound notebook that she kept on the coffee table by her chair.

"Dawn, we have worked through a lot and you have made amazing progress regarding how you react to aggressive men. What was different about Drew's approach?"

"Well, I need to be honest and tell you that I'd stopped the yoga, meditation, and brain-visioning regimen we'd created because after we moved, my mother and I charged around getting the house in shape and then had to get ready for school. I am exhausted and I wasn't ready to be confronted within minutes of getting to school. It looks like the old Dawn's way of reacting by attacking or making self-destructive decisions won out over what you and I had been working on for so long. I need your help with getting back into the new Dawn pattern as I deal with these idiots."

The rest of the hour was spent discussing how to take more control over how Dawn was to react to the individuals in Fair Shore who would want her gone. They agreed to get together in a week to see how she was doing.

Her visit with Dr. Francis put Dawn in a positive frame of mind by the time she and her mother met for dinner.

Talking animatedly in the car on the way back to Fair Shore, they didn't notice the crowd in front of their house on Davenport Street until they were almost there. Dawn saw them first. People surged toward them as their car approached their short driveway, making it difficult for Dawn and Erica to open their doors. Erica was finally able to push hers open, demanding those around her to back up and let them out. Two microphones were thrust into her face, reporters asking in tandem, "Mrs. Mortenson, what comments do you have about your daughter's unprovoked attack on Drew Winston, the star quarterback for the Fair Shore football team?"

Erica got out of the car and closed her door, asking the people crowding in on her daughter's side of the car to let her out. She was stopped by a large man gone to flab who spread himself out so she couldn't pass.

"So how do you feel, now that your bitch daughter just ruined our football season?" he shouted. "Drew is in the hospital in a coma and if he's not able to play this season we might not win the conference."

Erica looked at the man while focusing on trying to control her mounting anger. She pushed past him, similar questions cascading down on her from the angry mob. Dawn was inching her way toward the front door, staring down questioners, linking with her mother for the final push up their front steps. Dawn went to unlock the door. Erica, standing between her daughter and the crowd who had stopped at the bottom of the steps, stood with her hands on her hips, glaring back through the television lights at the crowd on her front lawn. Taking the time to look each of the accusers in the eye, she quieted most of the crowd.

As she heard Dawn open the door, Erica told her to close it behind her, reassuring Dawn that she would be in momentarily. Instead, Dawn remained outside, closed the door, and stood on the top of the steps beside her mother. Erica started to argue with her, but then changed her mind and smiled at her only child. Side by side, looking at the crowd spilling across their front yard, Erica stated in a calm and forceful tone, "My daughter was confronted by a group of twenty male Fair Shore students who blocked her way into her class this morning. They made lewd comments about what they wanted to do to her. Drew Winston, the ringleader, told them that they were not going to do anything to my daughter until he had chosen to find out for himself about her body and to use his words, 'do her good.'"

"This was a threat of rape, and rather than having a large group of people leave the scene thinking she condoned that thought, she pushed him away and unfortunately he fell into a stone water-fountain, which caused the injury that put him into the hospital. We will have no further public comment on this matter. If this 6'5", 215-pound All-American quarterback wants to press assault charges against my 115-pound daughter, we will be more than willing to repeat this and other details about how he and his friends treat young women. And I guarantee that our comments will reach a national audience of colleges that might not appreciate his actions."

Pausing momentarily to let her words sink in, she concluded, "One final thing. If you are not off our property in two minutes, I am calling the police. And believe me, I will press trespassing charges."

Erica opened the door and, along with her daughter, went inside, ignoring the questions that came from the reporters in the crowd.

Three

THE THIRD OF fifteen messages on the Mortenson's answering machine was from Principal McMullen's office, confirming their early morning meeting. After listening to all the messages and sending Dawn to her room to do her homework, Erica settled into her favorite chair in the living room and thought about her beloved daughter.

Raising someone so bright, beautiful, and headstrong in a marriage that had been falling apart since the time of Dawn's birth had not been easy. The fact that Erica's charismatic, alcoholic husband had a weakness for screwing star-struck followers and students hadn't helped.

Neither had the day when Erica had come home early from a meeting in Los Angeles to find her twelve-year-old daughter locked in the bathroom to keep her drunken father's best friend from raping her again. After calling 911 and having her daughter's assailant arrested, Erica had stabbed her husband in the neck with a fork when he commented, "She had to learn some time."

Four years of marriage counseling and attempts to reconcile had only allowed time for more infidelity and verbal abuse. Filing for divorce, she gained a huge settlement in exchange for remaining silent about his actions over the years.

As Erica sat and thought about what had happened at school and the facts about the situation, she felt comfortable with the way that she had presented them to the reporters in their yard. This wouldn't go further—the All American and Fair Shore High had too much at stake.

The meeting the next morning in Principal McMullen's office was brief. The principal sat in the high school conference room at the head of a long table, the town's attorney to his right. He opened by saying, "I'm glad we're all here so we can figure out the appropriate punishment for Dawn's unprovoked attack on one of the many scholar athletes in our school."

Upon hearing these words, Erica stood and looked directly at Principal McMullen. "I am going to say this once," she declared, "and then my daughter and I are going to leave. As I'd said to the press in our front yard last night: Drew Winston had said, in front of twenty of his friends, that he was going to rape my daughter. She felt a need to make it very clear that she would not ever let that happen. She was compelled to act, to defend herself in an aggressive manner because she was surrounded by a mob of male athletes who had already tried to intimidate her by talking about her body and what they would do to it.

"My daughter is now going to walk out of this room to her first-period class. If there is any attempt to stop her, or any attempt by any of Drew Winston's friends to block her access to her classes, we will slap a lawsuit on this school so fast and so effectively that the national media will have no choice but to take notice.

"When that happens, Mr. McMullen, the press that will descend on this town will quickly uncover the negative behavior that you and your colleagues encourage. That coverage will certainly jeopardize the positive reputation that your town has created for itself. It will also jeopardize the chances that your so-called scholar athletes have for attending colleges of their choice." Looking calmly at the principal, she concluded, "I am not at all concerned about what you can do to us. You, on the other hand, should be extremely concerned about what we can do to you."

Brian McMullen's years in the spotlight had instilled in him a confidence that would have predisposed him to attack this woman whose challenge struck at the heart of the institution and philosophy that had shaped his life since he was fourteen years old. Yet there was something about the way she handled herself and the facts of the situation that caused him to pause.

It took every ounce of his will to keep from saying something as Erica Mortenson and her daughter got up and walked out of the conference room. His focus on their departure was so single-minded that he didn't notice when his colleague spoke to him. Finally James Whitehead's hand on his left shoulder brought him back to the present. His answer to Whitehead's suggestions about what the next steps should be was immediate and dismissive. "We will do nothing at this point regarding this situation. Their time will come, but on our terms."

The attorney rose and walked out, leaving the principal thinking for the second time in two days about Dawn Mortenson, while looking at the inside of a closed office door.

Four

DAWN HAD AWOKEN early enough on most days to do a yoga and meditation routine that she had learned from a former Franciscan friar who had been her karate teacher when she was eight years old. Part of the routine had been incorporated into her therapy sessions with Dr. Francis. The morning that she and her mother had met with Principal McMullen and the township attorney had been no exception—the only difference being that she went jogging an hour prior to doing her routine, as a way of losing some of the pent-up tension in her body from the situation at school. She had watched the sunrise as she finished the last mile of her run. She felt particularly relaxed getting to the Honors Symposium after walking her mother to her car following the meeting in Principal McMullen's office.

Richard Phillips found himself staring at Dawn Mortenson as she took her seat in the center of the third row. He had been stunned the day before, as had all the other witnesses in the hall, by what had happened between her and Drew Winston.

The noise of the incoming students pulled him out of his reverie and back to the class. Looking around, he noticed Dawn looking at *him*. It seemed, he thought, as if she knew that he was thinking about her. Flustered, he busied himself by pulling the text out of his backpack and then, turning his back to the class, he wrote the words "PASSIONATE" and "PURPOSEFUL" on the blackboard in large, bold letters.

Raising his voice, he addressed the class. "I have some good news and some bad news for you. The good news, at least for some of you, is that we won't be starting our discussion of *One Flew Over the Cuckoo's Nest* today because of the distraction of yesterday that kept us from doing what I normally do before beginning our book discussions. The bad news is that we are going to do that exercise now. Please take out a piece of paper and write a page on the difference between these two words. You have twenty minutes, so move it." The obligatory groans followed the announcement of the surprise assignment, with the class quieting down when he added, "And this will be graded for clarity and coherence."

As the honors students got on task, Phillips pulled a sheaf of papers from his backpack and began to read them. When he looked up to check on the class, every head was buried in the assignment. His glance stopped on Dawn Mortenson for a moment, and then he went back to his task.

The second time he looked up she had put her pad aside and was resting her chin in her cupped hands while staring straight into his face. He held her glance for a moment, at which point she smiled slightly. Thrown off guard once again, he got up and walked around the perimeter of the classroom, ostensibly to check on how his students were doing.

After the papers had been completed, he led them into a discussion about what they had just written, pushing as many as possible to talk during the remaining class time. Most of the students focused on a literal discussion of the differences between the words by bringing up examples from their own experience. Dawn caught the attention of a number of students by quoting from the rock singer Neil Young. "I think the difference is summarized in a song by Neil Young when he talks about it being better to burn out than to rust."

Looking directly at Richard, she continued, "Most of the members of my mother's generation are rusted. They were energized and passionate when they were younger, looking to change the world. Now they have settled, with no possibility of burning out because they're not doing anything. They are purposeful about making money and not rocking the boat.

"Passionate people follow their creative spirit wherever it takes them, and they're not worried if it doesn't seem practical or purposeful, as long as they are alive. Passionate people are alive; most purposeful people are dead."

Her comment sparked a number of reactions, which culminated in Jan Ostraczyk saying, "I think the difference between the two was one that most of us saw yesterday," she said. "Drew Winston was purposeful in doing what he always does—that is his wiring, which is to hit on any good-looking girl that he doesn't already know. Purposeful has a pattern to it; it has a history or an almost predetermined or preordained aspect to it. It is what someone does. Drew hits on pretty girls.

"Passionate people react to the moment, when their beliefs are engaged. There is not the predetermined 'I am going to be passionate' character about passionate acts. They happen from a place of conviction, of outrage, of spontaneity.

"So Drew said what he'd said to Dawn in a purposeful way. Her reaction to him was passionate, unplanned. And I would guess that it came from a place of outrage at the sexism or assumption implied by his comments. Passionate people don't like to be taken for granted, so Dawn reacted in the first instance by telling him that he had a little brain, and the next day by tripping him. He was purposeful and she was passionate; preordained and predictable versus spontaneous and creative."

Richard listened carefully to all the comments, focusing particularly on Dawn and Jan. He noticed the three remaining varsity-letter athletes listening with particular interest to what Jan had to say, with Paul Withers, linebacker on the football team, catching the eye of Lennie Bartolo, the starting guard on the basketball team, as Jan was talking.

Jan stopped to catch her breath, and before she could go on or anyone else could respond, the bell rang.

"You all have your assignment for tomorrow. Be prepared because it is an important juncture in our first week together, with the next two weeks of class hinging on your understanding of what we discuss tomorrow."

As the students got up to leave, Dawn turned toward Jan; her path suddenly blocked by the backs of the varsity athletes who were moving with Jan toward the door. "Jan…" was the only word Dawn could direct her way before Paul Withers turned and snapped, "Not now, Miss Passionate. We want to talk with Jan about the important homework for tomorrow." Looking around for either one of Jan's friends from the first day of introductions, she realized that they had already disappeared from the room. She took a deep breath and walked slowly out the door, with only Richard Phillips left in the room to notice her exit.

Dawn knew exactly whom she wanted to talk to the next day in school, and she went right over to Jan Ostraczyk as she walked into Honors Symposium. "I really need to talk to you when we both have some time," she said. "I saw you a couple of times yesterday but you were always surrounded by the jocks. Can we get together?"

Jan jerked her head toward Dawn, spit out, "Yeah, I'll be in the northeast corner of the park after school," and kept moving quickly to her seat.

Focusing on her teacher, Dawn thought he looked tired, and noticed that he missed some points that were made about the action in *One Flew Over the Cuckoo's Nest,* choosing to let the class drift instead.

She lingered after class and went up to Mr. Phillips after many of the students had gone. "Rough night last night?"

He turned slowly to look at her, scowling before forcing a tight grin.

"Yeah, those papers you guys wrote yesterday were garbage and I spent half the night trying to make sense of them. Got a blinding headache today because of them."

Not sure if he was making fun of himself or his students, Dawn responded, "Sorry about that, I'll try to do better next time. We need all of you here to rein in this menagerie."

As she turned to leave the already half-empty room, Phillips called out to her, "Wait a moment; I'll walk out with you." He finished picking up after himself, wove through the desks to the side of the attractive senior, and they exited into the hall.

"How are you doing with the publicity about your confrontation with Winston?"

"I was mostly ignored yesterday, which is fine with me. I get a sense that the jocks are biding their time, waiting to see how he does, before hassling me too much. My mother and I are waiting to see if the adults reappear at our house, although my guess is that they took my mother's threat seriously, which most people tend to do."

"I didn't catch the TV coverage. It seems like I'm the only person in town who didn't."

Dawn laughed, "If I'm never on local television again that will be like the best. And thanks for asking. Gotta go."

Five

THE CURRENT FAIR Shore High, built in 1999, had not been around long enough to show the wear and tear of being attacked by over 450 students each day, or to gain the character that can envelop a school that has been shaped by generations of students. The English Tudor construction was what was initially striking about the school. Built on a hill, the school looked, by design, like a castle; the chief architect Terrence O'Shea smiling when townspeople referred to it as the castle on the hill.

The next aspect of the school that caught one's attention was the whiteness of its students. The almost exclusively white girls and boys who entered and exited the large front doors every day were the sons and daughters of the metropolitan New York City professional elite. Visitors commented on the homogeneity of the students, and those interested in looking a little more closely sensed a smugness in the students and their parents, a sense of superiority to surrounding communities.

Dawn thought fleetingly of these things as she moved purposefully through the wide front doors, hoping that her meeting with Richard Phillips hadn't forced her to miss Jan. Walking down the circular driveway that led to the front entrance, she cut across the nicely manicured practice football-field to the left, crossing Elmwood Street and walking two short blocks to the entrance of Van Orsback Park.

The entrance to the park was a broad black wrought-iron archway, the arch extending twenty feet overhead, merging on each side with a six-foot-tall fence that circled the entire park. At the uppermost point of the arch was a large and compelling diamond with the words *Van Orsback – 1901* scrolled in white lettering within the diamond. The Van Orsback family had owned over a thousand acres in Fair Shore at the turn of the twentieth century, donating the land that was now the park to the town, following the death of its last surviving member, Johannes Van Orsback, in 1901. The remainder of the family's land had been divided into large lots upon which mansions had been built, creating the residential reality from which much of the smugness of its inhabitants flowed.

Dawn had heard almost immediately upon moving to Fair Shore that "the park" was a major hangout for the students from the high school. It was only a leisurely

20

five-minute walk from the school, and its size allowed numerous groups, couples, or individuals to have relative privacy within a beautifully kept, natural setting.

Dawn didn't take time to notice the beauty, as she was moving at a quick pace toward the northeast corner. As she slowed to look more closely for Jan, she walked in and out of various cleared areas and around numerous bushes and plantings before seeing Jan sitting against a large oak tree in the farthest corner, looking toward the woods that stood outside the fence.

Not wanting to startle her, Dawn looped around so that she approached more directly in her sight. It was a good thing she had, for Jan had been lost in thought, not noticing Dawn until she was ten feet away and said, "Hi, Jan. You certainly picked a secluded spot."

Jan looked up sharply, responding to Dawn with a terse, "That was not by accident. Sit down and listen. I don't want to spend a lot of time here." Dawn didn't argue and promptly sat cross-legged in a position that allowed her to look straight at her classmate. She was struck by the redness in Jan's eyes and the suggestion of shadows forming beneath them.

"You have no idea what you have done. None." Jan hurled these words at Dawn, her anger a vibrant reality.

"You have messed up your life, my life, and probably a lot of the senior class's lives by your stupidity. Damn it, Dawn, what were you thinking, doing that to Drew? And then threatening to go national with what he did? There are a lot of folks here who are riding on his and the other guys' coattails, my cousin being one of them. He was expecting a scholarship when he graduates, after the football team ended this season ranked in the top five high-school teams in the country. And now that ranking is at risk because Drew probably won't play at all this season."

Dawn was watching Jan closely as her words grew louder, some redness expanding quickly from her throat to cover her entire face.

"We've got a good thing here. Not perfect, but something we are mostly proud of. Our academic and sports reputation brings Fair Shore a lot of positive attention. Our students are recruited by a lot of good schools, and it's expected that we will do well. There is no way you can imagine the pressure on our faculty and coaches. No way. And we're not used to random acts like yours that upset the plan for the year. Injuries on the field are expected and handled, but not what you did. That is unacceptable and you are going to get hammered, and I feel bad about that, which is why I was stupid enough to say I would talk to you on the phone. Boy did that go over well."

Jan jumped up so swiftly that Dawn thought for a moment that she was going to hit her. Flinching involuntarily, she braced herself as Jan stood over her. Instead,

Jan walked away, but then circled back to where Dawn continued to sit. Dawn noticed tears in her eyes, Jan's attempt to wipe them away as her back had been turned only serving to highlight the moisture on her face.

Squatting where she had stood, Jan hissed, "I like you Dawn, and that's why I agreed to see you now. And I can't ever see you alone again. I am in big trouble because of my support of you. So watch your back, don't trust anyone, and above all, don't do anything else to provoke them. And please don't try and talk with me in class or in school because I'll have to ignore you, which will make it even worse for both of us. I can't say anymore. I've already said too much. Please believe what I say."

Looking in both directions, Jan quickly began to walk away. Dawn got up and ran to cut off her classmate. Standing in front of her, blocking her way, she said, "You have to tell me more. This doesn't make sense. Who are you so afraid of? Why did Drew call me *Number 37?* Talk to me, damn it."

Dawn's resolve to block Jan's exit until she forced answers to her questions was quickly dissolved by the look of terror that crossed her friend's face.

"You cannot do this to me; you have no right. I put myself at great risk coming here and you must respect that." With tears flowing freely, Jan pleaded, "I can't stay here. You have to believe me." Dawn stepped aside and Jan ran past her and toward the park entrance.

Dazed by the level of her classmate's terror, Dawn walked slowly to a quiet corner of the park and sat in the lotus position, closing her eyes and relaxing her mind. She sat for more than two hours, breathing in deeply the smells of the well-manicured gardens. She finally roused herself and began the thirty-minute walk to her home. Knowing that her mother had a client dinner that night, Dawn took her time. Passing the Fair Shore Book Center, she decided to walk in.

The store, with a sign that billed it as the largest independent bookstore in Connecticut, stretched back and out of sight straight ahead and off to her right. Books stacked to the ceiling covered the walls, with seven-foot bookshelves dividing the large main room into dozens of subject areas. Having moved into town only a month before the beginning of school, Dawn had not had the time to visit the bookstore.

After pulling half-a-dozen books from various shelves, she turned off her cell phone, bought a cup of Red Zinger tea and a muffin from the café inside the store, and settled into an overstuffed chair wedged into a corner of the philosophy and religion section. Oblivious to those around her, Dawn leafed through her selections, becoming absorbed in Jess Stearn's *Yoga, Youth and Reincarnation*.

Looking around, she noticed a small group of people gathered at the entrance to the café. She decided to buy Stearn's book since she was into yoga, was seventeen, and believed in reincarnation. As she found her wallet, she heard the beginning of a song that she didn't recognize coming from the café area.

"You have live music?"

"Yeah, most nights," smiled the long-haired cashier. "This group, Max Lunatic, is one of the better local groups. They are all from the high school and they know their music. The lead guitar player's father was the singer for the Cosmic Chord back in the sixties. He owns the record store down the street. If you have some time they're worth a listen."

"Thanks, I'll do that." Dropping her purchase into her backpack, Dawn moved toward the music. Surprised at the size of the crowd that had formed at this early hour, she pushed to the far wall, leaned against it, and looked toward the four scruffy students at the front of the room. Wondering where they hung out at Fair Shore High, as she did not remember seeing any of them in her first week, she relaxed and listened, struck by how musically tight the band sounded. And then the lyrics of their third song caught her attention.

> *Our parents they don't get it, neither do their friends*
> *Hopeless conversations never seem to end.*
> *They don't know what's happening, yet they think they do*
> *We are all alone here, hey Fair Shore, screw you.*
>
> *Athletes run the show here, guess they always have,*
> *Man that gets so boring, makes us start to laugh.*
> *They don't like that sound here, laughing's not allowed,*
> *Cheering for their exploits, that's the sacred sound.*
>
> *New girl in the school, man, messed up all their heads*
> *Tripped their football hero, left him there for dead.*
> *Everyone's in mourning, don't know what to do,*
> *Their fear, it excites us, hey Fair Shore, screw you.*
>
> *Gonna play our music, usually don't get heard,*
> *When they hang around us, they all say we're absurd.*
> *At least we're alive man, and know how hope here sinks,*
> *And we feel pretty good 'cuz, you can't shape how we think."*

Dawn leaned against the wall and listened for the next half-hour as the talented band played a set of original songs for an enthusiastic crowd. When they explained that they were going to take a short break, she watched the four band members mingle briefly with the young people in the crowd. Dawn held back, waiting for them to break free. After five minutes they headed for the front door, Dawn following them. They went down the street, ducking into the alley that ran on the café side of the large bookstore. Noticing her as they turned, the singer motioned the others to continue on, while he stopped, asking, "What do you want?"

Dawn stopped five feet from him, waiting to respond. Being of equal height, they stared straight into each other's eyes until Dawn finally answered, "I wanted to introduce myself since you guys were singing about me. I'm Dawn Mortenson."

Tripper Cardone looked closely at Dawn's face, a smile forming as he did. "No kidding, you're the one who decked Drew. C'mon and have a drink with us in honor of you."

As Dawn turned into the alley, she saw the tallest of the four close the side door of a beat-up van and walk toward his bandmates with a six-pack. He offered a beer to each one as Tripper introduced Dawn.

"Hey guys, this is Dawn Mortenson."

"Yeah, I saw her watching us tonight and saw her the other morning kick the crap out of that fascist football hero. Great to see you. Want a beer?" Lou Malone held out a beer that Dawn took eagerly, popping the top and taking a long sip.

"That's Lou. He and I formed the band three years ago. I heard him playing guitar in the pit band at a school play and knew I wanted to work with him." Tripper chugged his beer, throwing the empty can against the wall and grabbing the last one from the driveway where Lou had just set it.

"Billy, who plays bass, is the quiet one, just right for those chicks who like the shy types." Billy smiled and nodded in Dawn's direction, long brown hair falling over his face. "Billy's also a damn genius. He's going to MIT after graduation, in electrical engineering. We brought him into the band to do all our technical work and make sure the audience could actually hear what we're playing. Gordon over there next to him plays a mean set of drums and has read more books than any other teenager I know."

Gordon, black as anyone she had ever met, smiled broadly toward Dawn with large white blazing teeth. "Hi Dawn. I had no choice with the reading. Both my parents are literature professors."

"And if you're wondering how the hell they let him into Fair Shore, he was recruited to play football and then quit the team as a sophomore. He probably joined our band to spite his jock friends, but he's never admitted it."

Gordon smiled widely again. "Yeah, Dawn, that was part of the motivation. And I figured our fearless leader here was going to make me rich with his plan for hitting it big in the rock-and-roll world, so I've put up with his crap for the past two years. Actually I just had to hang with someone as talented as he is at pissing off the jackasses in this town."

Dawn finished her beer while Gordon completed his introduction. Lou had already produced another six-pack from the van, with each of the five taking another can. As Tripper opened his, he looked at Dawn and said, "So that's us. What's your story?"

Dawn had remained standing as the band members sat on the ground or leaned against the van. "My mother and I moved here from Boston in July…"

"…where she had been a respected management consultant with Beckman Consulting," Lou Malone smiled and continued, "Dawn was kicked out of The Broadmoor School in Wellesley during ninth grade for insubordination, completing that year and grades ten and eleven in the public schools in Boston. She was an honors student, getting a black belt in karate her junior year after studying for years as the pupil of a former Jesuit priest and Boston College professor."

Dawn threw her half-finished can against the wall, grabbed her backpack, and turned to walk up the driveway. Gordon, who had been watching her tense up as Lou spoke, moved quickly to stop her. "Dawn, don't get pissed. Lou likes to show off. His mother is an investigative reporter and he finds out all kinds of personal stuff about everybody. The first night I jammed with these guys he told me about my grandfather who I had never heard of and how he was a great jazz musician. Don't take it personally."

"Of course I'm going to take it personally, Gordon. I thought I might be able to hang out with you guys, and within five minutes I'm being taunted with information about my past that is nobody's goddamn business. I don't need that garbage, man, I really don't."

Lou moved over next to Gordon, facing Dawn. "Dawn, I'm sorry. I do that all the time and I'm not even sure why. I wasn't taunting you; I was trying to impress you with what I had been able to find out about you. It was, in a perverse way, a compliment. Same reason I did it with Gordon when he joined the band. Don't go. People like us need all the friends we can get while living in this messed-up town."

Dawn wavered, wanting to trust and yet consumed by her frustration and anger. "You didn't have to impress me, Lou. Music is special for me, and you guys know how to play. That's all I needed."

"Have you, um, ever been in a band?" Billy asked. Everyone looked at him, leaning on the back door of the van.

"No I haven't, but I have sung in different choral groups and choruses."

"So you have a good voice?" Tripper asked, finishing his beer and motioning for

Lou to throw him another.

"Yeah, I'm not bad."

"And what songs that you love do you know how to sing?" Tripper, animated and intent on her answer, took a long sip from his beer.

"Music is a big deal to my parents so I was brought up on country and rock-and-roll; my mother was into rock-and-roll and my father into country, having been born and raised in Texas. I have a particular interest in good lyrics; songs that say something. I have really gotten into outlaw country or whatever you want to call it. My dad is a huge Kris Kristofferson fan, a fellow Texan, and has followed him since the '60s and so I have all his records and CDs. My interest in him moved me toward Steve Earle, another Texan, as soon as my dad suggested that he is comparable when it comes to telling stories about what's really going on in our world, the same as Kris. I have been listening to both of them the last few days to help me deal with the garbage going on and there are a few that I know that kind of speak to me and my relationship to Fair Shore. *The Revolution Starts Now* by Steve Earle is one of my favorites, and I know it by heart."

All four friends reacted immediately, led surprisingly by Billy who almost shouted, "You can sing Steve Earle? He's one of our favorite singer-songwriters."

"Sure. I don't know how well; I mean, I'm not a performer, but ..."

"You want to be a performer and sing *The Revolution Starts Now* with us when we go back in?" Tripper leaned forward expectantly, along with his friends.

Dawn looked with amusement at the earnest expressions on her new friends' faces. "Yeah, I could do that, though I can't guarantee what it will sound like."

"It doesn't matter. We'll explain the situation and the audience will groove on it." Lou concluded. "Do you have another you could sing?"

"You into Kristofferson? I could do *Don't Let the Bastards Get You Down,* which would seem to fit into what you guys are trying to do."

Gordon said, "We love Kris. Let's do it. We'll call it the Texas suite." His band mates nodded in agreement as they finished picking up the empty beer cans and putting them into a bag in the van.

Hands on her hips, Dawn looked at the band members. "So, you ready to kick ass?" She was met with a resounding, "Hell yeah" as they all moved together up the driveway and back into the bookstore café.

The Friday-night crowd had grown significantly in the half-hour they had been in the alley. All the seats were taken and people were standing packed against the wall. The group was composed mostly of young people, but Dawn was surprised to see a number of folks her mother's age in the audience. When she asked Lou about the kinds of people they attracted, he explained that a lot of kids came, and that despite the fact that more than one of their songs told adults to go screw themselves, a number of adults came regularly to their gigs.

As the band members tuned their guitars, Tripper stood next to Dawn. "We're going to do an original song and then do yours. You alright?"

Dawn, surprised at his question, responded, "Should there be something wrong?"

"It's just that performing can be intimidating, especially if you haven't done it before."

"It won't be a problem. I'm looking forward to it."

They both laughed, Tripper turning away to talk to the band, which quickly finished its preparation and launched without introduction into a song the audience knew well.

> You say that we're insane because your meanings we don't catch
> And our views are not supported by sound logic or your facts
> That our anger makes no sense since we have all the things we need
> That it seems so dumb to rail against your hatred and your greed.
>
> Well goddamn it parents and adults who think you know it all
> Your ideas of what is fair and right makes all of our skin crawl
> Cuz when looked at in the light of day, your reason makes no sense
> Unless we thought consumption rules, and we are not that dense.
>
> Your lives are hollow, damn it, and are guided by beliefs
> That we won't begin to follow, instead we'll take it to the streets
> Because we know that if we follow you our world will soon be gone,
> And we'll no longer see the sunset or the pale pink light of dawn.
>
> You must wake up and see that your beliefs are bankrupt now
> In light of all that's happening you need sweat upon your brow
> That shows you're thinking and are scared and have some thoughts about our fate
> As we your sons and daughters push for change 'fore it's too late.
>
> Our anthem now is simple, think you'll get it, listen close
> We need your help, let's work together; a new day's brilliance can explode
> Stop buying things you don't need; friends don't need to be impressed
> Use money wisely, solve the problems; pull your babies to your chest.

Support ALL people, not just those who look like you in every way
Random kindness to all people brings a new and loving day
Forego winning at all costs, for it now rules all your lives
Focus instead on these six words LOVE FOR ALL LETS US SURVIVE.

Many in the audience were singing along with Tripper as the song built to his shouted conclusion. Most erupted into loud applause and cheering as the song concluded.

The band waited for the applause to die down, sipping soda and water as they waited for Tripper to introduce Dawn.

"We have a *very* special treat for you now, something we have never done in the three years we've been together as a band. We're going to bring in a guest singer." Smiling broadly, he continued, "And this is not just any guest singer. She is someone we sang about earlier. We have never rehearsed these songs with her, so cut us all some slack, OK? Please welcome Dawn Mortenson."

A small percentage of the audience erupted into loud cheers as her name was mentioned. An equally small number yelled "No way" and "Sit down, bitch" as they booed. Most had no reaction, waiting to hear what came next. Dawn and the band ignored the audience as she walked to the microphone in the middle of the stage between where Lou and Tripper stood with their guitars.

"Good evening. I just met these guys about half an hour ago. We started talking about music and now we're going to do a Steve Earle song for you."

After Dawn sang *The Revolution Starts Now* and *To Beat the Devil* to a positive response, she sat down to the left of the stage as her friends played an energized second set, the concert ending at ten o'clock when the bookstore closed.

As Dawn helped the band break down their equipment, Tripper asked her if she was interested in going to a big party with them over at the Bainbridge estate. Hesitating for a moment, she replied, "I just need to call and tell my mother what we're doing. I think I can convince her that I am safe with you guys."

When she came back into the room Gordon asked, "No problem with your mother?"

"No, she trusts my judgment about people. Just wants to know who I'm with and where I'm going. Let's do it."

Six

JAN OSTRACZYK WAS ready for Friday night and ready to party. Jumpy since her first contact with Dawn Mortenson early in the week, she couldn't finish her dinner before she excused herself, explained she was running late to pick up Missy and Lois, and bolted out the front door.

She picked up her friends in her parents' Toyota, and they seemed to share her excitement. The fact that this was the first of many parties held each year at The Hills only increased their anticipation of a fun night.

The student parties at The Hills estates had begun in the early 1970s. Five of the seven families at that time had boys who played sports in the junior or senior high school, and they began hosting parties for their children and their friends to celebrate the town's athletic achievements. The parties were very popular and got larger each year, to the point that this year they were expecting 300 young people. The Bainbridge home was the focal point for this year's Kick-Off Bash.

Jan parked her parents' car on Sound View Boulevard, a five-minute walk up the street into The Hills. She, Missy and Lois walked quickly toward the music that was blasting through the trees surrounding all seven mansions. "It doesn't sound like the party has started yet. Maybe we should come back." "Yeah," Missy replied, "Not only should we leave, we shouldn't come back, since this is obviously the low-rent end of town, and I don't want anybody to hear that we set foot in this dump." The three friends laughed and walked past dozens of cars parked along Violet Drive before turning into the wide driveway that wound up toward the large home sitting on a small rise.

Their pace quickened as they got closer to the house, walking past knots of kids of all ages, including a number of former students who had graduated and were back in town for the yearly event. The massive double-hung iron doors were open and held in place against the house's front wall by red velvet cords, allowing those entering the party to walk straight into the Bainbridge's' front foyer. The foyer broke off into a library on the left, doors open there as well, and into a huge living room on the right, with hallways leading back to the other areas of the first floor. The wide center stairway loomed ahead, with a plush red carpet and gold railings glittering in the light of the cut crystal chandelier hanging above.

Young people were everywhere, sitting on the stairs, leaning on the railing, and draping over the antique couches in the living room, where a roaring fire cast grotesque shadows on the patterned red-velvet wallpaper.

"The fire was my idea. I thought it would add a medieval look to the party," Bart Bainbridge greeted the three friends as they entered his living room, followed by Charlie Huntington and Buddy Fontanella.

"What do you think, Jan?" he continued, putting his arm around Jan's shoulder, "Did I create that effect?"

Jan leaned into Bart. "I would be better able to tell if I had a drink," she said.

Smiling, Bart replied, "Let's you and I go and take care of that." Pulling her away from her friends, Bart moved out of the congested living room and into a room off to the side. Immediately losing sight of their friend, Missy and Lois began to go after her, but Charlie and Buddy moved toward them and cut off their path. "Come on, you two. Let's go get you something to drink."

Buddy guided Missy toward the bar that had been set up in the corner of the living room. "So did you all come together?" he asked.

Charlie led Lois out onto the patio, saying, "I want to show you what they have set up by the pool." Holding the shy senior by her elbow, he maneuvered her through the massive flow of young people, saying hi to most as he did. Not used to being the center of the action, Lois followed his lead, enjoying the attention. As they reached a thirty-foot-long bar with six bartenders in tuxedoes, he asked her what she wanted to drink, followed by, "I know you and Jan and Missy are inseparable. Who ends up doing the driving?" Drinks in hand, they sat together on a couch set up by the pool.

Rock-and-roll was pounding loudly from powerful speakers positioned around the inside of the house and in the backyard, as the party became more and more crowded and animated. The DJ platform was adjacent to the external living room wall with a view overlooking the expansive backyard. Johnny Cardone, Tripper's father, was controlling the song selection. His thinning black hair hanging down to his shoulders, Johnny was dancing and laughing as he watched his music choices push the assembled teens to throw themselves around and at each other.

Johnny had made and lost millions on classics such as *You Got It So Show It, Darker than Time,* and *Inside Everyone.* Numerous lawsuits had followed his band's break-up as members fought for control of the name and their former fans.

Johnny had formed one other short-lived group before opening Johnny Come Lately Records in Fair Shore in 1977. With one of the largest collections of rock-and-roll records in the world, he supplemented his income from his record store by DJ'ing six to ten mega-parties a year. Wearing a faded Sex Pistols T-shirt, cut-off jeans, and orange sneakers with no socks, he flailed around his sanctuary, pulling albums, 45s, tapes, and CDs from the shelves that surrounded him.

Noticing a large crowd gathering outside the glass-enclosed porch at the far corner of the mansion, he stood up on a box to see what was happening. Vicky Smithson, a junior with long, stringy, bleached-blonde hair, was standing on a small wooden coffee table to the right of the sliding glass porch doors, dancing slowly. Arms extended in front of her, she seemed fascinated by the movement of her fingers, weaving them together as camera and strobe lights exploded around her. Her clothes were nowhere to be seen as she swayed leisurely in tune with her hand movements. Johnny laughed and mumbled, "This is gonna be cool."

Taking a pull from his beer, he dove into a carton of records at his feet, selecting an album and announcing into his microphone, "This goes out to our mesmerizing blonde dancer over by the porch." As he turned up the volume on Sly Stone singing about doing what you want to do, he yelled, "All right," laughing loudly as he spun around and danced to the music.

Bart took Jan to the bar on the far side of the pool, telling the bartender named Daniel that she wanted a Scotch on the rocks, same as he was drinking. Before Jan could protest, Daniel pushed a large glass toward her, and Bart said, "All right Jan, I want to talk with you away from all this noise." Clicking her glass, he took a large swallow from his, and watched her as he tilted his head back.

Jan hesitated while the popular athlete took his drink, but then she put her glass to her lips as he lowered his. "C'mon Jan, let's party," Bart whispered in her ear and took another gulp.

"Yeah, let's party," she responded, looking him in the eye as she took a long swallow, coughing at the unnatural taste.

"I knew you would be a good partner for this party, and I was really hoping you would be here," he said in a low, soft tone, brushing her hair out of her eyes.

"Well I am definitely ready to party after this crazy week," she said, putting her arm around Bart's shoulder. Emboldened by his attention, she asked, "So whatdya want to talk about, big guy?"

"Actually, I wanted to talk about the need for everyone to loosen up with all the crap that went down this week, and I'm glad that you agree. So let's finish these drinks, get another, and see who else is here." Kissing her firmly on the cheek, he turned to the bartender and told him to make two more drinks, as Jan, flushed, looked across the pool.

Late arrivals, Dawn and the band had a twenty-minute walk to the Bainbridge estate from where they had to park their car. They passed cars in ditches, abandoned in front yards, and double-parked at intersections. Some groups of teenagers had never left their cars and were sitting on hoods, either in the woods or by the side of the road, drinking and snorting.

Moving up to walk beside Dawn, Tripper said, "I want to warn you that you are going to meet my dad at this gig." Before she could reply, Lou laughed and added, "Yeah, 'warn' is the right word. He is a nutcase. You can see a clear hereditary example of how fruit doesn't fall too far from the tree."

Gordon supported his friend's comment, "Yes, Tripper's dad is certainly not like any parent I have ever known or read about for that matter. There is a little of Kesey's McMurphy in him, with a splash of Donleavy's ginger man, Sebastian Dangerfield. But he knows how to get a party going with his music. There are some folks who came here from out-of-state just to hear him play tunes all night long." Explaining that Tripper's father owned a record store and also did a few DJ gigs a year, Gordon and the group kept walking toward the music.

Five minutes after arriving through the front doors of the Bainbridge mansion, the friends were drinking their first beers while talking to others from school. "Hey guys, how ya doin'?" All turned to see who had greeted them, and Tripper found himself face-to-face with Dale Winston, one of Drew's two older brothers. An All-American running back while at Fair Shore, he was now in his senior year at Syracuse, where he had been All-Conference during his junior year.

Dale was flanked by two of his Fair Shore teammates, Luke Pettibone and Archer Duquette. The trio towered over Tripper, Dawn, and the rest of the band.

"Hey Dale, I didn't figure to see you here tonight, what with football practice and all."

"Yeah, we finished up this afternoon and drove straight up to see my brother, have a few beers, and listen to your dad play his tunes. We'll be driving back early tomorrow morning for ten o'clock practice."

"Well I gotta figure if anyone would do that it would be a rock-and-roll fanatic like you. The band still together?"

Besides playing football, Dale had started a rock band in his sophomore year in high school that had gained some notoriety when it toured with Tom Petty the summer after graduation. Breaking up because of ego issues after that tour, they had assembled for local gigs a couple of times after that, but without their previous success.

"Nah, we're done; can't get that old groove back so we're all movin' on. I need to focus on football exclusively, anyway, if I want the NFL to take notice."

"You had a hell of a year last year," Gordon chimed in. "With the offensive line that's returning, you all should have another great season."

Turning to look at Gordon, Dale smiled. "Yeah, that's what everybody says. We'll see." Pausing to drink his beer, Dale continued, "You know, Gordo, I'm still sorry that you quit. You had it all, man."

Squaring his shoulders, Gordon quickly replied, "As you said, Dale, 'we all have to move on.'"

"That is actually why we came over," Dale quickly added. Turning slowly to look at each friend, ending with a cold stare at Dawn, Dale growled, "The bitch isn't welcome here, guys. She's got to go."

Everyone stood their ground while Dale Winston and Dawn stared at each other. As Tripper opened his mouth to reply, all were jolted by a louder noise than the rock-and-roll blaring from the speakers.

"All right, it must be alumni weekend at the Bainbridge playground. How the hell are ya, Dale?"

Grabbing the large football player by the shoulders, Johnny Cardone pushed him back, a big smile on his face. "Couldn't stay away from me spinning some tunes, huh, buddy?"

Not waiting for an answer, he turned to Dale's friends who had tensed beside him. "Hey Luke and Archer, how the hell are you?"

Having regained his balance, Dale Winston stood next to the man who had arranged his band's tour with Tom Petty. At 6'1" and 250 pounds, Johnny Cardone held his own in the presence of the three football players. Not letting on that he sensed the tension in the group, he waited for a response from the startled friends.

"You're absolutely right, Johnny. Couldn't stay away from you doing your thing," Dale agreed. Looking around with exaggerated interest, he continued, "And as always, you've got things rocking."

"That's my job, Dale, that's why old man Bainbridge is paying me the big bucks."

Johnny Cardone looked at Dale and Dawn and continued smiling while saying, "And I gotta tell you, the last two people I thought I'd see socializing were you and the young woman who put your brother in the hospital. That is pretty big of you to come over and welcome her, man. There was a time when you wouldn't have been that gracious."

Putting his arm around the reluctant Winston, he continued, "And there are some who wouldn't be welcoming her here tonight, I know. So the fact that you are over here showing folks who know you, which is just about everyone, that she is welcome, will go a long way toward making this my best party ever. Because, quite honestly," he said, still smiling, "I was expecting that if she did show up, some knucklehead would try and cause trouble or kick her out or pick a fight or some damn thing. If that did happen, I'd have to get involved and tell them that I am pulling my show if she isn't encouraged to stay. And man, I am stoked about making this the best party of the year and would have really been disappointed if I had been forced to go in that direction. Anybody who ruined my gig would go on my crapola list immediately and that's not a good place to be, ya know?"

Throwing his head back and chugging his beer, he threw the empty can into a garbage bin, bringing his gaze back to the group, before belching and saying, "Good seeing you all. Dawn, welcome to Fair Shore. Stop over later, OK?"

Without waiting for a response, Johnny turned his back on the group, winked inconspicuously at Dawn and Tripper, and lumbered over to his enclosure.

Both groups continued to stare at each other until Tripper finally said, "Nice seeing you guys. We're going to show Dawn around the grounds." Putting his arm around Dawn, he pulled her away from her eye-contact duel with Dale Winston and motioned for his band-mates to follow.

Purposefully steering Dawn and his friends out of sight of the three, Tripper pushed through the crowd and around the side of the house to a relatively quiet area. Everyone stood silently drinking beer, with Billy volunteering to get some more. As he walked toward the bar by the pool, Dawn looked at Tripper and said, "You guys were right. Your father is something else."

"Yeah, he is pretty unique. Growing up with him was quite an experience."

Dawn laughed tightly. "I can only imagine. No, on second thought I can't. Is he always that, um, forceful?"

Lou, also smiling, answered for his friend. "That was low-key compared to what you might see later, Dawn. He is like a large typhoon, a force of nature."

"And don't for a minute think that he didn't know exactly what was going on here," Gordon added. "He didn't choose to say what he did randomly. As the business writer and strategist Peter Drucker said, only monomaniacs with a mission get things done, and Johnny's mission tonight is to make this a great party where Dawn is not antagonized."

Billy returned with half a dozen beers, distributing them as he sat on a stone bench that curved around the sculptured walkway.

Dawn asked Tripper how his father knew Dale Winston and his football buddies, leading into a long discussion of how Johnny had gotten him hooked in with Tom Petty.

Gordon, Lou, and Billy left the two to talk, wanting to check out the party action. Left alone by the increasingly frenzied crowd, Tripper and Dawn talked easily about his father and the differences in how they had been brought up.

As the rest of Max Lunatic wandered around, they stopped to talk to various friends, watching as more teens took off their clothes to dance to the music, go swimming, or get to know each other better. Those with clothes on who got too close to the pool soon regretted it, because large guys would grab them and throw them into the water.

When it was close to 1:00 a.m., Dawn said she needed to go to the bathroom, and Tripper said he wanted to go see his dad. Agreeing to meet in a few minutes at his father's DJ station, Tripper walked Dawn into the Bainbridge study, where a short line of young people were waiting to use the bathroom. Not knowing anyone in the room, she sipped her beer and gazed at the original paintings that flanked the entrance to the bathroom.

As the line moved fairly quickly ahead, she heard a drunken girl in front of her saying to her friend, "Didja hear that Bart got Jan Oztrick drunk and that sheze getting gang banged buh half the football team in his parenz bedroom zweet? It's apparently quite a speshtayor scene."

Startled to full attention, Dawn listened intently for more information about her friend. The second girl giggled, "They probably picked her for that iniziation cuz she waz friendly wiz that Morgenzin chick." Turning to look in the other direction so she wouldn't be recognized, Dawn heard the original speaker say, "Yeah, the football team iz pretty riled bout whuh happened. I wouldn't want to do anythin to get targed by thosh guys." As the two entered the bathroom together, other teens exited, and Dawn spun away.

She moved from the study toward the front of the house, trying to get her bearings. Figuring that the master bedroom would be on the second floor, she remembered the long, winding center-hall staircase that led up from the large foyer by the front door. Weaving her way through the mass of drunken bodies, she soon got to the stairway that was the seating area of choice for dozens of young people. Not wanting to take the time to find another route to the second floor, she began saying, "Excuse me, I need to get upstairs" to the people blocking her way. Most shifted to let her by, and those who were too drunk or too intertwined with their partners were either pushed aside or stepped around.

Frustrated with the slow pace, Dawn walked carefully, not wanting to bring herself to the attention of any possible enemies. Finally reaching the second floor, she looked left and right down two long hallways. Noticing a small group gathered outside a doorway at the end of the hallway to her right, she moved slowly in that direction. The overpowering smell of marijuana hit her as she walked down the hall, passing by teenagers smoking outsized joints or personalized pipes.

Approaching the group by the door, she saw that it was open and that they were being stopped from entering by a tall, muscular, full-bearded man. Unbuttoning the top three buttons of her blouse, she was able to move over by him, murmuring as she rubbed her leg against his thigh, "I'd like to get into the action. Do you think I have what it takes?"

As he leaned down to kiss her, she jammed her tongue into his mouth, moaning as she pulled away, and moved quickly into the room before he could protest. Buttoning her blouse, she quickly zeroed in on the focus of everyone's attention. A large four-poster bed was bathed in light, with two half-dressed college-age boys standing to the right side and Bart Bainbridge standing half-naked at the head of the bed to the left.

Straining to see, Dawn heard the unmistakable sounds of sex.

Her anger mounting, she looked around the room, which she noticed was filled with twenty to twenty-five people watching the scene. Thinking quickly about what to do, she was concerned that there seemed to be only one way out, the way she had come in, past the bearded gatekeeper. Looking back toward the door, she noticed that the guard had stopped watching her and was talking instead to someone out in the hall.

Continuing around the bed, she saw two men on the mattress with Jan. Dale Winston was one and the guy Tripper's father had called Archer was the second. Crouching, she pushed between two startled teens into the lighted area by the bed.

"What the hell" and "Hey, bitch, get your ass out of here" greeted her surge toward the bed. Dale, accustomed to an audience, smiled over his shoulder at her, saying, "Hey, hot stuff, come for a taste?"

Addressing the startled and confused group of onlookers, Dawn said in a controlled tone, "This is over. I've come to take my friend home." When the only movement seemed to be that of the bearded man toward the bed, she screamed, "Move it, goddamn it! This is statutory rape. This girl is only seventeen. If all of you want to join Mr. Winston in jail, that's your business. My uncle is a reporter and would love nothing more than to get every one of your pictures on the front page of *The New York Times* connected to a story about the gang rape of a minor."

Staring at the crowd, she saw Bart Bainbridge move toward her. "She's bluffing," he said. "Janice would never press charges, and besides, she loves all the attention. I am getting this bitch out of here so I can screw her again."

Looking directly at Bart while watching Archer on one side and the bearded man on the other, she said slowly, "Do you really want to risk that, Bart? I understand you want to go to Yale like your father. My mother knows President Arturas; they went to grad school together. I can guarantee you that he has not one ounce of sympathy for this kind of action after his daughter was raped in New Haven.

"And she knows Coach Hutchins really well at Syracuse, Winston. She did some consulting for him when he was at the University of Richmond. You think he's going to want to hear this story first thing tomorrow before practice? Because I guarantee you he will."

As the bearded man and another man forced their way toward Dawn, she turned sideways and crouched, breathing slowly as she waited for their next move.

"Don't touch her, Donnie. It's over." Looking quickly to her side, she saw Dale Winston roll off the bed and put on his clothes. Standing to face her and putting on his shirt, he continued, "Leave the two of them alone. There's better meat out by the pool. I'm ready for a beer anyway."

As a couple of aroused teens protested, he cut them off. "I said that's it." Turning toward Dawn, he remarked, "I'm looking forward to the next time you and I meet. That is going to be one fun night."

Still crouched, Dawn replied slowly, "The only way you get it is when you have a gang to back you up, you piece of garbage." Stepping toward her, Dale then changed his mind, turned, and walked out the door.

Only when the room was empty did Dawn finally move toward her friend who was moaning and whimpering softly, eyes closed. Pulling her into her arms, she held her, stroking her hair. Watching the door and expecting more of the Winston brothers' friends to arrive, she said to Janice, "Jan, its Dawn. I am going to take you out of here now. Let's get your clothes on."

When Dawn got off of the bed to find her friend's clothes, Jan lurched the other way and threw up all over Bart Bainbridge's parents' bed. As she heaved, Dawn let her go while she gathered her clothes. Going into the master bathroom, she got a washcloth, ran cold water onto it, and came back in and helped Jan wash off her face. It took some time to coax her into her clothes since she was barely able to stand.

Tripper, Gordon, and Billy came charging in, almost running into the two girls standing by the door.

"Dawn, are you all right?" Tripper asked, looking at her as she struggled to keep Jan upright. "We heard what happened."

"I'm all right. Jan is another story. I don't know if she's drunk, stoned, or both, and I also don't know how many guys screwed her before I got here. Can one of you find her purse or anything else I might have missed?"

Gordon bounded to the side of the bed. "I've got her purse," he said, "and what I guess are her glasses." Billy looked under the bed and said, "I don't see anything else."

Tripper supported Jan's right side and, together, he and Dawn managed to get Jan out the door and down the hallway. Reaching the top of the stairway, Dawn noticed for the first time that the music had stopped. "What happened to the music?"

"When my father heard what happened, he shut his music down while we came upstairs. Lou went to get the van and should be somewhere near the front, I hope."

The stairway was still filled with teenagers, with a couple dozen milling around the foyer. Leading Jan out the front door, Dawn saw a larger group down by the pool, with Dale Winston standing with his arm around a tall brunette in a string bikini. Someone had set up a boom box by the cabana and music was blasting.

Dawn asked if anyone knew who Jan had come with to the party, and Gordon explained that had probably been Lois and Missy, her best friends. "I'll take a quick look around and see if they're here," he said. Jogging in the other direction, he disappeared.

Moving slowly down the front steps to the gravel driveway, Tripper pointed with his free hand up the driveway. "There's Lou." Stopping to wait for Lou's van to arrive, Dawn looked around at the groups of young people watching them.

"What is it with these people? It's like this is a normal occurrence," Dawn remarked. She noticed Tripper and Billy exchanging a glance between them.

"What are you doing? What's going on? Does this happen all the time here?"

"Take it easy, Dawn. Don't make a scene. We're almost out of here."

Stopping short, she pivoted and looked at Tripper. "What the hell are you telling me, 'Don't make a scene.' Are you kidding me? Maybe someone should be making *more* of a scene in this messed-up town! Tell me, goddamn it. Has this happened before?"

"It has happened at least five times that I can remember." Tripper looked down at his feet as he spoke.

Dawn could not speak. The bile in her throat blocked her ability to breathe. Focusing on Jan, she started toward the oncoming car. As Lou pulled up, Missy stumbled toward the van yelling, "Wait, ztop."

Everyone looked at her as she lurched to a stop in front of them.

"She's supposed tuh be stayin at mah houze tonight wiz Lose whose getting car. Will take care off hers."

Missy looked wrinkled, her normally starched clothes spotted and stained. Out of breath and scared, she spoke in quick bursts.

"I know what um dong."

As if on cue, Jan slumped forward and threw up on the driveway, inches from Lou's front bumper.

Dawn, stunned by what Missy was saying, took a moment to respond. Tripper and Lou looked at each other while Dawn finally spit out in slow, controlled words, "She has been raped. She needs to see a doctor. Her parents need to know."

As Dawn completed her statement, Lois pulled up next to Lou's van. Jumping out, she ran and put her arms around Jan. Missy helped her pull Jan away from Dawn, yelling, "Look what you did to her!"

Missy and Lois each took an arm of their friend and started to ease her toward the car. Dawn, stunned by the outburst, let Jan go and stood silently watching the actions of Jan's best friends.

Lou recovered first, stepping between the three girls and their car. "What the hell are you talking about? Jan was raped by Bart Bainbridge and Dale Winston and other guys after they got her drunk. Dawn stopped it from continuing and brought her down."

The response from Lois was immediate. "Dawn brought her down all right. She pushed Jan to talk about Drew Winston and the way things are done in this town, and she brought this attention onto Jan, who was just trying to be friendly. If she hadn't come here, this wouldn't have happened—guaranteed."

Lois got Jan into the back seat of her car while Missy took a long time to open the other rear door so that she could sit next to Jan. Then Lois slipped behind the wheel, put the car in drive, and took off slowly down the driveway.

Dawn, still stunned, stared after the car. Tripper walked over to her, put his arm on her shoulder, and said, "C'mon Dawn. Let's get out of here."

From the front seat, she turned to look back at the mansion, the last people she saw being Dale Winston and Bart Bainbridge, who were smiling and waving to them as they departed.

Seven

"ALL RIGHT, THERE'S her house. Let's see if she's home."

The members of Max Lunatic all walked up the stairs to Dawn's front door, with Tripper ringing the bell.

Dawn opened the door and asked, "Hey guys, what's going on?"

Tripper replied, "My father is doing Italian tonight, and we were wondering if you wanted to join us since your mom is out of town. You can have dinner, meet my parents, and then practice with us if you want. We all are in, like, total agreement, which is an extreme cosmic event, that we'd, like, really love you to sing a few songs with us at our next gig if you're into it. The way you sang, *The Revolution Starts Now* and *Don't Let the Bastard's Get You Down* at the bookstore the other night cemented it. You've got one hell of a voice and no doubt you know your music."

"How about I say yes to your dinner offer, and we'll talk about the singer part at rehearsal?"

"You got it. You need to get anything from your house?"

Grabbing her shoulder bag, she locked the door and followed her friends to the van, moving into the front seat next to Lou, as Tripper piled into the back with Billy and Gordon.

Lou, smiling, remarked, "Dawn, I'd just like you to know that I am doing a hell of a lot better, now that you're in the front seat instead of Tripper's sorry ass."

As Lou drove, each band member tried to make a larger case about how excited they were that she was there. When it became a hopeless babble, Dawn, laughing, yelled, "Enough! I feel appropriately honored. Now tell me, should I be really psyched for Tripper's father's Italian cuisine, or not?"

Gordon replied immediately, "Dawn, he is so into cooking, you have no idea. He can talk about a particular meal for an hour. Reminds me of how Melville wrote about clam chowder in Moby Dick, and I quote: *But when that smoking chowder came in, the mystery was delightfully explained. Oh! sweet friends, hearken to me. It was made of small juicy clams, scarcely bigger than hazel nuts, mixed with pounded ship biscuits and salted pork cut up into little flakes! the whole enriched with butter, and plentifully seasoned with*

40

pepper and salt…we dispatched it with great expedition.

Gordon continued, "Dawn, his dad knows how to do Italian, trust me. All those years on the road touring in a rock-and-roll band, combined with his heritage, created an ability to cook about half a dozen amazing Italian meals. Getting him to figure out how to put milk on cold cereal, on the other hand, is an impossible task."

Everyone agreed with Gordon's Johnny Cardone observations as they drove through quiet residential neighborhoods. "The other thing you need to know about the Cardone's," Lou said, "is that their home is a safe haven for a lot of kids in this town. We practically live there because we practice in their basement. There are other kids who show up a lot too cuz they know Tripper's parents will welcome them and be like mega-interested in what's happening in their lives. You don't find that kind of communication in a lot of families."

Lou pulled into a long driveway at the end of a tree-lined street. The large, old Cardone home stood warm and inviting to their left. As they walked toward the house, the front door was opened by a woman of average height with natural blonde hair falling loosely to her shoulders. A white cotton man's shirt hung down over faded jeans that covered worn sandals.

Coming down the front stairs to meet them, Melissa Cardone looked at Dawn and said, "So you're the young lady that's causing all the commotion, and none too soon for this macho enclave if you ask me. Dawn, I'm Melissa Cardone, den mother to this motley crew."

Melissa opened her arms, gave Dawn a strong hug and held her at arm's length while exclaiming, "Oh yeah, I understand why you are tying the men in this town into knots—attractive, sexy, smart, and strong."Turning toward the house with her arm around Dawn, she continued, "As you have probably found, the young women in this town, for the most part, don't have any spunk. They all defer to the young guys, who are mostly clueless." Turning to the boys following in her wake, she winked, "Present company excepted, of course."

Entering the front door, they heard Neil Young singing *Cowgirl in the Sand*. "That music is coming from our kitchen, where my husband, whom I understand you met briefly Friday night, is cooking the meal. Let me take you back to re-introduce you and let him know you're all here. Then we can sit down and wait for dinner to be ready."

They walked through a disheveled living room with stuffed furniture careening at odd angles, then moved into the library where there were books arranged the same way, some in precarious piles on one of three large desks. They pushed through double oak swinging doors and entered the huge old kitchen, where three large pots were bubbling on a massive stove and a mix of aromas embraced them.

Johnny Cardone, holding a large, round, crystal goblet half-filled with scarlet wine in one hand and a long wooden spoon in the other, was leaning over a pot, sampling the contents. His face lit up at the sight of his wife and Dawn, and he said softly, "Well, if that isn't a sight for a lover of women. Magnificent. Dawn, if my son or one of those reprobate band mates of his has not told you at least twenty times today that you are one stunning young woman, then let me be the first. A toast to you, young vision of beauty, and to my gorgeous bride standing there by your side."

Holding his glass to the light, he saluted his wife and her charge, draining the glass before putting it down on the counter by the sink.

"We didn't have much of a chance to talk this past Friday because of the horrid actions of Dale Winston and his posse. This evening we will have brilliant conversation and amazing food. Now be gone, both of you. You will distract me from creating another masterpiece."

As Johnny turned again toward the stove, Melissa led Dawn through the kitchen and into the backyard. Standing on the porch that wrapped around the entire house, they looked out onto an acre of land that became a forest surrounding the property on three sides.

Dawn caught her breath. "This is unbelievable. What a wonderful yard."

"Yes, the house could have been one room and we would have bought it because of that yard. The forest behind it is state land, so there will never be any development behind us. We have our quiet place where I can paint and write, and Johnny and Tripper can do their own writing and playing. We are lucky to have found such a space in this increasingly crowded commuter town."

"The boys will find their way back here before too long. Would you like to join me for a little red wine before dinner?"

"Yes, thank you."

Melissa went back inside, returning with a newly opened bottle. She pointed Dawn toward a group of stuffed yard-chairs to their left. "I love these chairs positioned this way at this time of day. They catch the sun as it falls behind the pines."

Sitting on one of the sofa chairs, she motioned for Dawn to sit in the seat next to hers as she poured a glass for each of them. Taking a slow sip, she sighed, and looking toward the setting sun, said softly, "We are artists, Johnny, Tripper, and I. We so need this space to create, uninterrupted by the fools that surround us."

"Is art important in Fair Shore? It seems like there are way too many galleries on Sir Francis Place for a town this size."

"Yes, art is very special here in Fair Shore. It is not necessarily art for art's sake, however. Much of it is purchased to show others how well-off you are. There is a well-known corporate bigwig who owns one of the largest homes in town. He paid an artist friend of mine a $50,000 retainer to teach him what he needed to know so he could sound well-informed about art. That kind of foolishness goes on all the time in this place. This town didn't used to be as bad as it is now. There has always been an elitist attitude in Fair Shore, but it's more hard-edged now, more combative and brazen.

"I grew up here, you see. Born and raised not five minutes from this house. Then I left for college, went on the road with Johnny after my first year, and came back to protect myself from the excesses of the music business. This space was for me. Back then Johnny couldn't have cared less. Now he doesn't know how we could have ever lived without it."

Dawn was drawn to the lilt in Melissa's soft voice. Sipping the wine, she felt herself relax in a way that she hadn't done since school had begun. Sensing this, Melissa asked, "Do you have a sanctuary, Dawn? Someplace you can go to be safe and centered?"

"Actually, I am very lucky. My relationship with my mother is very strong. Any time I'm with her I feel safe and I can relax. Also, my training in martial arts and yoga lets me get to that centered state pretty quickly, even if I'm not in a good physical space."

She looked around at the bucolic setting. "I don't have any physical space like this, though. This is amazing."

"You are welcome here any time, Dawn."

"Thanks, Mrs. Cardone. I appreciate that more than you know, I mean with all that is going on."

"Please call me Melissa. And I hope we see you in our home a lot. As it stands now, we host a big Sunday dinner once a month throughout the school year, so that as many of Tripper's friends as possible can come here for the afternoon and relax. We probably average forty or fifty young people for any given dinner. They are good people, Dawn, they really are. And they so want to be listened to and respected for what they think and do. It's a shame, really, that many of them feel they have to get out of their homes to receive that respect. Well, we love to have them and we get more back from them than we can ever give."

Sitting back, they both drank their wine and enjoyed the last rays of a beautiful fall day.

"All right, who wants more?" Johnny was standing at the head of the massive dining room table, brandishing a long-handled serving fork like a rapier. Hearing no reply, he exclaimed, "You heathens cannot possibly be thinking that you are done eating this amazing food. C'mon, c'mon, c'mon, pass your plates up here for more linguini. This meal has just started." When nobody moved, a pained look crossed his face as he implored Dawn, "Please, save my last small bit of dignity by having some more."

After it was obvious that Johnny was not going to convince anyone to eat another bite, everyone cleared the dishes and moved into the living room, where Johnny and Tripper led the whole group in singing, very unevenly, a number of rock-and-roll classics. Johnny then put his guitar down and, looking at Dawn, said, "You are our guest of honor here tonight and are also new to our town. What burning questions do you have for this august group?"

Dawn, though caught by surprise, didn't take long to answer. "When I had my first run-in with Drew Winston he referred to me as Number 37. What did he mean by calling me that number?"

"Goddamn him." Melissa blurted out the expletive before Dawn had finished her question. She walked to the kitchen door and back, before saying, "A very small percentage of football players have kept score of the number of Fair Shore High School girls they have screwed. A few years ago Joseph Bruschi wrote a few articles for the newspaper on the issue. His articles triggered the creation of sensitivity workshops for all the students in the school. They actually may have made things worse, as some of the girls who normally wouldn't have put up with that garbage decided to do it to rebel against their parents, and some guys who hadn't paid much attention decided to go along to try and be cool. Discussion of it had stopped recently. It's a very small group of popular athletes, and unfortunately their popularity bestows a mantle of legitimacy to their actions."

Johnny, leaning forward, said, "Somehow I don't think old Drew is going to be getting any Number 37 for a while."

Dawn waited for a moment for the laughter to subside before continuing, "Nothing much surprises me about this place. My next question is about what has been happening this week. It would be very helpful if someone would explain the meaning behind all the activities that are leading up to the first football game. What is such a big deal, that we have national network coverage of this craziness?"

Melissa looked over to Lou, "Lou is kind of the Fair Shore historian, since his family has lived here awhile. Want to take a stab at that question, Lou?"

"Every fall," he replied, "since the early 1800s, there has been a celebration in Fair Shore of our gifts. It was an acknowledgement by the residents, who felt that this town was a special place to live in, that it was better than larger towns up and down the coast. By the 1930s, that celebration began to be tied to our sports success, something that has been a tradition in Fair Shore since football, baseball, and our other sports have been introduced.

"Then about 1950 the large head that you see as you walk into the high school was sculpted by one of our alumni in the form of our mascot, The Beast; and then after that a more, like, official schedule of events was created. There's a lot of fanfare leading to our first game, and then there's a whole crapload of activity that builds up to homecoming weekend in late October and our football game with our archrival, Grand Shore. We've gotten national coverage for a lot of reasons, like being near to the media capital of the world and also that our town is pretty awesome when it comes to PR. The David-versus-Goliath trait we have is like a huge plus, cuz we are usually a much smaller school, I mean in respect to student population than the teams we usually beat. Like, Grand Shore has eight times our student population. Those are the historical facts that I know. Does that help?"

"A little I guess. This celebration seems to be mostly about male athletics, is that right?"

"Yes, it is," Melissa answered. "Although equality for female athletics is now a legal reality in this country due to the 1972 Title IX legislation, they don't get the same attention in Fair Shore as the male athletics. The glory lies with the guys, as you have seen."

Warming to the discussion, Dawn continued, "And how do the women in the town react to this? Have they ever tried to create more balance? "

"Sorry to say, but what you saw on Friday night is like the norm in this town. Girls, who try to change the status quo, if they're lucky, will only get shut out of the dating scene. But if they're not lucky – whoa – they can get punished in a lot of different ways. What happened to Jan is not a first."

Dawn sat back on the sofa, mumbling under her breath. Billy looked at his watch, motioning to Lou that he had to be getting home since it had gotten too late to practice.

As they started to move, Dawn sat up. "Hang on just a minute. I've got one more question. How about if we come up with an alternative event on homecoming weekend—one that celebrates inclusion, diversity, a social conscience, the success of girls and guys—in *all* that we do, not just athletics? And we could use music as one of the draws; like we could focus on the music of people who have literally tried to change our world. Hey, I got it," she shouted, growing more excited. "We could focus on the socially conscious musicians that Richard Phillips is focusing on in his senior symposium class. You guys could play, we could get other good groups, and we'd shine a light on something other than self-centered male athletes. Whatdya think?"

Melissa verbalized her support immediately, Johnny said that he should be able to recruit some musicians, and Gordon stood up and said, "I am with the activist and music executive Danny Goldberg on this one. He said in his book, *Dispatches from the Culture Wars: How the Left Lost Teen Spirit*, "I discovered that music could mirror my feelings and magically make me feel more powerful and less alone." So if this event can make women or anyone else that feels alone in this town more powerful, you can count me in. Anything that makes those idiots see that they are not *all that*, will get my support."

Billy mumbled, "If you get to the point where you need me to, uh, create spreadsheets or organize all the, um, moving parts that this event might need, just let me know; I'm pretty good with that kind of stuff."

Dawn got up, saying, "I'm going to think this whole thing over and get back to you all really quickly."

"Dawn, I am home all afternoon tomorrow," said Melissa. "Give me a call and I'll help you flesh this out."

"I'll definitely do that."

"Thanks for the ride, guys, and for an awesome evening. You were right. Tripper's dad knows how to cook. And I am psyched at the thought of singing a couple of songs with all of you in three weeks. That will be fun. See you in school tomorrow."

Eight

"MAY I HELP you?" The white-haired woman sitting at the desk outside the mayor's office was forceful and direct in asking her question.

"Yes, I am new to town and was wondering if there is a press kit or some kind of schedule of activities relating to all the celebrating that leads up to homecoming weekend."

"Yes, Ms. Mortenson, we have a department that coordinates our Fall Celebration activities. It is down at the end of the hall to your left."

"Thank you. And how did you know my name?"

"I read the paper and watch television, dear. It was not the most difficult deduction I will make today."

Dawn picked up the packet of information outlining all that the town was doing. Putting it into her backpack, she walked across the street to the Fair Shore Public Library, where she spent an hour and a half researching Fair Shore's history from both her laptop and the local publications in the library that weren't online.

At five-thirty she went two blocks up the main street in town, into the office of the local newspaper, *The Fair Shore Quill*.

"Hi, is Joseph Bruschi here?"

"He is out covering a story. I expect him back in a few minutes. Can I help you with something?"

"Thanks for the offer, but I'll wait. I need a few minutes with him, if he can spare them, when he gets back."

"No problem."

Dawn stood for a moment looking around the newspaper's main working area. Cubicles with computers filled the space, and small offices lined two of the four walls. A glass-enclosed case to the right of where she was standing caught her attention, since it looked like an athletic department's trophy case.

Walking to it, she was surprised to find dozens of plaques, trophies, laminated newspaper covers and testimonials to the successful reporting of *The Quill*. She picked up a pamphlet entitled, "The Proud History of *The Fair Shore Quill*," and stood reading, so caught up in the story that she started when a dark-complexioned man of her own height stated her name.

"Dawn, I understand you were looking for me. I'm Joseph Bruschi." Extending a hand, he asked, "Should we go to a conference room where there is privacy, or do you only have a quick question?"

When she hesitated, he said, "I prefer conference rooms myself. Why don't we walk over to that corner by the large plant?" Motioning to a door twenty feet from where they stood, he stepped ahead of her, opened the door, and let her in.

"Would you like some coffee or a soda or water? I think that's probably the full array of choices."

Smiling, Dawn said, "No, thank you. I realize you're busy and I don't want to take up too much of your time."

"Actually, my deadline is not imminent and I have a good handle on my story. Please take your time and tell me what's on your mind."

"I just spent the last few hours in the library reading about Fair Shore, trying to understand what I've walked into. When I read your articles, I got the feeling that you were a straight shooter who isn't bound by the powers that be. Actually, the feeling was that you kind of pride yourself on being an outsider. Did I get that right? "Yes, I'd say so, partly because I am not from here, and partly because I have always seen myself as an outsider, wherever I've been. It's kind of my personal and professional identity. My first job out of college was at *Rolling Stone*, which helped to create that kind of attitude."

"All right, that's good. Then can I talk with you off the record and be sure that it stays that way?"

"Yes, I can assure you that anything we discuss today will not be repeated to anyone else, unless you are talking about harming yourself, others, or destroying public property. Then I am obligated by law to act on that information. I cannot, however, guarantee that, if you mention something that could be an important story, I wouldn't follow my instincts about that piece of information, again, while ensuring that you would not be mentioned as a source."

Frustrated with his answer, Dawn got up and walked to the one window in the room. She took a couple of slow breaths while gathering her thoughts.

"Dawn, you have to understand something. I am the last person in this town who wants to create any more trouble for you than you've already created for yourself. I applaud the guts you've shown in confronting the athletes that dominate the scene here. I really do. I also know that you have created a ton of trouble for yourself, and quite honestly, I'm not surprised you're here. If you have questions that I can answer—that will help you to help yourself—then I encourage you to ask them. The choice between siding with the predatory Winston brothers and their town full of admirers; or with you, the members of Max Lunatic, and their small circle of friends, is a no-brainer. Besides, I usually go with the underdog—and you are outnumbered big time in this town."

Joseph leaned back in his chair, waiting for Dawn to make her decision. Turning to look at him, she said, "I need help with what I have learned about how young women are treated here. Within forty-eight hours of my arrival in school, I was given a number—Number 37—by Drew Winston, and I was told later that this number meant I would be the 37th student that he would have slept with. I was also told that the guys here publicize the number of girls they've slept with, and that when the guys talk to each other, those numbers are understood to be one of the ways that girls are talked about here – by their damn number. And then Jan Ostraczyk was gang raped at the Bainbridge party this past Friday, and I found out that this kind of thing goes on all the time in this town, and is not challenged or written about, apparently.

"So please help me understand what…the…hell…is…going …on…in…this…goddamn…town?"

Dawn collapsed into the nearest chair after asking her question.

Now it was Joseph's turn to get out of his seat and stand at the window. Talking with his back to Dawn, he began quietly, "This is going to take a few minutes."

Dawn did not reply; she stared at him instead, with a fevered intensity.

Joseph turned to look at the inquisitive student. "You have hit on a very sore subject for me, one that I have turned over in my mind for years. On a base level I have chosen not to write about this stuff in the depth that is necessary, because I would lose my job. I almost had lost my job when I had written about this topic a number of years ago. It is that simple. My boss, the publisher of the paper, is one of the staunchest supporters of the way things are here, and he would reject any article that I were to write on this subject, and I'm convinced that he would tell me to leave. I love it here and don't want to go. Nor can I financially afford to have that happen. He pays very well."

He paused to drink from the soda he had brought with him into the room, self-consciously twirling the hair on the back of his neck with his free hand.

"There is a very sophisticated structure in place in Fair Shore that supports the way things are. Think of Fair Shore as a corporation. Corporations spend massive amounts of money on creating an identity in the larger world and on products or services that support that identity, or, as some would call it, the town's brand. This identity could be as an international financial services leader or as a producer of products that make good things happen for individuals. The happiness of everyone in that corporation is based on how well-received the product is, and how much the consumers believe in the corporate identity. If the products are well-received and the image is respected, then more products are bought and everyone in the company benefits.

"OK, let's apply this to Fair Shore. The Fair Shore identity is that of a place where successful people live, are developed, and are sent out into the world. A number of products support that image—amazing houses, clean beaches, and a small and upscale town proper. The most visible product, and the one upon which the whole corporate infrastructure depends, is the male Fair Shore scholar athlete. The message for years has been clear: If you move to Fair Shore and pay a lot of money for a home here, your children will be successful—as epitomized by the male athletes who gain national attention and go on to star in the professional sports leagues. Fair Shore has graduated more guys who have played professional sports than in any comparable town and in many major cities."

Stopping to sip his soda, Joseph was glad to see that he was keeping Dawn engaged.

"So, a massive public-relations and advertising strategy has been created around this image of success, and everyone in town benefits from it. Our last two mayors have been executives from major PR firms, for Chrissake. Our property values are the best of any town in this very affluent state. Fair Shore generates more positive publicity than the rest of the towns in this county combined. Colleges and universities want to attract our students, and major employers want to hire them. We generate college scholarships for a broad group of students. We have corporate internships during high school for any student who is interested. And we generate more money from the sale of sports-related clothing and paraphernalia than some of the professional teams.

"Everybody is seen as winning, male and female alike. It is a great American success story. Fair Shore residents have paid top dollar to join this winning team and are disinclined to raise any questions about the unsavory practices that support its continuation." Catching himself lecturing, Joseph explained, "I'm sorry Dawn, this is obviously a topic I have given a lot of thought to and I guess I got on my soapbox about it. Did I help you with your question?"

"So, when a girl is raped, it's not reported or dealt with by the authorities because nobody wants to disturb this money-making machine? Is that what you're saying?" Dawn flushed and, clenching her fists, turned to hear what the reporter had to say.

"It's not that simple. There is also a feeling, which is certainly not exclusive to Fair Shore, that boys will be boys. There are usually…"

50

Dawn exploded from her seat. "And you choose to support this? You choose to do nothing so you can stay part of the family? Goddamn you. Goddamn all of you." Grabbing her backpack from the floor, she turned toward the reporter. Lowering her voice and speaking in measured tones, she said, "Let's only hope, Mr. Bruschi, that the success of this 'everybody-wins' model spreads to towns all across America. Let's only hope that within a few years, tens of thousands of young women are raped without comment so 'boys can be boys.' Congratulations, Mr. Bruschi. You are doing a totally amazing job of creating your legacy."

As she turned and headed toward the only door in the conference room, Joseph moved quickly to stop her. "Dawn, don't leave. Let's talk further. Maybe I can help."

"Go to hell. I thought there was hope with you because of some of the writing you've done. That series you did on the woman who overcame serious car injuries and went back to being an engineer after everybody said she would never work again was powerful. I saw some passion in that one."

"She is a remarkably brave young lady."

"And there are a lot of them out there, but your silence is ensuring that they will have to fight that much harder to create the stories they were born to tell."

Before he could reply, she had stormed out of the conference room, down the hallway, and into the street. Staying where he was, he took out his notepad and wrote feverishly for a few minutes before hurrying to his office. He closed the door so nobody could hear him and dialed a number he knew by heart.

As soon as Dawn arrived home the phone rang. It was Melissa Cardone.

"Hello, there. I have some great news. I have a hold on the Adams Amphitheater at the edge of town for whatever concert we might want to do homecoming week-end. It's a natural outdoor setting where they have fitted in seats and lighting. It stretches out into a field and can accommodate thousands. It's perfect. Johnny and I also made some calls to musician friends we know and have the possibility of pulling together at least two very popular Connecticut groups who might be able to make that Saturday. We might even be able to get an A-list singer-songwriter to come, and she would definitely draw a large crowd.

"In addition, there is an acting troupe that has a great reputation around here who would perform for free because of the concept, and I know another group of performers who juggle and do trampoline. They're terrific and would draw parents and kids. There is also a very wealthy woman who owns one of the largest catering companies in the country. She is so excited about the concept that she will donate enough food for a couple thousand people. I've got a bunch of other calls out, but that's all that's firm at this time."

Dawn found herself getting increasingly excited as Melissa talked. When Melissa had finished, Dawn said, "Damn, Melissa, I feel like a slacker here. You really have been making progress."

"Well, I got taken over by your vision and ran with it. That kind of activity is just what this town needs to shake it out of the bad place it's in. I will have a complete idea of what we have by this weekend. How about if we get together at my place on Sunday for a full-blown planning session?"

"That works for me. My mom will be back by then and you'll get a chance to meet her."

"Terrific. And just to make sure I haven't gotten ahead of myself, I am looking at this being an all-day Saturday kind of a celebration. That's what you were thinking, right?"

"If you think we can fill that time with activities that will pull attention away from the homecoming football game and the party afterward, then that is exactly what I meant."

"Oh, don't you worry, Dawn. We're going to focus some attention on the crap that goes down in this town. I have one other detail to mention. I've asked everyone to keep this quiet until we finalize our plans. Didn't want to give those who will oppose this too much warning. I encourage you to do the same with the folks you approach."

Dawn hesitated before saying, "That makes sense."

"Good, then I'll see you at our place for lunch around noon, and we'll have as much of the rest of the day as we need to push this forward. I plan to invite some others that we can trust."

"Awesome, and how about inviting Billy since he volunteered and is apparently this big-time computer whiz?"

"I had him on my list."

"Cool, my mother and I will see you then. And thanks."

Nine

"YOU'VE GOT A nice shot."

Dawn, startled, dribbled the basketball off her foot and toward the short blonde woman who had made the comment. Dawn had sought out the solitude of the gym to work off some of her tension.

The stranger picked up the ball, dribbled to her left and took a 25-foot shot that fell noiselessly through the net.

Dawn smiled. "You're not so bad yourself." Moving to close the gap between them, Dawn extended her hand, introducing herself as they shook.

"I'm Pat Roberts, the woman's field hockey, basketball, and softball coach here at Fair Shore High. And I definitely know who you are."

Dawn grimaced at the remark. "I'm hearing a lot of that lately."

"Dawn, believe me, that is a good thing. I graduated from this place ten years ago and nothing has changed. Now that I am all of a couple of months into my job here, I hope to make some changes in how female athletics are seen. What you represent is definitely needed here."

Pat sensed Dawn's reluctance to talk. "Want to go one-on-one?"

For the next half hour the coach and the student went full force at each other, pushing and elbowing and fighting for every advantage. Pat Roberts, an All-Conference guard in college, had the quickness and ball-handling ability, whereas Dawn had the height and strength.

With both sweating freely, Pat finally said, "I'd say that was a draw. I have a team to go coach. Want some water?"

Pausing to catch her breath, Dawn readily agreed, following the coach into one of the corridors off of the gym. They took their cups into Pat's office. "Have a seat for a minute and cool off," she said, "while I try to do the same before going to the field. You pushed me harder than anyone has in a while."

As they drank their water and toweled off, Pat looked at Dawn. "What's your organized sports experience?"

"I played all three that you coach, as well as track and field, when I had a run-in with my softball coach at my former school."

"How did you do in each sport?"

"I started as a freshman in all three, and was captain of each that I played my sophomore and junior years. I love sports and have had good teachers."

Smiling, Pat said, "It's not just the love and coaching, Dawn. You're obviously very strong and coordinated, and, I would surmise, not one who takes too well to losing."

Dawn returned her smile. "You're right, coach, on all of the above; and I have to be honest with you, I am really sick of talking about myself."

"Then I will ask you one more question. My goal, and the only reason I came back to this place, is to bring the women's sports program to the same level as the guys'. If you played for me, you could help me make that happen this year. You interested in considering that?"

Dawn contemplated the question. "I need to think that one through. I am going to be very involved in a few activities and don't want to get distracted from them. Let me think about it and I will come by tomorrow and give you my answer."

"I couldn't ask for more; and I have to run. I am here after class. Field-hockey practice starts at four o'clock, which is where I am heading now. Stop by anytime and let me know your answer."

As the coach gathered her things, Dawn looked at the one small plaque on a shelf behind the desk, hesitated and then asked, "Can you use a goalie?"

As a huge grin covered her face, Pat responded, "The two-year starter graduated, so that position is up for grabs."

She reached for a gym bag and moved over to Dawn. "Let's get your uniform and equipment, and I'll introduce you to your new teammates. They are a good group—a little short on the talent side, but willing to bust their humps to do well. I think you'll like them."

Pat Roberts disappeared down the hall. Dawn looked around the office, threw her empty cup into a wastebasket, and sprinted after Coach Roberts.

Dawn's entry onto the girls' field-hockey team at Fair Shore High— after her meeting on the basketball court with Coach Roberts—had been almost as eventful as her first two days of school. Three of the girls who dated football players, along with Jan Ostrazyck's friend Missy Hinthrop, had gotten up to walk out when Coach Roberts introduced her to the team. The coach moved quickly to block them, saying, "I'd hate to lose the four of you; it would be a big blow to our chances to win the conference title this year. It would also be an act of betrayal to your friends and teammates who have supported you all through your problems and difficulties over the years.

"I do want to be very clear, however, regarding what you are thinking of doing. If you walk out that door, you will have chosen to quit the team and will under no circumstances be allowed to return. The only way we can win as a team is to work out any differences we have among ourselves and not run away from them. Dawn has been asked to try out for this team because she was a three-year field-hockey starter at her former school and was the captain during her sophomore and junior years. She knows how to play. I hope you decide to see whether she helps us, as our teammate—and not from the stands." Three of the four decided to stay, but Missy left quietly when the coach had finished.

After warm-up drills, Dawn was put into goal for the red team and stopped every shot that came her way during a full-length game simulation scrimmage. Determined to show her new teammates that she belonged, she was so focused that every ball shot at her seemed the size of a grapefruit and she stopped it with seeming ease. When the scrimmage ended, she self-consciously stayed on the fringe of the players who huddled around Coach Roberts, until Ernestine, who was in three of her other classes, pulled her over to stand beside her, at their coach's right side.

Practices since that day had gone well. Dawn excelled in goal, and the entire team came together in a way that generated excitement that had never before existed in a Fair Shore girls' field-hockey team. Most of the girls on the team had befriended Dawn, with the exception of Brittany Swanson and the others who had intimate contact with the football team.

Dawn was particularly aggressive on the field four days before the team's first game. Noticing the shift in her style, Coach Roberts took her aside and asked if everything was all right. In reply, Dawn asked if she could see her after practice.

"What's on your mind, Dawn? You were working real hard to get rid of some kind of demon out there, kind of like when I first met you on the basketball court."

"I'm having a real problem with a lot of the things that are going on in this town. But a major one is that the football team has this huge town-wide celebration leading up to their homecoming weekend pep-rally and homecoming game and dance, but the girls don't have anything. So the question that I have for you is this: What is keeping us from getting up on stage with the football players at the pep rally? Why don't we make the case that we deserve as much attention as they do, and then take it?"

Her coach listened quietly to what Dawn had to say, getting up from behind her desk when she was done. "That's a good question and it's actually one I have been pondering as well, having decided to wait until next year to bring it up, after we have a few women's championship banners hanging in the gym. But now that you have raised it in the way you have, I don't see any reason why I can't try and make that happen. It is going to take some maneuvering, and I have some leverage I am going to need to use; but as soon as I know anything I will let you know. It could be a couple weeks.

Dawn, stunned with the quick and positive reaction to her suggestion, got up slowly to shake her coach's hand. "Thanks for listening, Coach. I really appreciate it."

"Not a problem, Dawn."

When Erica Mortenson arrived home that evening, her daughter grabbed her and spun her completely around. Laughing at Dawn's enthusiasm, she asked, "What is going on with you? Is this more of what you told me about on the phone, about the homecoming weekend?"

"Mother, you wouldn't believe how quickly we've moved on this. Actually, it isn't we; it's really Tripper Cardone's mother, Melissa. And the girls' field-hockey team coach is way cool. You would love her."

"I want to hear every word. Talk to me while I change out of my business clothes and tell me all that's happening. I also wanted you to know that we have both been invited by one of my clients to a large party tomorrow, the last big Saturday afternoon party before the football season starts. He thinks it would be a good place for you and me to get to know some of the important folks in town. Do you have any plans for tomorrow?"

"No, I don't. I've got to tell you, though; I'm kind of not enthused about meeting any townspeople right now, with emotions running so high about Drew Winston. Who is going to be there? Can we be sure that people are not going to get on our case?"

"Ronald and Renee Jeffers are decent people. They are a little full of themselves, maybe, but nice people. He particularly said that it would be good for people to meet us so they can see that we don't have two heads. I think it will be fine. If not, we leave."

"All right, I will make sure to wedge that date into my full social calendar."

Laughing, mother and daughter walked together up the stairs to Erica's bedroom, talking animatedly.

Ten

AS ERICA AND Dawn waited in the line of five cars for the valet attendants to come park their car, they watched the guests ahead of them exit their cars and go into the Jeffers' home. Although the invitation had said a casual lawn party, the guests were dressed anything but casual.

"Other than the host and hostess, will you know anyone else here?"

"Probably not too many, and that will make it more interesting. Are you nervous, honey? That's the third time you've asked about the guests."

"Like I said yesterday, after the reaction of the town to the incident, I am gun shy, yes. Part of me wants to just disappear for a while."

"I understand—which is why I appreciate your accompanying me. It helps me, and it shows the town that we have nothing to hide. All right, here we are."

As Dawn and her mother got out of their car and headed through the front door, a short, dark-haired woman in a white silk pantsuit approached them.

"Hello there, you two. Dawn and Erica, I'm Renee Jeffers." Renee guided Dawn and her mother through the foyer of the Tudor estate in the posh Eagle's Nest section of Fair Shore. They were immediately assaulted by the noise of more than a hundred guests.

Erica remarked to Renee, "This must be the hottest ticket in town from the sound of things."

Renee leaned close to Erica and whispered, "Well, it would be a lot quieter if Johnny Cardone wasn't here. But what do you expect from a rock-and-roll drug addict? I never would have invited him but my husband insisted that it would be cool to have him, even though he doesn't fit into our circle."

Wanting to get onto safer ground, Erica exclaimed, "Your home is amazing. Did you do the decorating yourself?"

"I came up with the concept, and then Sergio made it happen. He is so exquisite. He has decorated all seven of the estates in The Hills since I recommended him to Tish Bainbridge. Dawn, dear, there are some young people in the backyard. Johnny Cardone's son is one of them. I understand you are friends. He seems like a very nice boy, although I don't see how he has a chance of surviving with a name like Tripper. There are some other young people we invited who are surrounding my son. Have you and Whitney had a chance to meet in school?"

"No, we haven't met. And I'm fine right now. I'm sure I'll …"

"Yo, Rich baby, what's shakin', man?" Cut off in mid-sentence by Johnny Cardone's bellow, Dawn looked in the direction of the noise. Johnny was hugging Richard Phillips with one large arm.

Johnny was ready to continue when Richard asked, "Where's the better half, man?"

"I don't know where she went. Wait, there she is, over by the bar." Johnny pushed Richard toward his wife while he stood still and scanned the room.

"How are you doing, gorgeous?" Melissa looked up at Richard, smiled, and quickly took his arm. "I'm fine, and we have to find a seat; I've been standing since we got here."

Melissa maneuvered Richard over to a love seat in a corner of the crowded living room. She did it calmly and with authority, much the same way she maneuvered her husband through his tumultuous life.

Melissa said, "It's good to find a voice of sanity in this place. Johnny and Renee are already at it. He wasn't here five minutes before he made some crack about her designer Sergio and the "in" color of the month. Jesus, he knows how to get to people, doesn't he?"

"Of course he does, which is one reason that you married him. The great mediator needed someone to keep herself in practice by mending the fences he knocked down. Poor metaphor, but you get my point."

Melissa acknowledged his compliment with a nod while looking toward where her husband was embroiled in an animated discussion with a knot of people.

Richard watched her closely, something many men had done over the years. Her long, straight blonde hair; bleached Scandinavian complexion and riveting blue eyes led many to believe that she was a model. She had, in fact, been a part-time model before she met Johnny Cardone, rock-and-roll legend, when they were both nineteen.

"You look tired, Melissa."

"Yeah, I'm beat," she responded, while continuing to watch her husband. "Johnny has been particularly wired lately, with all the Mortenson hoopla."

"So, Rich, you finally stole her from her ingrate husband. Congratulations."

"Hi, Joseph, it's good to see you." Melissa and Richard greeted the reporter at the same time, both with big smiles and both reaching to hug him, which led to everyone's bumping into one another.

"Hey, hey, hey, let's get this right. I mean, we're not the most coordinated crew here, but at least we can do a three-way greeting without killing ourselves, can't we? There, that's better. Anybody hurt, anybody bleeding?"

As the three friends disengaged, smiling as they did, Joseph's brow furrowed, and, looking at Melissa, he asked, "You OK?"

"What is it with you guys? Can't I lose a little sleep for a couple of nights without everyone thinking I'm on my deathbed?" Melissa got up and took off toward the bathroom, leaving Joseph looking puzzled in her wake.

"What the hell is going on, Rich? It's not like I told her she looks like a piece of crap."

Richard and Joseph had known each other since getting their Master's degrees together at Columbia in the late sixties—Richard's in Counseling and Joseph's in Journalism.

"I'm not sure, man. Johnny has been wired lately, and she has missed some sleep. To top it all off, you and I both asked her how she was *really* doing within sixty seconds of each other, which put her over the edge. So the lesson in all this is quit asking people how they *really* are and just say, 'How ya doin?' while walking by without breaking stride. I mean, it works for most in this room."

At that moment everyone in the room heard Johnny Cardone yell at Ronald Jeffers while pointing his finger in his face. "You wouldn't know what passion is if it bit you in the ass. Your life is controlled by the interior decorator color of the month. What was the most recent thing you talked about, Ronnie, that didn't relate to a possession? The bumper sticker on your Jaguar says it all: HE WHO DIES WITH THE MOST STUFF WINS."

Catching his breath for just a moment, Johnny continued, "You told me once that you risked your future by joining the protesters who shut your college down. You said you agonized, then acted. That was passion—not talking while you drink a crystal glass of Chivas about which of Steve Turner's sculptures you're going to invest in next month. You're the poster boy for all the yuppie swine in this room."

Johnny straightened as he moved to the left toward the sliding glass doors leading to the sun deck. Nobody stopped him. When conversation in the room began to pick up, Melissa emerged from the bathroom and almost ran into Dawn standing next to her mother. "Hi, Dawn, how are you? Is this Erica?" Dawn and Erica hesitated before answering, both still reeling from Johnny's outburst.

"Yes. Melissa Cardone, this is my mother Erica. But more importantly, Melissa, Johnny just yelled at…"

"Where the hell were you when your barbarian husband screamed at Ronnie?"

Renee's scarlet face was inches from Melissa's as she struggled to control her rage. Pushing past Melissa, she reached her husband who was getting another drink.

"What happened?" Melissa asked the Mortensons. Erica responded first.

"I'm surprised you didn't hear anything. Johnny laid into Ronnie and then stormed out the sliding doors into the backyard."

"Unfortunately, I am not surprised by his getting on his soap box. This kind of self-congratulatory yuppie gathering drives him straight up a wall." Melissa excused herself and went out the same door Johnny had exited, looking for her wayward soul mate.

The house continued to fill with a mix of Renee's and Ronald's friends from town and co-workers from their investment bank and law firm. Johnny's outburst was soon old news as he remained outside and away from most of the guests.

Staying close to her mother, Dawn was pleasantly surprised that she hadn't yet been accosted by anybody. She introduced Erica to Joseph Bruschi, explaining how he had helped her in her research of Fair Shore. Richard came over to join the discussion, and the four took over a corner away from the noisy center of the room. Dawn chatted with the other three for a few minutes and then wandered outside to look for Tripper.

"EXCUSE ME." The large room full of adults turned as one, and looked again at Johnny Cardone, standing next to Renee Jeffers and holding in his extended left hand an object that most could not make out.

"I have been hearing from different guests here that I shouldn't have insulted the host as I did a few minutes ago. So I have come with a peace offering that I know you both can appreciate. Here is a check for $5,000 to buy something nice to spruce up your home."

Johnny brought his hand down to give the check to Renee, who said, so all could hear, "Thank you, Johnny, but I wouldn't consider taking your money."

Her husband, standing next to her, turned slowly as he sensed what she was going to say, and pulled the check from Johnny's outstretched hand. Renee looked at him and then at Johnny, threw her hands in the air, and moved toward the bar. Smiling as he watched both hosts retreat, Johnny said, "Nice job, Ronnie. Looks like you've had a lot of practice grabbing other people's money."

Pausing for a moment to scan the room, he continued, "I have only two more things to say and I will let you all go back to your wheeling and dealing. First, a few of you have asked me what I meant earlier by the term 'yuppie swine.' Yuppie swine are individuals whose primary focus in life is on their own comfort and impressing as many people as possible with the purchase of expensive things they don't need. Another way to put it is that yuppie swine are self-centered, shallow, image-conscious and materialistic.

"Having answered that question, I would like to make a toast." Reaching down and picking up the bottle of beer that had miraculously stayed standing at his feet, he shouted, "Here's to conspicuous consumption—and the plundering of our children's world." Turning slowly, he exited once again into the backyard.

The room was slower to jump back into the party than after Johnny's last pronouncement, a fact that Renee noticed immediately. Coming over to Erica, Richard, and Joseph, she declared, "All right, enough talking among yourselves. I need you to mix with the others and distract them from Johnny's antics." Taking Richard firmly by the left arm, she pulled him with her toward the larger crowd. Turning back, she yelled, "Now move it, goddamn it."

Erica looked at Joseph and said, "We've been commanded. Shall we mix and mingle?" She offered her arm to the reporter, and the two replenished their drinks at the bar before wading into the gathering.

Within minutes of walking into the crowd, she was separated from Joseph and pulled over by a short, well-built woman with severe, darkened eyes and five-inch heels. "I have been admiring your pin. I have a Delacroix that I paid $7,500 for that looks just like it. Did you get that at his gallery on Fifth Avenue?"

"No, actually, my daughter made it in jewelry class in eighth grade." Smiling a stunning exclamation point to her answer, Erica moved toward the door to the backyard.

"Well, Whitney, I've got to give it to your parents. They are putting on one hell of a bash," Tripper finished his beer after complimenting the only child of Ronald and Renee Jeffers. Every young person at the party was sitting either on a lawn chair or on the grass in the farthest corner of the Jeffers' expansive backyard. Two coolers of beer and soda had been brought down by the staff at Renee's command. Tripper and Whitney sat in a circle with Dawn, Lou, Eric Regis from the baseball team, Jason Levy a neighbor, and Ernestine O'Malley from the field-hockey team.

"Thank you. They've planned this event for months. It's very important to them both, and they want everyone to be impressed—I mean—to enjoy themselves." Whitney, not used to being the center of attention, blushed at what he had said, and the fact that he had to say it at all. Sipping self-consciously from his soda, he laid back in a stuffed lawn chair.

Dawn leaned forward, saying, "This town seems to do a lot of really big parties. I mean the Bainbridge's and now this. Does this go on throughout the year?"

Eric stood to get another soda, his large muscles straining against the blue blazer that he was wearing over a pale-blue silk shirt, unbuttoned to the middle of his chest. "In case you haven't noticed, Dawn, there is a ton of money in this town. Add to that the fact that there are a lot of very nice estates that the adults in this town want to show off, and you end up having a lot of parties."

"The need to show off is, like, totally one of the key drivers of what goes on in this town," Ernestine remarked as she stood up from where she had been kneeling on the ground and swung her arm in an arc to take in all the party attendees. "Like I mean, look at these people. Look at how they're dressed. Did you see Mrs. Whitlock? Like she must be wearing half a million dollars of jewels for a casual party. What the hell would she be wearing if this was a formal? And did you see the cars that are being parked down the street? Or that are in the school parking lot each morning? I bet you didn't know that Fair Shore can lay claim to having both the largest BMW and largest Mercedes dealerships in New England. In the same damn town! And then the pressure to look impressive carries down to the kids. It's, like, no wonder so many of us are screwed up. I know a dozen girls in this town who have been hospitalized with anorexia. Three of my best friends are addicted to diet pills.

"And what about the percentage of Fair Shore kids who go to private schools? I mean, Fair Shore High attracts smart kids. How many editorials in the newspaper talk about our town taxes being astronomical, but that's OK because look how well our students do? But we all have very close friends who are off at boarding school, prep school, whatever you want to call it. Which raises the question, Whitney, what are *you* doing here? I thought you were at Groton?"

Caught off guard, Whitney was completely incapable of speaking. As Ernestine rocked back and forth in anticipation of his answer, he mumbled, "My parents thought it would be best for me to come back to Fair Shore High for my last two years."

"Yeah, look at this dump," Ernestine said. "They must not be able to pay boarding school tuition, room, and board." Expecting an incredulous laugh from her host, she was surprised when he blushed and got up from his chair saying, "I need to go to the bathroom."

As he walked toward the house, Ernestine said, "Cool, now I get the comfortable seat," and settled into Whitney's chair.

Dawn, not exactly clear as to what had just happened, asked, "Hey, what's going on here? Are the Jeffers hurting for cash?"

"Let's just say that they are a little overextended. This party was as much to encourage investors in Mr. Jeffers' firm as it was to entertain their friends and neighbors," Jason replied. "My parents are clients of Mr. J's firm and know it's not doing well. And to answer your question from before, Dawn, this won't be the last party this year by any stretch that is hosted to shore up overextended Fair Shore residents."

"So, Gene, do you honestly want to know why I ranted inside about yuppie swine, or are you jerking my chain?" Johnny moved to within a couple of feet of Gene Hibbard, an investment banker with one of the major Wall Street firms. An avid record collector, Gene had frequented Johnny's store for years, where the two had become friends while chatting as Gene bought records, tapes, and CDs.

"Yes, I'd like to sit here and get a real idea of why you are so out of control about what you are calling yuppie swine. We've got our beers, it's a gorgeous day, and I'd really like to understand."

As Johnny sat down he looked to his left and moaned, "Oh goody, here comes a duo for the ages."

Gene looked up to see Bernard and Samuel Cassidy, third-generation owners of one of the largest law firms in Fair Shore, striding aggressively toward them. "Jesus, Gene," Bernard shouted, "You trying to convince the rock-and-roll has-been to take you out of his yuppie-swine category?"

Johnny stayed seated while Gene got up to greet his long-time business acquaintances. "No, Bernard, I'm just catching up with a friend."

"So my question to your friend is: did he brainwash his son to talk his drivel? Because he's over there in heavy conversation with the young people who are here, and I wouldn't want to think he's wasting their time in the same way that his father did earlier. Life's too short to listen to that kind of garbage."

Bernard finished his Scotch and dropped his glass to the ground. Johnny smiled, saying, "Did I hit a nerve, Bernie old friend? Did one or all of the phrases 'self-centered, shallow, image conscious and materialistic' apply to you?" Struggling up from his chair, Johnny waited for a lunge that didn't come.

"Don't waste your time with him, Bernard," Samuel said. "C'mon, let's get another drink." Taking his brother by the arm, Samuel attempted to steer him toward the house. Stiffening, Bernard stopped, looked at Johnny and said, "It's not so much you that's the problem. It's the fact that you couch your crap around a concern about our children when you obviously didn't care enough about your son or he wouldn't have had all the drug problems that he had. The fact that he could be encouraging our children to do the drugs he is obviously so fond of makes me…"

Johnny bellowed and lunged toward the attorney. Expecting his move, Bernard stepped sideways and hit him hard on the side of the head. Johnny reached out his left arm as he began to fall and pulled his adversary down on top of him. Johnny reached his right arm around Bernard and rolled over on him and punched him twice in the face before Samuel kicked Johnny on the side of the head. Gene tackled Samuel Cassidy while Johnny fell to the side, Bernard twisting to hit him once in the face before Johnny rolled out of his reach.

As Erica stood just outside the back door enjoying the last rays of sun and her glass of Chardonnay, she heard Johnny's yell from the shadowed reaches of the large backyard.

Joseph slipped past Erica and joined a large group of guests who ran toward the commotion.

Half a dozen guests reached the area at the same time. Johnny was lying on his left side, blood flowing from his mouth and a cut over his left ear. Samuel was helping up his brother, who had a cut over his right eye that was trickling blood. Gene, standing between the two adversaries, said forcefully, "It's all over, folks. Just a little misunderstanding."

Joseph knelt by Johnny and asked if he was all right. "I'm fine, and would be a lot better if swine like the Cassidy clowns disappeared for good." Joseph, turning to see if Johnny's words had sparked a reaction from the lawyers, was relieved to see that they were already walking back to the house.

"C'mon, Johnny," he said. "Let's get the hell outta here."

As he helped Johnny stand, Melissa and Erica arrived together, Melissa putting her arm around her husband without saying a word. Joseph looked at her and said softly, "Let's get you and Johnny home before there's any more trouble."

"Thanks, Joseph, that's the best idea I've heard in a while. He's been an accident waiting to happen."

Ronald Jeffers surveyed the scene, figured no major damage needed to be accounted for, and began shepherding his guests back toward the house. "C'mon people, the fisticuffs are over. Let's go back and have some of the food from the most expensive caterer in Connecticut."

Joseph turned to Erica and asked, "Erica, could you help Melissa get Johnny to their car while I go find Tripper?"

Turning toward the house, he almost ran into the Cardones' only child. "Hi Tripper. Your dad got into a fight with the Cassidy brothers and we're getting him home. Are you OK to drive?"

"Whatever." Moving toward his mother and father, he asked, "Dad, you all right?" Melissa replied, "It looks like he'll be OK. Why don't you go get our car and meet us out front?"

Johnny didn't speak or argue about being led from the yard. As they neared the corner of the house, he said, "I'll meet you all at the car after I mend fences with the Jeffers."

Joseph immediately responded, "No way, Johnny. We're not letting you deal with any more people. You're going home with your wife and son, and that's the way it is."

Johnny turned and Joseph expected him to charge through him toward the house, but after pausing a moment, he smiled, "Yeah, probably the best move. Let's do a Kerouac."

Eleven

FAIR SHORE EXPLODED when, a week after the Jeffers' party, the lead article in *The Quill* provided details of the plans for the full day of Saturday activities during homecoming day.

First Annual Fall Family Celebration

The Fair Shore Board of Realtors and Chamber of Commerce and a number of Fair Shore civic groups are sponsoring the First Annual Fair Shore Fall Family Celebration. Designed to provide a wide variety of family activities, the Saturday celebration will complement the Fair Shore High School football homecoming festivities.

Musical performances at the Adams Amphitheater from noon to midnight will feature music of Bruce Springsteen, Neil Young, Roger Waters, Joan Baez, Melissa Etheridge, Steve Earle, Kris Kristofferson, Green Day, the Dixie Chicks and Mary Chapin Carpenter. Connecticut bands led by Fair Shore favorites Max Lunatic will sing the songs of these social activist performers who have fought for justice and equality in their words and deeds.

Local merchants will be providing discounts on merchandise. Carnival rides, clowns, balloon animals, face painting, magicians, jugglers and many more attractions are scheduled at Woodland Park adjoining the Adams Amphitheater and throughout the downtown area.

It is the goal of the organizing committee to provide a wide range of family activities for Fair Shore alumni who are back for the weekend attending the football homecoming festivities. In addition, there is a desire to showcase Fair Shore to surrounding communities as the vibrant, family-oriented, and inclusive town that it is.

Dawn laughed out loud when Tripper brought the paper to her as she and the band met for lunch. "This is so cool, Dawn. You did it. Talk about front and center. This is going to create some excitement in this change-nothing town."

"I am so psyched to be playing the songs of those cool musicians at the amphitheater in front of what I hope will be a ton of people. It'll be awesome." Lou was pacing around as he talked, his excitement forcing him to move.

"Lou, I am so glad you are psyched; I really am. But as for me I'm wondering what kind of new garbage I'm going to have to deal with over this. It won't take much for the jocks to figure out that I was involved in some way."

Dawn noticed that her friends were looking past her as she spoke. Before she could turn to see what they were looking at, Tripper said, "It looks like you are going to find out real soon there, sweetheart. Let's all just stay cool here, all right?"

Bart Bainbridge, who was leading the half dozen athletes that included Buddy Fontanella, stopped five feet from Dawn and the band.

"You're really something else, Mortenson. It wasn't enough to sucker-punch our best player. Now you want to draw people away from what is always the biggest football weekend of the year. What the hell are you trying to prove, anyway?"

Dawn had chosen to step in front of her friends, where she stood sideways, arms hanging loosely by her side, facing the muscular, three-sport athlete.

"Hi Bart, how are ya? I'm not sure what you're talking about."

"That's crap, bitch, you know exactly what he's talking about." Buddy moved next to Bart, looking down on Dawn and her friends. "It was your idea to create this fall weekend so that it drew people away from our game with Grand Shore. You're jealous of all the attention the football team gets, and this is your way of trying to do something about that. Well, it isn't going to work. The stands are gonna be packed for that game and the party Saturday night will be the best ever. So you are just wasting your time."

Gordon moved forward and stood next to Dawn. "Hey, guys, how have you been?"

"I wish the hell you weren't involved in this, Gordo. You're a good guy and I hate to see you brought down with this troublemaker."

"The question I have for all of you," Tripper said, "is this. If you agree that all your activities are going to be packed, then why did you take the time to come out here and threaten our friend? It looks to me like everybody wins with the weekend that's planned. You all get your crowds, and those who wouldn't have come to watch you guys have an alternative.

"And believe it or not, guys," Tripper added, "not everyone in this town loses sleep over how you guys are going to do against Grand Shore."

Bart chose to ignore Tripper's questions, snarling, "We wanted you to know that we are on to what you're trying to do and that you're going to be in for a few surprises. Let's get out of here, guys."

Bart turned and his teammates followed, with Dawn and the band watching in silence as they left. When they were out of sight, Lou whistled softly. "Well, there's your answer. They aren't a happy group."

"And I wouldn't take them lightly, Dawn," Tripper added. "You've got some Neanderthals on that team, but you also have some very bright guys. And the fact is that this has hit their parents, too. They live vicariously through these guys in a big way."

Dawn, more agitated than during the confrontation, colored noticeably before saying, "You're starting to make this sound like some kind of covert operation is going to be taking place. We're talking about having some fun on a weekend that will draw positive attention to the town and take hardly any people away from their game and their activities. C'mon guys, lighten up. This will blow over and everyone will win."

"Dawn," Gordon replied, "you're a smart person, but you are either being naïve or headstrong when you talk like that. You have no idea how big a deal homecoming weekend is to this town. Anything that takes away from the total absorption of this town in their current and past football heroes is a big deal to these folks. Bart's threat is real, and you need to take precautions accordingly."

"What are you saying, 'take precautions'? What do you want me to do, get a bodyguard?"

"All I am saying," Gordon continued, "is that you need to be careful. You saw what they did to Jan, and if you are caught alone they could pull the same stuff with you. You obviously know how to handle yourself, Dawn. That's not the issue. If you're by yourself and a bunch of them are there, you could be in trouble."

"He's r..r..right, Dawn." Billy stammered. "What he is saying is, um, logical. These guys are used to being the center of attention, and, uh, anything that takes away from that is a threat. If you need someone to g..g..go anywhere with you, give any of us a call."

Touched by her friends' concern, Dawn blushed and said, "Guys, I think it's so sweet that you're worrying about me, I really do. But I won't do anything stupid, I promise. C'mon, we've got to get to class." The five gathered their things and returned to the building as the warning bell sounded.

"Erica Mortenson, please."

"Who's calling?"

"This is Ted Erickson from Fair Shore High School. It's about her daughter. It's an emergency."

"One moment, I will interrupt her meeting."

"This is Erica Mortenson."

"We know what you and your daughter are trying to do. If you continue, we will destroy you. This is not a hollow threat."

Hanging up before she could respond, Erica immediately called her daughter. Dawn was walking to her last class when her cell vibrated and she saw her mother was calling. She quickly moved into an empty classroom.

"Hi, Mom. Everything OK? You never call me at school."

"I wanted to make sure you were all right. I just got a call at work threatening you and me. Has anything happened in school today?"

"Yes, I'm fine, and yes, it did. Some of the football players were not happy with the announcement of the weekend activities that compete with their football exploits. They let me know about it, and I promised Tripper and the guys that I would be careful, just as I have told you. OK?"

"All right. You're coming home right after class today?"

"Yes, I'll walk home with friends, and I'll lock the doors until you get home. I'll be fine, Mother. No worries; really."

"I am calling the chief of police, and I am going to tell him about the phone calls at home and now this incident."

"Sounds like a good idea. I've got to get back to class. See you tonight."

Twelve

"YOUR CALL WAS a very pleasant surprise." Richard, driving, looked over to Erica Mortenson sitting in the passenger seat of his Audi as she smiled and continued, "I am not a spur-of-the-moment type of person, in general, but the stuff that is going on has me more needful of company than normal. The timing of your call was perfect with Dawn at band practice with her friends."

"Well, I'm glad you are interested in meeting my crazy New York comrades."

"So you didn't have a line of other women that you are seeing who could have gone with you?"

Richard looked to his left before moving into the passing lane and he drove fast down the West Side Drive into Manhattan. "I'm not seeing anybody in particular right now. My fourth divorce was finalized only a few months ago and I'm laying low after that disaster."

"So, we're birds of a feather then, both recovering from disastrous marriages. You see, we have a lot in common."

"Well, I don't know about that, but the disastrous marriage part I can attest to in spades. I have obviously not figured out how to get the marriage thing right. Four attractive, bright women with whom I had magical times during our early years together all ended up hating me and wanting out of the relationship. Damn, let's change the subject; these flashbacks get me down."

"All right, tell me who I am going to be meeting tonight."

"These are three of my closest friends from Columbia. Along with Joseph, they are the guys I have stayed in closest contact with since the sixties and seventies. Jason is a banker who works in international finance. He is married to Marianna who also works in that area. Ian is in advertising and is married to Heather, who is a model, and Barry is a writer who is dating Shakira, who's an attorney at one of the large law firms."

Three hours later, Erica opened the door into the living room of her home. Dawn was startled. "Hey Mom, I didn't expect you home so soon from your date with Richard."

70

Erica stood still, dropping her pocket book by the front door and placing her jacket gingerly on the coat rack. She stood looking at her daughter with a distracted look on her face.

"Mother, are you alright?" Dawn got up from the couch where she had been reading and looked more closely at her mother.

"Could you get me a glass of water please, and I will tell you what happened."

As they sat side by side on the couch, Erica said, "It was a horrible evening. Richard got totally drunk and ended up vomiting in the bathroom. As he was doing that I got an earful from his friends, who in no uncertain terms told me to run as fast as I can, that he not only has a drinking problem but that he has hurt many people in his life in his self-centered desire to get what he wants. And, oh yes, he blames himself for the death of his brother who died in a car accident that occurred because Richard was drunk. He was also apparently complicit in the death of two Columbia students who were part of the student activism group he was leading during the protests of the sixties.

"And I need to go to bed; I have a major headache."

As Dawn settled into the front seat of Tripper's old Ford the day after her mother's date, she smiled and said, "I'm psyched to see you."

He looked over at her and responded so softly that she needed to lean closer to hear, "I feel the same way. It will be weird being together without the rest of the band being within arm's length."

Smiling mischievously, Dawn asked, "Are you going to be all right with that arrangement? We can give them a call and ask them to meet us at Watson's."

"Actually, I wanted to change the plan and go to my place and chill out. My parents are both out for the night, and we would have the entire place to ourselves. It would be cool." Tripper, having watched Dawn as he made this suggestion, stopped talking as he noticed a quick frown cross her forehead. Observing her hesitation in responding, he added, "It's not a big deal. We can go to Watson's if that's a better vibe for you."

"No, let's go to your place. You just caught me off guard after all the props you had given Watson's and how hot the jazz is there."

"If you want to listen to hot music, you will definitely find it in my father's music collection. He has over 30,000 records, tapes, and CDs." Tripper started the car and pulled away from the front of her house.

"You're right about your father's collection. He has everything." Dawn sipped from the beer Tripper had gotten her from the refrigerator in the basement of his house, as she looked at one of four walls full of albums in his father's music room.

Tripper smiled up at her from one of two large, worn leather chairs that were the only furniture in the sound-proofed room. "He inherited a pretty cool collection of old blues and jazz albums from his Uncle Salvatore who died when he was thirteen. He had already begun to play guitar, so that gift pushed him to really immerse himself in music, and he has collected albums and tapes from all over the world ever since."

As Dawn finished circling the room and looking at the titles on all four walls, she fell into the other leather chair, spilling some of her beer on the rug. "Damn, that was stupid. Where can I get a cloth and clean it up?"

Tripper chuckled, saying, "Don't worry about it. The reason my mother had this God-ugly mud-brown rug put in this room is to hide the stains from all the beer and wine my father has spilled here over the years. What kind of music do you want to hear?"

"How about a female rocker? You pick."

Dawn sat back and watched Tripper jump up and move with purpose to different sections of the collection, pulling seven records from a variety of locations. "I've picked my favorites by the artists that we're playing at the homecoming weekend concert. Does that work for you?"

"Great idea. I love them all."

As Melissa Etheridge filled the room from the speakers on each wall, Dawn got up and pulled the other leather chair next to hers. Tripper sat down next to her after grabbing two more beers from the cooler that he had brought up from the basement.

"Did your interest in music come naturally, or were you pushed in that direction?"

"Actually, my mother discouraged it and my father was neutral. He thought it was cool that he and I could talk music and he could help me learn the guitar. He shared my mom's concern that I would get pulled into the crazy music business, and neither of them wanted to push me in that direction. It was obvious when I was a little guy that I had musical aptitude, so I ended up following that talent, but with some real double messages from my folks."

"Is Max Lunatic your first band?"

"Yeah. I'd played guitar for some other groups in the New York City area, but nothing permanent. We created Max three years ago and we've stayed together. They're good guys, and we all like and trust each other. With all the crap that goes down in this town and the music business in general, we know that we've always got each other's back. You can't buy that kind of trust and friendship."

72

"I felt that the first time I saw you guys at the bookstore. It's a vibe that the audience can feel." Pausing to sip her beer, Dawn asked, "How'd you come up with the name Max Lunatic?"

Tripper smiled widely, jumping out of his chair as he did. "Come on, I'll show you." Reaching down, he grabbed Dawn's hand and pulled her up and out the door to the second floor hallway. Turning to his left, he took half a dozen steps and opened a door to a wooden stairway. "Watch your step; they are steep. I'm going back to get the cooler."

Dawn took a long pull from her beer before heading up the stairs. Stepping gingerly through the small doorway, she slowly climbed the stairs, holding onto the smooth handrail that snaked up and around the winding stair path. A single light bulb lit the way as she climbed fifteen steps to another door. As she pushed it open, she walked into a light-filled room.

As her eyes got used to the shift from darkness to light, she saw that she was in a room that took up an entire floor of the nineteenth-century structure. Floor-to-ceiling windows and two skylights filled the room with light from the full moon overhead, which was complemented by soft light from ceiling fixtures twenty feet above her head. Every inch of wall space that was not filled with windows was filled with books. Thousands of volumes, many leather-bound editions from another time and place, drew her to them. As she looked at the books, she realized that Melissa Etheridge was now playing through speakers in this room as well. Tripper stood by the far wall, smiling at her movement among the books.

Dawn looked reverently at the books in front of her, running her hand over some of the leather spines. Pulling one of the volumes from the shelf, she opened it carefully and turned a few pages before putting it slowly back in its place. Turning to Tripper, she whispered, "This is an amazing space."

Moving toward her, he guided her across the deep blue carpet to one of the three couches scattered around the large room. Sitting down, they faced each other as he replied, "My mother's family has consisted of writers, philosophers, teachers, and artists since at least the mid-eighteenth century. She is the last surviving member that we know of, and so she's gathered all of the volumes that were left from her ancestors. She and I spend a lot of time up here reading."

Dawn smiled at her friend as she heard the obvious love for his mother in his voice. Looking around the room while she took another sip of beer, she asked, "So how did this place lead to your calling your band Max Lunatic?"

Tripper got up slowly from the couch and walked to the wall behind where they were sitting. Reaching up, he took a worn volume from the shelf. Sitting close to Dawn, he replied, "It was this book that did it. It is one of my mother's favorite books, and she thought I would like it also. Man, was she right. Herman Hesse is now my favorite author and *Demian* is probably my favorite book. In it Hesse writes about the importance of self-awareness and self-fulfillment. One of the main characters in that book represents the quest to live the examined life; his name is Max Demian. So the first part of the band's name came from him.

"Roger Waters has been a major influence on me. He is quite simply a damn genius. His song *Brain Damage* is probably my favorite song. Since, as you know, it talks about the threat of lunatics to our sane world, I thought combining the two would be cool. Hence the band name Max Lunatic. It has worked out well."

Dawn took the book that was offered and noticed the worn cover and pages. "It looks like this edition has gotten a lot of use."

"Well, I have probably read it a half dozen times, and no telling how many times my mother has come back to it. Are you familiar with Hesse?"

"Yes, I've read *Siddhartha*. You've now gotten my curiosity up about Max and the other characters in *Demian*."

"Go ahead and take it with you. I'm sure my mother wouldn't mind."

Dawn thanked Tripper and looked through the book before putting it down on the table next to her end of the couch. Looking over at him, she asked, "So tell me about you, now that we have some time alone. How has your self-awareness journey been progressing?"

Tripper finished his beer, got up and pulled another from the cooler, asking Dawn if she wanted one too. She nodded, draining the one she had brought up from downstairs. As Tripper settled back down on the couch, he opened his beer and said, "I'll give you the greatest-hits version, and if you want more details you can stop me, OK?"

"That works for me."

"I am the happiest I have ever been. That's not because I don't think the world is really messed up, or that I don't have my problems. But I'm graduating on time, and that wasn't seen as a possibility a couple of years ago. The band is really creating some good music and we are really tight as friends, and I have met a lot of cool people over the last couple years that I like to chill with. That includes you, in case you didn't catch that."

"I bet you say that to all the girls."

"The difference is I mean it this time. The key for me, though, is my relationship with my parents. We had some rough times back about five years ago. My mother and father were really going at each other, and I got in with the wrong crowd and got into some pretty heavy stuff. That's how I got my name, which was actually one that I coined for myself so I could have my own identity and make the

74

girls think I was cooler than I was. Pretty messed up, huh?"

"Doesn't sound so bad to me. So where are you with the drugs now?"

"I'll smoke a little weed every now and then, but I am off the hard stuff. My best friend, Elliott, died from an overdose, and I never did hard drugs again. He was fourteen years old, man, and I was the one who found him alone in his bedroom." Tripper got up to move around the large room, Dawn staying seated while he paced. He stood in front of the windows, looking out at the lights of Fair Shore. After five minutes of silence, Tripper walked around the room a couple of times before sitting down heavily where he had been sitting before.

"My family really came together then. I hit emotional zero, and my parents stopped their fighting and were there for me. We did a lot of things together and still do. They helped me pull through. Then I started Max and the music began to pull me out of myself and back to some pretty good friends. I gotta tell ya though I still wake up in cold sweats feeling Elliot's clammy body in my dreams."

Pausing again, he drank his beer and looked past Dawn to the wall behind. "In some perverse way, his death helped me with the self-awareness that you asked about. I spent a lot of time thinking about every possible question beginning with the word *why*. I began to read Hesse and authors like him and started to sort out some stuff about what I was trying to do in this crazy world. So Elliott pushed me to think about personal stuff that probably wouldn't have happened if I had kept on the tripping-out path."

Smiling self-consciously, Tripper mumbled, "Well, that's the greatest-hits version, complete with laps around the room."

After talking for another thirty minutes about what it was like spending his whole life in Fair Shore, Tripper asked Dawn, "So what about you? What are the major things that have gone on in your life?" Dawn looked at him quickly, seeing that he really seemed interested in hearing what she had to say. Standing in front of the windows, she sipped her beer, reluctant to turn and talk.

Tripper came up behind her and stroked her hair, saying, "What's going on? It couldn't be that bad." Dawn stayed where she was, saying bitterly, "You don't know what you're talking about and therefore have no right to say that."

Tripper stumbled backwards as if he had been pushed away. Standing ten feet from Dawn, he looked at her back, noticing the tensed shoulder muscles. Deciding not to respond, he sat back down on the couch in the spot were Dawn had been sitting.

"I was raped by my father's best friend when I was twelve. I crawled to another room and locked myself in to keep him from screwing me again. My father said he didn't see where it was a big deal, since I looked eighteen and had to learn sometime. My mother stabbed him in the neck with a fork and would have killed him while he lied there on the floor if I hadn't pulled her off.

"Although we went for family counseling, our relationship as a family was over, and my father began to drink heavily and spend weeks away from home with other women. My mother filed for divorce, and he spent tens of thousands fighting it. When she won and got the financial settlement she wanted, we left Boston and moved here.

"I was way ready to get away from Boston. A half dozen times during ninth and tenth grade I dressed up and went into some Boston bars when my mother was away on business trips. I picked up and screwed older men and then called their homes to get them in trouble. Those were not the best years of my life. I'm sure as hell not proud of them.

"The three things that kept me from breaking down completely were organized sports, karate, and yoga. I was able to put most of my anger into those activities. Man, I gotta tell you, I beat the crap outta a lot of guys during karate practice. Unfortunately, some of it was definitely misplaced, and I hurt some good friends, like my karate instructor, whose jaw I broke during practice. And I was so looking forward to starting clean in a new place, and then I'm face-to-face with Drew Winston my first thirty seconds in class, goddamn it."

Dawn had told her story in a monotone until the last two words, which she spit out as she smacked her clenched fists against her sides. Tripper stood up, saying, "It's going to be all right. There are a lot of really cool people who are on your side." Reluctant to touch her, he stopped three feet short of where she stood. Dawn turned as he spoke and walked into his arms. Kissing him tenderly, she pulled him to the floor, where they were still lying together after hearing his parents call up the stairs for him two hours later.

Thirteen

TWO WEEKS AFTER promising Dawn that she would look into equal representation at the pep rally during homecoming weekend, Coach Roberts took her aside after her third-period class. "I couldn't hold off until practice to tell you. All the fall sports—both male and female—are going to be represented equally at the pep rally this year; it will no longer be billed as the football homecoming pep rally. I made my case to Howard Rowley, the Athletic Director for the district, and he argued against it, but I finally got him to come around after I told him that I was also going to bring my uncle, the Superintendent of Schools, into the conversation."

Dawn shrieked and grabbed her coach, both of them jumping up and down in their excitement.

"Oh my God, this is awesome! This is so cool!"

"Well, I wanted to show you that we old folks could also get something done around here. I'll see you at practice."

The entire field-hockey team was energized when Coach Roberts told them of the change in the pep-rally emphasis. Dawn noticed that some of the girls who had been distant with her looked at her in a more positive way when their coach explained that the change had been Dawn's idea. The practice that afternoon reflected the energy that the change had created.

Coach Roberts gathered the entire team together at the end of practice. "Damn, you all were on fire today. How about dinner at my place tomorrow after a shortened practice? That way you won't miss too much study time." The team shouted its approval as it ran off the field.

The enthusiasm in Coach Roberts' home the following evening was beyond anyone's expectations. The coach spoke to it after they had finished the chicken and risotto and cleared the table.

"I've got to tell you, if the energy you all are showing in practice and this evening is any indication, the teams we face this year don't stand a chance."

Every member of the team stood and cheered, raising their soda and juice glasses high in the air.

"As I've said since our first practice, if each of you chooses to do the best you possibly can, and then takes it up another notch, we will have a great season. You have already gone beyond what I'm sure many of you had thought possible, and it's paying off." Sipping her cranberry juice as the cheering erupted again, she waited for it to subside before saying, "And beyond the athletic part of what you're doing, there is also a strength of character that's showing through. I'd like to particularly thank Brittany, Ingrid, and Molly for deciding to stay and work together as a team. I know that was a tough decision, since you are all dating football players who were upset with what happened between Dawn and Drew. Well, you chose to take the tough road and stay, and work through your feelings. I know it has helped the team—and I hope it has helped you."

Ernestine, sitting across the room, looked directly at Coach Roberts, saying, "Yeah, well, if the guys weren't such jerks we wouldn't have *any* problems on this team or in this school."

"Listen, the guys around here can be really stupid and chauvinistic and self-absorbed. My guess is that is how girls see guys they know all around the world." All eyes shifted to Molly Edwardson, a two-year field hockey starter, currently dating Brent Wood. "I also believe that most of the football players are good guys. I obviously feel that way about Brent. They can be really sweet and considerate and do some nice things. Look at the surprise party they had for Mimi on her seventeenth birthday. That was Phillip's idea."

Ernestine tapped her right foot rapidly as she listened to Molly. Before she could respond, Brittany Swanson stood and said, "Listen, we could talk about nice things and stupid things that the guys have or haven't done for the rest of the week. Bottom line for me is the fact that their success in this school has helped many of the female students, big time. Fair Shore has a reputation for graduating accomplished scholar athletes, and when you tell someone you're from Fair Shore, they figure that you're like, extremely successful. That's what counts for me. I also know that I need to get home because I've got a huge English paper due and it is not where it needs to be."

Coach Roberts seconded the popular senior's comments, thanking the team for coming. Ernestine was still mumbling as she walked out with Dawn and the other girls. Striding toward Dawn's mother's car, she was the first to notice that it was boxed in by two cars that had parked bumper-to-bumper with it. Ernestine stopped ten feet from the car and yelled, "Goddamn it, Bart and James are such jerks. They've boxed in Dawn so we can't get out." As they all looked around to see if the football players were in sight, Ernestine sprinted back toward her coach's home, picking up a brick that she had noticed was set in the garden to the right of the stairs. She headed purposefully toward the Camaro that was pushed up against Dawn's back bumper.

Stepping back from the car, she cocked her arm and threw the brick through the window on the driver's side. As glass exploded, a number of the girls jumped at the sound. While they stood stunned, she reached through the shattered window and lifted the door lock, letting herself into the car. Within moments, the car started, and those who had walked toward the car had now moved back and onto the sidewalk. Smiling wildly, she jammed down the accelerator, and the car squealed fifteen feet backwards before she slammed on the brakes, shut off the engine, and walked back to join her teammates.

Continuing to smile, she looked slowly at each. "James and I spent a lot of time in that car. Once he showed me how to hot-wire it."

As Ernestine looked around at her teammates, she expected to be vilified for what she had done. Her muscles tense, she was stunned to see smiles on most of their faces.

"All right then," she said contentedly, "maybe next time they will show a little more respect when they stop by one of our gatherings." Walking around to the passenger side of Erica's car, she let herself in as Dawn started the engine and led the line of cars away from Coach Roberts' home.

Ernestine was leaning against her locker, talking with Mike Rudolph, starting center of the football team. Friends since grammar school, they laughed at a joke Mike had just told.

"You bitch, I'm gonna kill you." Both were startled by James Mason as he rounded the corner, sighted Ernestine, and screamed. Attempting to push past his teammate to get at her, he was startled when Mike grabbed him and pushed him away, standing between the two. "What's your problem, Mason?"

"The bitch ruined my car, man. She threw a brick through the window and I'm gonna make her pay." Lunging at Ernestine, he was once again pushed back by his teammate who said, "I don't care what the hell she did to you or your car. You touch her and you're dealing with me, Mason."

James stood straight and clenched his fists, wild-eyed and ready to charge. At that moment, Todd Benson appeared next to Mike, creating a wall between the enraged student and his target. "Listen to me, Jimmy," Todd said in a loud voice. "I don't give a crap what she did to you or your stupid car. Beating up a girl just isn't cool. Get your shit together and let's get to class."

A large group of students had gathered around the three football players. Todd noticed Principal McMullen moving through the crowd, so Todd told his teammates he was coming, then took off in the other direction. Mike stayed in position while James hesitated momentarily and then followed Todd, snarling at both Mike and Ernestine as he did. By the time the large principal reached Mike and Ernestine, most of the crowd had dissipated, and Ernestine was closing her locker and walking arm-in-arm with her friend down the hall. Principal McMullen smiled as he reached her locker, proudly thinking that his mere presence had broken up the commotion.

Fourteen

"WE CAN'T LET this happen, guys. I heard what Coach Oates said about choosing our battles and not fighting a good guy like Howard Rowley, who does have the authority to let girls' teams take part in our rally. But we have to do something or else we're going to become second-class citizens around here."

Bart Bainbridge stopped talking and continued to pace nervously on the well-manicured baseball diamond in the hollow on the north side of Fair Shore High. A dozen members of the football team were sitting around him, having gathered there after practice. All stayed focused on their captain, waiting for him to continue, as they knew he would.

"So I have a plan for showing up Dawn Mortenson and her supporters. We will hold our own football pep rally on the front lawn of the York's. They're cool with that idea and understand that their lawn is about as close to the size and shape of a football field as there is in this town.

"We'll build a stage, and we'll come exploding out of a tunnel and go through some formations for our fans, with our cheerleaders doing their thing, and bringing in the best music our money can buy so we can really get our fans pumped up for us. We'll invite former star football players to come to our blast, and maybe we'll do a little light scrimmage and they'll get up and speak. Most people will come to our rally, and their rally will have only the candy asses. The entire town will see who the real athletes are. So we've got to get moving on this. Are you with me?"

Expecting unanimous approval, Bart was surprised when Charlie Huntington asked, "What did Coach Oates say about this? I think he and the other coaches would be required to be at the school-sanctioned rally."

"I already thought of that and ran this idea by him, and he said that he couldn't officially support it. But then he gave me the thumbs up as he turned to walk away. My father's gonna pay the entire cost of our rally and is gonna donate workers from my uncle's construction company to do all the set-up for it. We will have ourselves one hell of a party."

"You know, Bart, you're not just going up against Dawn Mortenson on this. There will be a whole lot of teachers and students who support this all-inclusive idea." Brent Wood sat on the grass looking up at Bart as he offered his thought. Paul Benjamin chimed in, "Yeah, like we might not get the cheerleaders, since they might support the female teams. Even if they wanted to, they might be required by their coach to stay and cheer for the other teams." Paul stood to argue his point, looking confidently at his long-time friend.

"So, guys, when did the three of you lose your balls?" Everyone looked at Buddy Fontanella, who was recognized by the Fair Shore football coaches as the strongest athlete they had ever coached. He was also described as one of the most violent. Stories of his attacks on people, both on and off the football field, were legion. Charlie started when Buddy stared at him. Paul, relaxed, stood his ground but didn't reply. Brent did the same while continuing to sit.

"Since when did it matter what other people thought was important in this school? The male football players at this school are the ones who have given this place a national reputation. Do you think the idiot teachers and administrators would be pulling down the salaries they're paid if we hadn't performed the way we have? We attract people to this town and we keep them here because we know how to kick ass. The faculty and administration are not going to ruin a good thing. Rowley got boxed into a corner by that bitch coach he has the hots for and he did what he needed to do. We're doing what we need to do, and they won't try to stop us. So quit acting like such pussies and get with the program." Buddy was vehement.

Charlie, Brent, and Paul stayed silent as Bart said, "OK then, we're ready to go." Bart grinned at his friends. "We've got to get moving on the planning of this. Let's go to my house and start making this show happen."

The group got up and walked slowly toward their cars, with Charlie, Brent, and Paul talking to a number of other teammates as they brought up the rear.

Erica and Dawn were both working in their living room that night when Dawn's cell rang shortly after ten o'clock.

"Hi Ernestine, what's up?"

"I just wanted you to know that some of the guys on the football team are organizing their own pep rally to compete with the traditional school event that has been opened up to girls' teams. They're calling everybody to encourage—and in some cases threaten—them to come to the York estate to see the football team acknowledged in the right way.

"They are getting very aggressive with this, Dawn. They're calling the members of the field-hockey team and telling us to come watch them rather than be honored ourselves, and they are doing the same thing with the cheerleaders, pushing them to cheer at their alternative rally and not ours. I've already called Coach Roberts and wanted you to know too. Somehow I didn't think they would be calling to ask you to come to their shindig, although they're probably arrogant enough to try."

Dawn, brow furrowed, listened intently to what her teammate was saying. "What did you say to them after they made their pitch to you?"

"I told Buddy Fontanella to go screw himself. I said that I was going to be up on stage taking part in the acknowledgment that the field-hockey team finally deserved and working my ass off to make sure that as many of my friends were there to see me as possible."

Dawn laughed, replying, "I would have paid money to see the look on that big ape's face when you said that."

"Oh, he was not pleased. I can tell you that."

"Which of the cheerleaders let you know they had been called?"

"I'd rather not say. She was scared to even call me, concerned that the guys would try to get back at her if it seemed like she was trying to weaken their efforts."

"Do you think there is a real possibility that some of our teammates would give up being honored on stage to go to the guys' party?"

Erica had put down her work and was listening with interest to her daughter's side of the conversation.

"Yes, I do. Dawn, you still don't have a real, gut sense of how the guys have ruled this town. Unquestionably they are the kings, and everyone, especially the parents and the school faculty and administration, has bought into that fact. I could give you dozens of examples to prove it. This one will give you an idea. Every Friday the cheerleaders are required to clean out the players' lockers. They also have to put pictures and flowers and notes in the lockers to 'inspire' the team. Each cheerleader is also required to help at least three of the starting players to 'relax' during the season. If a girl who is trying out for the cheerleading squad verbalizes her refusal to do that, she doesn't make the squad. Veronica Cheswick decided last year that she wasn't going to do the relaxation drill with one of the players and she was off the squad the next day, replaced by a sophomore who helped three players relax with her that same night."

"I had heard rumors about that stuff."

"Oh, they're true all right, and those are not even the worst."

"So what you're saying is that the guys have a chance to pull off their rally and make it more successful than ours."

"You're absolutely right, and I want you to know that I will do anything I can to make sure that our rally rules."

"Let's talk about the team we need to pull together to make that happen." Grabbing the pad that she had been using, Dawn settled into a conversation that lasted an hour.

"Ernestine, this has been amazing. So we will both talk to the people on each of our lists, and get as many of us together as possible at my house at six-thirty tomorrow night, for pizza and planning. OK, let's get some sleep. One final thing, Ernestine; be careful. Now that you have made yourself known as the enemy, there is no telling what crap they might pull. As I've told you, they've been calling our house and making threats. So watch your back girlfriend."

That week, three different people came up to Dawn and explained that they would not be able to help in the way they wanted to because of personal developments about which they would not elaborate. The Mortensons got a first-hand idea of the scare tactics that were being used when Erica received a call threatening to divulge sordid and embarrassing information from her divorce. She told the caller to go ahead and make it public so she could use it to emphasize the kind of tactics the supporters of the football team were resorting to in order to have their way.

Coach Robert's response to the tactics was a completely different situation. She took Dawn aside for a brief conversation that Friday, explaining that she would have to back off from her involvement. "Dawn, these folks are playing for keeps. I received a call from someone who had some information from my past that they threatened to reveal if I stayed visibly involved. This is information I just cannot afford to have made public. This information was very hard to find. You all have to be very careful."

Ernestine was able to get commitments from all but five of her teammates that they would attend the sanctioned rally, but was not completely confident that the commitments would hold.

Distractions notwithstanding, the team was extremely focused on their first field-hockey game that Friday against Edgewater, which turned out to be just as well, for they battled to a zero-to-zero tie in regulation time against one of the strongest teams in Connecticut. They won on a goal by Ernestine in overtime. Dawn was emotionally exhausted after the game, having made numerous acrobatic saves, the last on a point-blank shot by Edgewater's All-American forward forty seconds before Ernestine scored the game winner.

Dawn slumped in front of her locker, too tired to take off her uniform. Since she was the last to make the team, her cubicle was in a far corner of the locker room, distanced from the teammates who were celebrating their important victory.

Letting herself go, she stayed slumped and alone while her teammates yelled and carried on.

Ingrid Bjork turned the corner near Dawn's locker to go to the equipment room, stopping when she noticed Dawn sitting alone in the corridor in front of her destination. Hesitating, she considered either going back with her teammates or forging ahead to the equipment room, but she opted to walk quietly toward Dawn and sit in front of an empty locker across from her.

Dawn looked up slowly, focusing on Bart Bainbridge's girl of the moment, startled out of her torpor by Ingrid's lovely face. Looking straight into Ingrid's pale blue eyes, Dawn held her gaze and produced a small, tired smile.

Ingrid stared back, looking over at her slumped teammate. Dawn continued to look into her eyes, her frustration with all that had happened in Fair Shore channeling through her gaze.

"You played an amazing game in goal today," Ingrid finally said. "I've played a lot of field hockey and I don't know if I have ever seen any better."

Dawn continued to stare, no longer from frustration, but from curiosity.

"Thank you," she replied.

Ingrid broke her stare, looking at the floor, and then back toward Dawn, who asked, "Why are you dating Bart Bainbridge?"

Ingrid paused, surprised by the question. "Oh my God, are you serious? Like, he's one of the top catches in this place. All my friends are, like, so jealous that I got him away from Melissa Packer." Pausing again to look hard at Dawn, she continued, "You're, like, kidding, right? That question was really a joke, wasn't it?"

Dawn smiled while looking into Ingrid's eyes. Seeing that she was, in fact, being serious, she lowered her gaze and said quietly, "No, I wasn't kidding."

Staying slumped and resting her elbows on her knees, she expected and half hoped that Ingrid would leave.

"Dawn, explain to me why you asked that question."

Looking again at Ingrid to see if she was being honest or just wasting her time, Dawn sat up and stretched her back and neck.

"Ingrid, let me ask you a few questions. Have you been with other guys while you've dated Bart?"

As Ingrid paused once again before answering, three of their teammates walked over and stood next to where they were sitting. Ingrid asked them to leave, to which Dawn reacted immediately, saying, "I'd like them to stay, if you don't mind." Distracted, Ingrid motioned them to sit.

"To answer your question, no, I have never been with any other guy during the five months Bart and I have been a couple."

"Has he ever slept with another woman during those five months?"

"Bart has probably slept with half a dozen girls during that time."

"Second question. What would he do if you slept with someone else and he found out, just as *you* have found out about his other escapades?"

"That's easy. He would kill whatever guy was stupid enough to do that, and dump me."

"Have you ever told him how you felt about that double standard?

"Of course not. Are you crazy? I'm lucky to have him. We are *the* couple here at Fair Shore High. When we walk into a party dressed to kill, everyone wants to be with us and always tells us how great we look together. I love him and want to marry him. Why would I do anything to jeopardize that?"

"Next question. Does it bother you that he's leading the movement to squash the importance of our team's accomplishments?"

"I can tell you that it bugs the crap out of me that those macho idiots are pulling this scam because they might have to share the stage with a group of successful women. Who the hell do they think they are, for Chrissake?"

Ernestine burst through the circle of field-hockey players who were now surrounding Ingrid and Dawn.

"What's the matter with you all?" she continued. "We're good. We're damn good. And because the women in this school have finally gotten permission to be up on stage with them for their precious pep rally, they go and decide to have their own so they don't have to share the stage with us. Damn them all."

Dawn smiled as her friend made her impassioned speech, saying, "Hi Ernestine. Come on in and don't be bashful." As a few of the team laughed, Dawn looked around for the first time and noticed that almost the entire team was sitting or standing around her.

"What do the rest of you feel about the guys' creation of an alternative rally?"

The next fifteen minutes were filled with energized discussion, during which Dawn listened and helped everyone to feel comfortable in saying what they felt. "So what I hear is that most of you want the rally to include all the fall teams, represented equally. But you're worried about going against the guys on this because you don't want them to come down on you or cut you out of the social scene that seems to revolve around them and their parties. Am I getting this right?"

The group murmured agreement. Standing, then moving to face her teammates, she announced, "I'm going to show you another perspective, and it will only take a couple of minutes. Please bear with me.

"According to the *Tao Te Ching*,

The spirit of the fountain dies not.

It is called the mysterious feminine.
The doorway of the mysterious feminine
Is called the roof of heaven-and-earth.
Lingering like gossamer, it has only a hint of existence;
And yet when you draw upon it, it is inexhaustible.

"What if we decided that we were the center of the social structure here and that we could decide what events we wanted to host and where we wanted to go?

"How many of you have dated a guy who told you that he would meet you at a certain place and time and didn't show up? C'mon, let me see hands." Most of the young women in the locker room raised their hands.

"OK, how many of you reacted to that by telling that same guy you would be somewhere at a certain place and time and didn't show? Anyone? Nobody.

"How many of you have been told by your guy that he needed some space and was going to see other people and you said, 'Yeah, that makes sense. There are a few guys I was interested in getting to know as well. This is a good idea.' Nobody, again.

"OK, here's the punch line. Guys are going to keep treating us like crap until we start showing that we're going to look after ourselves as well. There is nothing that gets a guy coming back to you faster than the knowledge that you aren't sitting around waiting for his call. It's a matter of respect. If you act in a way that shows you respect yourself, other people will respect you more. I know half a dozen situations from where I used to live where a guy said he needed his space and his girl said that was a good idea because there were guys she wanted to see, and in *every case* the guy changed his mind by the next day.

"Look around you for a minute. C'mon, look at your teammates. This is a talented group that's also creative and smart. How many of you have seen Irene's paintings? Really beautiful and creative art. Four of you that I know of are applying to Ivy League. Jennifer is going to Stanford. And we just beat one of the best field-hockey teams in the state. We are very talented, so why not act like it?"

Dawn, watching the group, noticed most nodding their heads in agreement.

"So, why don't we have a party tomorrow night to celebrate our victory?"

"Oh my God, are you crazy, Dawn? We, like, can't do that. Jeremy Knox is having one, and all the guys will be going to it."

"Damn, Jennifer, haven't you heard anything that has been said?" Rachel Woodley, red-faced and agitated, continued, "Let's get on the phone with our friends and invite them to our celebration and see who comes. I know Todd better get his ass there, or I'm shutting him off."

The laughter that followed Rachel's comment was spontaneous and real.

Rachel, encouraged by the response, continued, "And when Todd comes, Will Bryant and that whole crew will follow. C'mon, let's try it. I'll volunteer my place if you all help with the food and stuff."

The organized frenzy that ensued concluded with most of the team members committed to a party at eight o'clock the following evening. Dawn purposefully stayed in the background as the others came together in shared excitement. She noticed with surprise and satisfaction that Ingrid was volunteering to take part. When the group began to disperse, she went up to her. "I see you're going to the party. Aren't you worried about how Bart will react?"

"Sure I am. But at the same time, what all you guys were saying made a lot of sense. If he chooses not to come with me, I'll hang out at Rachel's for a while and then head over to Jeremy's."

"That's great. And thanks for starting all of this by coming over to talk."

"I hope we can get to know each other better really soon. See you tomorrow tonight."

Within moments the locker room had emptied. Sitting for a few minutes more and reviewing the last hour, Dawn slowly peeled off her uniform and went into the shower, humming Steve Earle's *The Revolution Starts Now* as she let the steaming water cleanse and relax her.

Fifteen

RACHEL WOODLEY'S HOME, built in the 1840s on four acres of land, was packed with young people when Bart Bainbridge arrived by himself at ten fifteen that night. Forced to park his Porsche five minutes away from the party, he walked deliberately toward the music. Bart was confused by the phone call that he had gotten from Ingrid, explaining that she was at Rachel's and hoping that he would come over. Equally confused by her refusal to respond to his threat that she'd be spending the night without him, he was not confused about what he would do when he saw her.

He walked briskly up the front walk, stomping up the ten steps to her porch. Brushing past a knot of teenagers, he entered the front foyer and turned left into the living room. Stunned by the large number of classmates that had decided to come to this party rather than the one he had just left, he scanned the room for his girlfriend.

"Hey Bart, great game this afternoon." The football team had beaten Clifford Wells High, 55–13. He turned toward Tracey Stafford, a junior on the field-hockey team with whom he had slept intermittently over the last two years. "Thanks, Tracey. Where's Ingrid?"

"Last I saw her she was dancing in the backyard."

Reluctant to deal with the large number of people that he knew in the living room, he retreated out the front door and walked around toward the back of the house. Groups of teenagers were spread out across the yard and up on the porch that circled the house. As he turned the corner into the backyard, he saw that lights had been placed on top of tall posts to form a square of illumination in which fifty people were dancing. Stopping again to find his girlfriend, he saw her immediately, dancing with one of his teammates, Nat Brandon, a junior starter in the defensive secondary, who had run an interception back for a touchdown that afternoon.

"Hey, Bart, how the hell are ya? I was keeping your girl warm for you until…"

Bart walked directly up to where Nat and Ingrid were dancing and punched him in the mouth, knocking the solidly built athlete to the ground. Turning to

Ingrid, he said, "You're coming with me. We need to talk." Pulling roughly at her as he grabbed her left arm, Bart was surprised when Nat put his large hand on Bart's and reasoned, "There's no need to get rough, Bart. Nothing was going on; we were just having fun while she waited for you."

Bart released his grip on Ingrid's arm while Nat let go of his hand. Staring at each other, Bart smiled and said, "Of course nothing was going on." His right hand moved so quickly that Nat did not even have the chance to move before he was smashed on the left side of his face. Two other rapid punches had him lying on his back.

As Bart turned to reach for Ingrid, Nat, wiping the blood from his face, charged his teammate, and both staggered five feet into one of the many gardens that surrounded the house. Landing on top of Bart, Nat punched him four times before he was pulled off by three classmates.

Although Bart's instinct was to get up immediately and continue the fight, he stayed on the ground, thoughts racing through his head. At eighteen, he had never been physically challenged by a teammate, and certainly never by a girl he was with, having been fawned over and deferred to ever since he stepped onto a football field in elementary school. Realizing that a yard full of people were watching and that Nat Brandon was poised to continue the fight, he slowly got to his feet, saying, "Hell of a tackle, Brandon. Where does someone get a beer around here?"

Waiting for a sucker punch that didn't come, Nat pointed toward a long table twenty feet away. Bart, standing tall and moving with a slow, purposeful swagger, headed toward the bar.

Dawn had stopped dancing with Brian Rossity, captain of the men's cross-country team, to run to Ingrid's side, as she expected the fight to continue. Turning to her teammate, she said, "Jesus, Ingrid, what was that?"

"Bart saw that I was dancing with Nat and punched him. Nat hit him back, and Bart went to get a beer."

"Do you want to go over to him?"

"No, I'll let him calm down a little first." Smiling at her friend, she said, "Besides, he can come to me, right?" Laughing loudly, Dawn quickly agreed.

The dancing had resumed immediately after Bart left the dance area. Red Holcum, a three-year starter on the baseball team, approached Dawn, saying, "You're not getting out of dancing with me that easily, Dawn."

Scott Donovan, the number-two runner on the cross-country team, came over with him, asking Ingrid if she wanted to dance. "Aren't you afraid of what Bart would do?" she asked, surprised by his request.

"Didn't you know that all runners are lean, mean fighting machines? I'll be even harder on him than that wimp Brandon was."

After dancing for twenty minutes and seeing no sign of Bart Bainbridge, they all agreed they wanted something to drink and headed to the makeshift bar. As they got their beers and sodas, Ingrid asked a couple of people if Bart was around. Her teammate Christy Thomas, who was working the bar area, said, "He left a few minutes ago; said he was going back to Jeremy Knox's place."

After getting their drinks, Dawn took Ingrid aside and said, "You look confused. What's going on?"

"I'm surprised that Bart didn't stay and not sure what it means. I think I'm going to drive over to Jeremy's and talk with him."

"Do you think that's a good idea? Like you said, he could really lay into you."

Smiling mischievously, Ingrid replied, "Actually, Dawn, getting laid into by Bart Bainbridge tonight might be just what I want and need."

Swatting her shoulder softly, Dawn laughed, saying, "He'd better watch himself or he won't have energy to go to church in the morning."

Ingrid stayed for a few more minutes, leaving at 11:05 for the five-minute drive to Jeremy Knox's home. Dawn sat on a bench located on the side of the house bordered by the woods of the county park system. Watching the party, she felt satisfied with her growing friendships with some of her classmates and teammates, and with the success of the field- hockey team's impromptu party. Deciding to call Ingrid the next day to find out how the remainder of the evening had gone, she got up and went inside to see if Rachel needed any help.

Ingrid was surprised to see, when she approached Jeremy's house, that there seemed to be fewer people there than at Rachel's. As she walked around, she also saw that there were significantly more girls at Rachel's party than at this one. Smiling to herself, she asked the first person she saw if they knew where Bart was. "He was in the living room sitting by the kegs."

As Ingrid walked toward the living room entrance, she passed her friend Brittany Swanson. "Hey, Brit, how's this party going?"

"Um, it's actually pretty slow. Why don't you come in the back with me and I'll get you a beer."

"That's OK; I heard Bart is in the living room."

Before Brittany could say any more, Ingrid had turned the corner and walked through the door, immediately seeing Bart leaning back on a couch with Janet Weston lying on top of him, kissing him deeply as she stroked his left leg. Eyes opened, Bart saw Ingrid as soon as she walked into the room. Pushing Janet to the side, he got up and walked to his girlfriend.

"Hello, love. You got here just in time. Janet and I were going to go upstairs and your arrival makes for a nice threesome. Can I get you a drink before we go up?"

Noticing that the dozen people in the room were all watching their exchange, Ingrid whispered, "We need to talk, and it would be better outside."

"Anything you have to say can be said in this room, Ingrid. We're among friends."

Pausing momentarily, Ingrid replied, "I have no interest in going upstairs or even being with you, Bart. Actually, you can stay with Janet as long as you want because we are through." Ingrid, tears forming as she spoke, turned and walked out the door. Bart, smiling, looked at three of his teammates, saying, "I guess I should be concerned, huh, guys? Like she won't be coming back for more tomorrow."

Turning to sit back down on the couch, he suddenly changed his mind and strode out the door. Catching up with Ingrid, he looked to see if anybody was watching. Noticing they were alone, he grabbed her shoulder and spun her around, slapping her twice in the face before she could put up any defense.

Moving closer to her, he grabbed a handful of hair at the back of her neck and pulled her face close to his. "You just made a big mistake, my love, and now you'll pay the price. You are not going to like being out on your ass as we celebrate our senior year." Raising his hand to hit her again, he was pulled back by Jesse Dawkins, who had followed him from the house.

"That's enough, Bart. Let her go." Squared off against his long-time friend and football teammate, Bart stood silently as he let the words sink in. Ingrid began to back away with the teammates staring at each other. Seeing her movement, he spat on the ground at her feet before turning and walking toward the house.

Dawn called Ingrid's home three times the next day, getting an answering machine every time. She finally decided to stop calling and talk with her in school on Monday.

Dawn went to school early that Monday morning, hoping to catch Ingrid before class started. Turning the corner as she approached her homeroom, she nearly ran into Jan Ostraczyk going in the other direction.

"Jan, how are you?" she exclaimed. "I heard you were transferring."

"Hi, Dawn," she replied in a low voice. "No, I'm back, and I really need to focus on school and nothing else, OK?" With dark shadows under her eyes and shoulders hunched down over baggy jeans and an oversized sweatshirt, she looked like she was trying to ooze into the floor.

"Fine, no problem, I'll leave you alone. If you need anything, call me at any time. I've missed you."

Hesitating momentarily, Jan turned slowly away, looking back quickly before walking out of sight.

Dawn kept her eye out for Ingrid as she went through her day, not necessarily expecting to see her until field-hockey practice. Walking into the locker room, she got a lot of high fives and praise for coming up with the idea of the field-hockey party. Coach Roberts did the same, saying to her as they walked onto the field that it had been a great idea and that she was sorry that she hadn't made it, but appreciated having been invited. After practice had started and she didn't see Ingrid, Dawn asked a couple of teammates whether they had seen her that day, and they all said the same thing—that the last time they had seen her was at their party Saturday night.

Dawn and her teammates went through the most energized practice of their short time together, as they prepared for one of their biggest games of the year that Wednesday against the defending state champion Cougars from Oak Knoll High. Coach Roberts pulled them all together after practice, just before they hit the locker room, and beamed, "You all were amazing today. If you play on Wednesday with the focus and energy you showed today, Oak Knoll doesn't stand a chance. See you all tomorrow."

Taking Ernestine aside, Dawn asked if she would give her a ride to Ingrid's after they showered. As they drove over, Ernestine asked, "Do you think something happened to Ingrid?"

"I don't know. You saw what happened with Bart and Nat at the party. I wouldn't be worried if she'd been in school today. But with her out, I want to see if she's all right."

"Got it."

When they pulled in front of Ingrid's home, Ernestine said, "We've got company. That's Bart's Porsche."

Looking toward the house, they saw Bart banging on the front door. As they got out of the car, they could hear him yelling, "Open the goddamn door, Ingrid, or I'll throw a chair through this goddamn window and follow it in." Intent on his assault, he didn't hear them approach.

"Hey, Bart, having a problem figuring out that doorknob?" Startled, he turned to see Dawn and Ernestine at the bottom of the stairs, smiling.

"Get the hell out of here; this is none of your business."

Dawn initially thought to walk up the stairs and stand next to Bart. Dr. Francis came to mind in that moment, so she decided instead to stay at the bottom of the stairs and focus on her breathing. Ernestine stayed five feet behind her, dialing a number on her cell phone.

Dawn looked at Bart, saying, "We wanted to see our friend also, since she wasn't in school today. Any idea why that might be?"

"Get out of my face, bitch, and stay out of this if you know what's good for you."

"I never know what's good for me, Bart, old boy. That's why my life is so exciting. So many jackasses, so little time."

Keeping her eye on her adversary, Dawn tried to hear what Ernestine was saying. She shut off her cell phone after only a few moments, saying, "I've called the police, and they said they'll be here in a moment."

Bart looked at Ernestine to determine if she was lying. Not able to tell, he walked with exaggerated slowness down the stairs to his car, started it up, and accelerated onto the street, tires squealing. In a moment he was out of sight.

"Did you really call the cops?" Dawn asked as he left.

"No, but I figured pretty boy wouldn't want to call our bluff."

As they laughed together, the lock on the door turned and Ingrid opened the door. Dawn and Ernestine froze at the sight of their teammate's swollen face.

"Ingrid, what happened to you?"

"Come in quickly so I can lock the door."

Sitting in the library of the Victorian home, she told them the whole story, tears falling as she talked. Ernestine got up and began to pace while Dawn sat still, focused on her friend's words.

When she had completed her story, Ernestine exploded, "We're going to nail that slimy bastard. My parents are good friends with the owners of the paper and..."

Dawn held up her hand, looking severely at Ernestine.

"Now is not the time for that kind of talk, Ernestine."

The agitated senior stopped short, as if she had also been hit. She began to argue, until she saw the expression on Dawn's face, to which she responded with a "Goddamn it," and sat down in an overstuffed chair near the huge fireplace.

Turning again to Ingrid, Dawn said softly, "Thanks for trusting us. It will stay between us. How do you think you want to handle this?"

Ingrid closed her eyes and lowered her head. "I'm not going to do anything about it. I've already told Bart we're through and I'm going to leave it at that."

Ernestine bolted from her seat, yelling, "Not do anything? You were beaten! We've got to nail him." Dawn stood and faced her, veins bulging in her neck. "Ernestine, this is Ingrid's decision, so shut the hell up."

Ernestine seethed as she looked up at Dawn. Pacing back and forth while Dawn and Ingrid stayed still, she finally threw herself down on the couch by the door, saying, "Fine, you're right. Whatever." Gripping the pillows on either side of her, she looked as though she were holding on so as not to shoot through the roof, while her friends continued their conversation.

Sitting back down, Dawn looked at Ingrid and asked, "How about your family? What did they say?"

"They don't return from their trip until Thursday, and by then it should be healed. I won't go to school until then. So as long as you both keep this between us, nobody will have to know."

Ernestine let out a low moan as if she were caged.

"All right, then that's how we will handle it. Do you want to stay here, or come over and stay at my house so that Bart doesn't come back and threaten you? You'd have the place to yourself. My mother can be trusted, and if Bart did somehow find out or guess you were there, you'd be safe since my mother has contracted with a security firm to watch the place because of the threats we've been receiving."

Ingrid reacted with shock at the mention of the security firm, to which Dawn responded, "It's no big deal, and they'll probably be sent away after the homecoming weekend. The point is that you would be safe."

Ingrid didn't hesitate. "I'll gather my stuff really quickly and let's get out of here. I'll call my parents and tell them I got lonely and took you up on a really nice offer. Thank you." Looking at Ernestine she said, "I really appreciate your anger, Ern, I really do. But right now I've got to do it this way."

"I understand; I do. It's just that the crap these guys get away with makes me nuts."

The remainder of the week was a blur of activity. Bart drove by Dawn's home on Tuesday, and seeing the security guard parked there, did not return. Ingrid went back to school on Thursday, face healed and all the assignments she had missed because she said she had the flu, completed.

The field-hockey team defeated Oak Knoll 2–0, the first time they had been shut out in over ten years. They followed that victory with their third shutout in three games that Friday, while the football team squeaked by Canaan 6–0, as Bart Bainbridge had one of the worst games in his athletic career. Ingrid had told him for the second time when she returned to school that she never wanted to see him again, that she had taken date-stamped pictures of her bruised face, and had recorded his threatening voicemail messages for proof of his beating her; and that if he tried to either see or touch her she would go to the police and press assault charges. He walked away without saying a word.

Sixteen

THAT MONDAY, WITH less than two weeks until homecoming weekend, the football players' efforts to create an alternative pep rally were cancelled. It was done quietly, after a huge majority of the football players voted to go to the traditional rally. The school was electrified as the word spread, many coming up to Dawn and congratulating her. She purposefully acted low-key, blunting all acts of celebration over which she had control. She was very firm with her key organizers, telling them to take the high road and not gloat.

Most listened, with the exception of Ernestine O'Malley. As soon as she heard the news, she went looking for Bart Bainbridge. Finding him in the cafeteria with half a dozen of his teammates, she marched up to their table. Standing on the bench of the table next to his, she shouted to the whole cafeteria, "Ladies and gentlemen, can I please have your attention? I wanted to make sure that everyone here has heard the news that the football players, represented by Bart Bainbridge and his posse at this table in front of me, have been shown that they are not as big and bad as they think they are. They have caved in regarding their efforts to set up a football-only pep rally and will be joining the officially sanctioned rally where they will be introduced with—oh my God—all the other fall sports teams."

As Bart started to get up, she stepped from the bench onto his table, forcing those sitting there to scramble to keep their food from being knocked over. "And one final thing. I'd be remiss if I didn't personally congratulate the football team's fearless leader, the aforementioned Bartholomew Bainbridge, for his three-interception effort against lowly Canaan this past Saturday. Great job, Bart."

Before he or any of his teammates could respond, Ernestine stepped down from the other side of the table and walked out of the cafeteria, leaving Bart standing red-faced in her wake.

Dawn was incensed when Ernestine told her what she had done. Pulling her into an empty room in the gym, she closed the door and said, "Damn it, Ernestine; that was exactly what we didn't want to happen. You've provided a rallying instance for the hard-core football players to use to keep their crap going. You've also made it more likely that they'll do something stupid."

"Oh, like Bart and his crew need provocation. Or have you forgotten Ingrid or Jan and what they did to them?"

"No, I haven't. I think of Ingrid and Jan and the others every day. But we can't bring ourselves down to their level. When we do, we become just like them, and it makes everything more difficult."

"All I did was point out what everybody was already going to hear."

Pausing momentarily, Dawn continued, "The major reason I am so pissed is that you have made yourself a target. I am scared for you, Ernestine, and I beg you to stop antagonizing them and focus on protecting yourself. Will you do that?"

Ernestine crossed the room to the windows overlooking the athletic fields. "Don't worry about me; I can take care of myself. Besides, I've known these guys for a long time. They know my dad would kill them if they did anything to me. They might talk about doing something, but they won't act—I guarantee it. So let's get to practice and keep this run of ours going, all right?"

With the announcement that the large majority of the football team had voted to support the sanctioned pep rally, the buzz in the high school shifted to whether the concert and related weekend events would decrease participation in the home-coming football game and traditional post-football-game party.

A coordinated effort to generate interest in the music of the ten featured singers/musicians was a major focus of the remaining time leading up to homecoming weekend. Johnny Cardone put a full-page ad in *The Fair Shore Quill* that included biographical information about them and a list of their recordings. He also put all of their albums, tapes, and CDs on sale for half price.

Joseph Bruschi wrote extensive pieces on each of the ten, documenting how they had written and performed songs that provided insights about the human condition and the need to treat everyone with respect.

At the same time, he and Richard Phillips wrote a joint series tying the writing of the ten to social activism. Titled *A Guide to Understanding and Changing the Human Condition*, it mirrored the work Richard was doing in his Honors Symposium. This guide was made available for free to anybody who picked up a copy at the town library, *The Quill* headquarters, or at Johnny Cardone's record store.

Richard Phillips changed the order in the syllabus so that he could focus the efforts of his Honors Symposium on the social relevance of the ten artists' music, playing their music and passing out their lyrics, and having students write reaction papers to what they had heard.

Richard introduced one or more songs from the artist of the day in each of the classes leading up to the Friday night pep-rally. He spoke about the meaning of that music to him and then led the class in a discussion of the meaning of the music to them. During these exchanges, he tied the discussion into other themes that they had discussed in previous classes.

The weekend before homecoming was traditionally a time of great excitement in Fair Shore. The combination of it being the first of six conference football games in a row that determined entrance into the state tournament, as well as the excitement of the build-up to homecoming weekend, usually led to an exciting time for all.

This weekend was no exception, but of course the success of all of the athletic teams significantly broadened the interest of all of the students and townspeople.

All six of the fall high-school teams entered weekend competition undefeated, the field-hockey team having won their fourth game that Wednesday, 8–1 over Lincoln Crest. The disappointment in the locker room over giving up their first goal of the season was more than balanced by the fact that their win put them in first place in their conference. In addition, there were reporters from four newspapers who wanted to interview the field-hockey team; this was actually the first time that *The Quill* had any competition.

Saturday was a perfect day for sports, with clear skies and cool fall temperatures. Five of the six teams responded accordingly, with the field-hockey team winning their fifth game by a score of 9–0. The men's and women's cross-country and soccer teams also won impressively.

The football team lost their first conference game in four years, 24–17. Bart Bainbridge recovered from his disastrous performance the week before to throw for two touchdowns and run for over a hundred yards. The defense, however, could not hold the Fighting Bengals of Cedar Ridge, who ran for over 300 yards and won the game with under a minute on the clock, their first football victory over Fair Shore in their thirty-three games together.

The Fair Shore stands, jammed with the usual-capacity football crowd, sat in simmering silence as the final gun sounded. The Cedar Ridge players seemed as stunned as their hosts, with the hugs and high fives surprisingly subdued.

When Dawn heard the score, she immediately called Ernestine and her other friends who had been active in the preparation for the alternative homecoming activities. Her message to them was the same, to be careful for the remainder of the weekend, since the hard-core football players would be looking to punish someone— so anyone working actively on the alternative activities would be likely targets. All agreed except for Ernestine, who told Dawn that she had every intention of rubbing the loss in their faces if given the chance.

Having committed to working with Melissa, Erica, and other key members of the planning committee on that night and again on Sunday, Dawn called Lou and asked him to keep an eye out for Ernestine if he and the band went to any parties that involved members of the football team. She also encouraged him to be careful, a suggestion that prompted the laugh-filled reply, "OK, Mom."

Buddy Fontanella's arrest that night did not, unfortunately, surprise anybody who knew him. The fact that it happened because he had driven his father's brand new Cadillac into the side of Ernestine O'Malley's car did.

The call that Dawn received that night, telling her that Ernestine was at the emergency room of Fair Shore Hospital was also not a surprise— until she found out that Ernestine had been nowhere near the football team's party. She had decided to listen to Dawn and not go near the team, and was driving through town when Buddy saw her, turned his car, and rammed her on the driver's side. The EMT crew that arrived five minutes after the crash said it was a miracle that she not only survived the crash but that she was able to walk under her own power into the emergency room.

The same could not be said for the All-State tackle. He suffered severe lacerations to his head and neck and possible damage to his left eye. Witnesses at the scene stated that he had deliberately turned his car with the intent of ramming Ernestine. Buddy was taken to the emergency room and stayed the night for observation. Ernestine was driven home by her parents an hour after her arrival.

The Fontanella incident was like a tire iron to the head of the football establishment at Fair Shore High. Coach Oates gathered every football player onto the field that Monday afternoon after classes concluded.

"I am going to be up here for no more than two minutes, and you all better damn well listen to every word I say—and then act accordingly. We have a rich tradition of football excellence at Fair Shore, dating back to the beginning of football play in this state. Our actions over the next five days will go a long way toward determining if you all have made a decision to tarnish that reputation.

"We need to concentrate 110% on our game with Grand Shore on Saturday. I have never, in thirty-plus years of coaching, lost two football games in a row. We cannot afford to be distracted by any of the other events that are being planned for this weekend. If I hear of *anybody* doing *anything* to interfere with *any* activities that are taking place this coming weekend, I guarantee that you will never play football here again, ever, and I will do my best to run you out of this school." Pausing to control his emotions and to ensure that his final statement was clear, the legendary coach cleared his throat and concluded, "I love Buddy Fontanella like a son, and, irrespective of the results of the police investigation regarding his actions Saturday night, *he has played his last football game for Fair Shore High.*

"It is your choice, gentlemen, whether you choose to enhance or denigrate the honor and tradition that is Fair Shore High School football."

Turning his back on over one hundred assembled athletes, he stalked off the field, leaving the control of the practice to his coaches.

The mood in the entire school loosened, with the final days of preparation for the big weekend seeming almost anti-climactic to many. The Friday afternoon pep rally was a monster success, including extended ovations for all of the fall athletic teams. The moment that was a vindication for Dawn and her allies, and a bitter note of reality about the changing times for the football team, came during Principal McMullen's opening remarks:

"The Fair Shore fall athletic teams have never been so healthy. Five of the six teams enter the weekend undefeated, with the women's field- hockey team winning its fifth game by shutout. The lone exception is the football team."

The screaming and yelling by a number of the women in the audience after his remarks were, by all accounts, over the top.

The town was unusually quiet for a Friday night. The traditional pre-game parties had been cancelled, and the football team was ordered home with a first-ever 11:00 p.m. curfew that not one player violated. The organizers for Saturday's festivities also went to bed early, many of them getting up before daybreak. Prayers by all for good weather that Saturday were met with cool temperatures and clear skies.

The turnout for the alternative activities was beyond all estimates. The organizers scrambled for more food, portable toilets, and volunteers, as an enthusiastic mix of adults of all ages and young children and teenagers descended on the town. The Adams Amphitheater was filled to capacity for both the afternoon and evening of music, and the musicians all arrived and played sets that were energized and drew in the crowd. Some of the groups played together spontaneously. Johnny Cardone jammed on at least one song with each of the bands, while doing a particularly moving set with his son and Max Lunatic.

Fans of the football team saw two things that none of them had seen in all their years of attending Fair Shore High School football—empty seats for their game with Grand Shore and their second loss in a row, by a score of 10–7. The crowning insult to the football program came that evening when half the normal crowd of students came to the traditional football homecoming dance, the remainder having opted for rock-and-roll and food from fifteen nations.

The only down moment of the weekend for Dawn was Richard Phillips' disjointed and dispirited presentation at the opening of the concert. She didn't see him after criticizing him for his poor speech, which suited her fine. When the concert ended at midnight because of a state ordinance, many of the musicians and audience members moved the show over to the Cardone house, where music played until after sunrise.

Dawn and Erica left the party at 2:00 a.m., exhausted from the activities of the day and the emotional turmoil of the weeks leading up to their victory. The standing ovation they both received for their efforts was spontaneous and heartfelt, and both went to bed feeling extremely satisfied with their success.

"I spoke with Richard after you yelled at him yesterday," Erica said, looking sideways at her daughter as she buttered her toast. "I'm having lunch with him on Monday."

Dawn stopped chewing her granola and yogurt, staring incredulously at her mother.

"Mom, I thought you had decided to stay away from him. What did he say that got you to agree to change your mind?"

"He said that you were right about his speech, and that he has decided to quit drinking, cold turkey. He says he's tired of disappointing people like you."

"Yeah, well I know personally that's not the first time he's used that line."

"I don't know, honey. I came close to believing him."

"Drunks are good at getting people to believe in their latest lie, but you should know that better than most."

"I also think, Dawn Randall Mortenson, that if he had his preference between the Mortenson women, he'd pick you. He was really devastated by your attack."

"Come on, Mother, listen to yourself. He's not, as you said when I asked you recently, worth it. We'd put so much effort into this weekend and then he gets up there and sounds as convincing as a single lump of cottage cheese. If he's so interested in having our love and respect then he would have done a better job of preparing for his speech."

"Well, I think there is more going on here than meets the eye. I think the reason you're so pissed is because you're attracted to him and don't want to admit it."

"Of course I'm attracted to him, Mother. That is not the issue. I've always been attracted to brilliant losers. Look at the guys I've dated. The issue of attraction comes in second to the issue of betrayal for me. He betrayed us big time and I have enough crap to deal with than to waste my time with someone like that. I really do hope you have a good time; I just don't want to be anywhere near him."

Erica swallowed her toast.

"I can't argue with anything you're saying, and I'm going into this with eyes wide open. Thanks for your thoughts. I'll only be home a couple of hours after our lunch before I get on a plane for that three-day business conference in Vegas. Will you be home between three and five?"

"Probably not. Ernestine and I are getting together with a couple friends to go over how the weekend went, then have dinner and wind down after all the craziness. She'll be staying with me while you're gone."

"Excellent. It will be good for you to have some companionship for that period of time. And you're sure you feel all right with my cancelling the security guard, since we haven't gotten any calls lately and it seems like the focus on you has subsided?"

"I'm positive everything will be cool. You just enjoy your conference and do well with your speeches."

Erica's lunch with Richard was uneventful, his primary focus being to convince her that he had really stopped drinking and hurting and disappointing people. Erica came back to an empty home, as she had anticipated, and left in plenty of time to catch her flight.

Seventeen

"WELL, IF THERE was any doubt in your mind about how successful the weekend was that meeting should have blown the doubts away. Everyone was so wired!" Ernestine leapt out of her car as soon as she parked it in front of Dawn's house.

Dawn, smiling broadly, opened her passenger-side door and answered, "I am not arguing with you. Everyone seemed genuinely happy with how it had gone. God, the football team must be pissed, with losing two games in a row and having empty seats in the stadium. It is so cool that they are finally playing second string to some of the other teams at school."

Both the seniors laughed as they ran up the steps. Dawn paused as she reached the front door. "Damn it, there is a light on in the kitchen that I know I didn't leave on. I don't like how this feels, Ernestine. I want to hold off going in. Come on; let's get back in the car."

"Jeez, Dawn, everything is all good. Besides, I really need to go to the bathroom. Nobody is going to hassle the two of us, and, I mean, I *really* have to go."

Smiling as her friend started to shift back and forth in exaggerated discomfort, Dawn unlocked the front door. Before she could turn to switch on the living room lights, she was grabbed and pulled into the house, her mouth covered with a wet chloroform-soaked cloth. Ernestine was grabbed from behind and drugged, and both were carried through the living room as a van pulled into the driveway and up to the back door. The girls were placed in the van by the two large men who had grabbed them, and who had then climbed into the van and slammed the door.

After some time, Dawn began to gain consciousness, but all she could see were shadows. She tried to hear, but any sounds were muted as if she were listening through gauze. Closing her eyes, she breathed deeply in an attempt to regain full consciousness. As the minutes went by, she began to hear more distinct sounds, but she continued to keep her eyes closed until she could make out what was happening. Her eyes jumped open when she heard a highly intense scream; she looked toward the sound and saw vague figures on the other side of the room. Not being able to clearly see the figures, she was startled when a voice near her right ear said,

"Well now, Ernestine, look what your scream did. You woke your friend from her golden slumbers."

Turning toward the voice, she looked at a canvas hood covering a head not six inches from her face. Starting, she tried to pull away and realized for the first time that she was tied to a chair, arms bound to the back of it, feet loosely bound to the front legs. Looking intently at the hooded figure, and beginning to be able to see more clearly, she turned back toward the location of the scream. Two other hooded men were standing in front of Ernestine, who was nude, straining against ropes that held her spread-eagled on a four-poster bed.

"Well, well, Dawn, darling. You are the lucky one, taking longer than Ernestine to wake up, for now you are going to be able to watch what we are going to do to you, while we do it to your loud-mouthed friend."

Dawn listened intently to the large man who was speaking so close to her face. As if reading her thoughts, he snarled, "It won't do you any good, darling, to try and recognize my voice. You've never met any of the three of us, so strain to recognize our voices all you want; it will do you no good. Once we finish our business with you, we are out of Fair Shore, never to return."

"Then I will spend every waking hour once I get out of here searching for that voice until I find you and bring you in, you pig."

"Nice thought, but you are not really going to be able to put your thoughts together too well after we are done with you. You see, I'm a research scientist in pharmacology. I've got a doctorate and a medical degree and I'm paid a lot of money to study drugs and how they impact people. I've created a cocktail for you that's powerful enough to leave you without any brain function while neutralizing any trace of the chemical and replacing it with alcohol and heroin. When we let them find you, they will find a beautiful vegetable that will become a living example of what not to try and change in this town.

"And I want to thank you for making it so easy for us. We wanted to grab both of you since you have both been such obvious leaders of this little weekend activity, and your decision to stay together tonight made it so much easier for us. I really appreciate your cooperation."

As Dawn listened, she looked around the room, realizing that she was in an expensive old home with perfectly finished floors, high ceilings, and floor-to-ceiling windows. She looked out of the closest windows, onto trees and blue sky.

"Ah, darling, you are the inquisitive one, aren't you?" cooed the leader. "Trying to get your bearings, I see. Let me help you. This mansion we are in is up on a hill, removed from prying eyes or ears. Even if we were close enough to be heard, the walls and windows in this particular room are sound-proofed, so you could scream for hours and nobody would hear you.

"We are on the fourth floor, so that if we did have visitors, there is no way they would be able to hear you."

Cold panic gripped Dawn for the first time, as the intent of her abductors and the hopelessness of her situation forced itself onto her. Ernestine began to cry as the reality hit her as well, tears falling down her face and onto her naked body.

"Well there we go, Ernestine; you finally understand. Good girl. I knew you were a quick study, and a realist. Your friend here is also very smart, but much too idealistic to acknowledge that the fairy-tale life she could have led is over. Such a shame, too; she could have made one of the Fair Shore studs a wonderful trophy wife. Now, none of them are going to want to sit with her night after night and watch her drool."

Dawn focused again on the speaker, saying calmly, "My mother will not rest until she finds you. No matter where you go or what you do, she will spend whatever it takes in time and money to find you. You will always be looking out for her if you do this."

"Actually, we have taken that into consideration. You are right; she is very accomplished and has access to significant financial and investigative resources. Which is why we have our secret weapon downstairs, waiting to come up. You remember Buddy Fontanella, don't you? Well, he is out on bail and we have allowed him to help us with this little caper. His semen is going to be in both of you before I administer the drugs that will take away your brain function.

"When you're found he will be there as well. He and Ernestine will be dead from an overdose. He'll be the perfect suspect in what will look like a drug-and-alcohol-crazed sex romp that unfortunately went a little overboard. We will be free and clear, and he will take all the blame. Your mother will certainly have her doubts, but nowhere to turn for clues. I have taken a lot of time thinking this through in the weeks since you've begun to make our lives miserable. Now, we're going to have to tape both your mouths before we go get Buddy. We wouldn't want you to suggest anything that would cause him pause, for he is a big ox."

The men moved quickly to cover the girls' mouths with duct tape, wrapping it all the way around their heads so they could not possibly force it free. Dawn moved her hands and feet as inconspicuously as possible to try to work them loose. Ernestine, on the other hand, was paralyzed with fright in the midst of a panic attack that had her face turning scarlet.

Dawn turned at the sound of one of the doors in the room opening, and saw Buddy Fontanella filling the door frame, his face as red as Ernestine's, a patch over his damaged eye. He looked with uncontrolled lust at Ernestine spread-eagled on the bed. Dawn had been picked up in her chair and moved to within fifteen feet of the bed, so she could watch Buddy with her friend. Looking around as she was being moved, she saw little else that she hadn't already noticed.

Her plan finalized in her mind, waiting for the right moment to act, she watched the movement of all the inhabitants of the room. Buddy looked at her briefly, coming over to leer down at her before moving slowly toward the naked senior. Taking off his shirt as he walked, he exposed rippling shoulder and arm muscles and a protruding gut.

As the three hooded men moved with him toward the bed, Dawn moved her feet from out of the rope that had bound them and stood up as straight as she could, still attached to the chair with her bound hands. With all the men focused on Buddy's walk toward the nude seventeen-year-old, they didn't notice Dawn's movement. Ernestine had noticed, and for a brief moment their eyes met, Dawn nodding in her direction before turning and running as best she could, toward the floor-length window nearest to where she had been sitting. As the men heard her movement, they turned to chase her. They were not fast enough. When she was three feet from the window, she turned sideways and hurled herself toward it, ensuring that the chair hit the window with full force.

James Masterson, the owner of the estate that adjoined the abandoned hostage house, saw her fall as he was walking his dogs on the hill overlooking the property. Looking over, he saw her hit the ground, her body and the chair that held her breaking completely upon impact with the driveway.

A self-employed financial advisor who worked from home, he dropped the leashes of his two golden retrievers and reached toward his belt for his cell phone, dialing 911 for assistance. Explaining what he had seen and where it had happened, he ran toward Dawn's broken body. As he finally reached her, he bent over her to check her pulse; then he heard a noise behind him. He looked up the driveway toward the four-car garage at the top of the hill and saw three hooded figures running toward a Ford Expedition.

Realizing that they were trying to leave and that the only way to do that was down the driveway on which he knelt, he paused momentarily before scooping up Dawn's bleeding body and running toward his own home. He did not have to run far. The Expedition roared past where he had just knelt, unconcerned with what he was doing.

Just as the truck turned and lurched out the gated entrance to the estate, it ran into the side of one of two police cars that had arrived simultaneously at the scene, pushing the police car twenty feet onto a manicured lawn on the other side of the tree-lined street. Within five minutes, three additional police cars and two ambulances were on the scene, and the three men sat handcuffed in one of the patrol cars.

Officers moved quickly toward the front door when they saw Buddy Fontanella running across the large backyard in the opposite direction of all the action. It took three cops to wrestle him down and handcuff him. They left one officer with a gun pointed at his head, while the others moved cautiously up the stairs toward the fourth floor, guns drawn. Reaching the landing and hearing Ernestine's muffled screams, they burst into the room to see her lying tied to the bed, having ripped one bloody ankle free.

The media coverage that followed had been unprecedented in Connecticut history. Joseph Bruschi won multiple awards for his coverage of the story, which included the arrest of seven Fair Shore football team supporters in the kidnapping and attempted murder of Dawn and Ernestine. The mastermind of the kidnapping was Dr. Edward Thornton, a former Fair Shore football player and a research scientist.

Dawn somehow survived her fall, and had over two dozen operations to fix her broken body. She had been unconscious for fourteen months.

PART TWO

—⁓⁓—

"Like art, revolutions come from combining what exists
into what has never existed before."
Gloria Steinem

"Do one thing every day that scares you."
Eleanor Roosevelt

"Never doubt that a small group of thoughtful committed citizens
can change the world. Indeed it's the only thing that has."
Margaret Mead

Eighteen

"MMMMMEHHH."

Erica Mortenson jerked awake, twisting toward what had been fourteen months of lifeless form in the hospital bed near the window overlooking midtown Manhattan.

"Aaaaah, water!"

Dawn Mortenson, hair matted from sweat and lack of movement, rolled slowly onto her side, facing her mother.

Erica quickly handed her daughter a water cup from the table near her right elbow. Dawn tried taking the cup and missed it, water spilling on her and her bed. Before Erica could position the cup so that her daughter could reach it, Dawn leaned back, and with a second, softer movement took the cup and drank deeply, spilling half of it on her light- green hospital gown.

"More?" she asked, beginning to realize she was talking to her best friend. "Mother, mother?" Lunging to her other side to see what was there, she lurched back to look deeply into her mother's face. "Mother? Where? Oooooh. Whaz going on?"

Dawn's mind desperately searched for data that would help her understand her situation. She was slowed by her mother's embrace, Erica sitting on the side of the hospital bed and lifting the upper half of her eighteen-year-old daughter into her arms, tears cascading down her face, deep purple bags under each eye, her four hours of sleep a night showing clearly. Thinking she should call the medical staff, she decided to hold her daughter's head to her chest, softly stroking her red hair, cut short for the multiple operations that had been needed to put her body back together again.

During the fourteen months that it had taken for Dawn to regain consciousness, she had become famous. Her fight to gain equality for women's sports in Fair Shore, Connecticut had created local prominence for her. When she and Ernestine O'Malley had been kidnapped by a group that did not want to see the male dominance altered, and she had chosen to risk her own life to save her friend, she was embraced nationally as a heroine.

Dawn fell into her mother's arms, resting her tortured brain as her mother stroked her hair. Erica couldn't talk, her relief of having her daughter back overwhelming her. Three minutes of intense connection followed, before Erica started talking, continuing to hold her daughter against her chest.

"Dawn, you have been in a coma for over fourteen months after you threw yourself out the window of Dr. Edward Thornton's estate, trying to save Ernestine." Erica's tears slowed her speech, neither woman doing anything to stop them. "Your fall was seen by a neighbor who ran over and pulled you out of the driveway where you had landed. He called the police on his cell phone when he saw you fall, and they subsequently caught the three adults and Buddy Fontanella.

"Ernestine is all right and has visited you regularly. All the men who were part of the plot to kidnap and hurt you were caught. There were seven and they are all in jail."

Inhaling deeply, Erica pulled her hand to her face where her one- handed effort to clear moisture from her face did no good at all. Dawn, watching her failed efforts, moved back from her mother's embrace, lying back down on the pillow while Erica blew her nose and reached for more tissues.

Her mother wiped her face while Dawn's head revolved very slowly, studying her home of fourteen months for the first time. Her observation was interrupted by the arrival of Janice Howley, the Head Nurse on G-3, who had spent the most time with Dawn and her mother, staying long after her shift to sit with Erica and watch together for the smallest signs of recovery.

Stopping short just inside the door to the room, she put her hand to her mouth before exclaiming, "Oh thank God you are awake!" Looking at Erica, she continued softly, "You have her back, Erica."

"Yes we do, Jan. Dawn, Janice is the Head Nurse here at University Hospital. She spent hundreds of hours with you."

As Dawn began to respond, she lurched forward with savage blasts of pain tearing through her body. Erica gasped and Janice moved purposefully toward her patient. "This is normal, Erica, for someone who has been unconscious for so long." Looking at the screen that was monitoring Dawn's vital signs, Janice paged Dawn's medical team.

As Dawn jerked in her bed, Janice turned to Erica. "She will be fine. Please sit over in the chair by the window. This room will be filling quickly."

Erica followed Janice's directions. Two individuals hurried into the room with a gray-haired, dark-skinned woman following close behind. This stately woman quickly took charge, and for the next sixty minutes Erica watched doctors and nurses who had operated on and had attended to her daughter talk with her and do whatever was necessary to understand her physical and mental status and transition her to a stabilized condition. After the intense hour, Dawn was medicated and sleeping, and the African-American doctor asked Erica to sit with her as the other staff left the room.

"I could not be more pleased with her status after her two dozen operations and all these months of unconsciousness. She does not seem to have lost any mental functioning and her psychological state is extremely realistic and appropriate. Physically, she is way ahead of where she should be if she were a normal eighteen-year-old, which she obviously is not. Her martial arts training, athletic conditioning, and physical and mental strength have served her well. The bottom line is that, in my thirty years of reconstructing broken bodies, I've never seen anyone as far ahead in her recovery as Dawn seems to be. She is one of the strongest patients I have ever seen."

Listening to the world-renowned doctor saying these words, Erica erupted into tears, sobs controlling her body as the months of worry began to leave her. Dr. Baldwin put her arm around the relieved mother and let her cry, offering her tissues when her sobbing slowed. After a few minutes Erica stood slowly, picking up the tissues that had fallen around her and throwing them into a trash can by the door.

Turning to Dr. Baldwin, who had also risen, she said, "You have no idea how much I appreciate what you have done to bring my baby back to me. I was told that you are the best when we arrived, and you and your team have certainly proven that to be true. Since she is medicated and you expect her to sleep for five or six hours, I'm going to go across the street to my hotel room and clean up and make some calls to let some people know she's all right. I'll be back very shortly, and look forward to the conversation that the three of us will have about how her recovery will progress." As tears began to form again, Erica waved her hand in front of her face and turned and left the room. Dr. Baldwin took one final look at her sleeping patient and quietly exited.

Erica walked very slowly through the hospital waiting room and out the main entrance into the tumbling snowfall. Pulling the collar of her navy blue winter coat up around her ears, she waited for the light to change to walk across the street and down a block, to the hotel in which she had been living for over a year. Walking through the lobby of the hotel, James O'Neill smiled at her and said, "Evening, Ms. Mortenson." Smiling back, she replied softly, "James, she's awake."

His face broke open into a huge smile and he jumped in the air. "All right, oh man, that's so great! Oh Erica, I am so happy for you." Catching himself calling the older woman by her first name, he stopped and looked around the lobby at the half a dozen guests who were staring at him. Seeing the smile on the face of the woman he had watched slogging through the hotel for months on end, he thought, "Screw it." He ran around the counter that shielded staff from the guests and threw his arms around the startled fifty-two-year-old, lifting her in the air and spinning her around before putting her down. Then he stepped away and said, "I am so happy for you and your daughter. This is the best news I have ever heard."

Erica stood stunned, looking at the handsome young man in his twenties whom she had gotten to know during the months of caring for her paralyzed only-child. Tears began to form and she knew she didn't want to begin to cry in public. Waving her hand in front of her face for the second time in ten minutes, she mouthed a "thank you" to the desk clerk and took off toward the elevator. Not able to contain himself, James shouted at her back, "She is so lucky to have a mother who cares as much as you." His words pushed her toward the elevator as she stabbed at the button, glad that the door opened immediately, letting her into the privacy that she so needed at that moment.

The tears came suddenly as the elevator door closed quietly, increasing in magnitude so that, by the time she reached the door to her fifteenth-floor suite, she was sobbing uncontrollably. Fumbling for the key in her purse, she found the plastic rectangle, inserted it into the lock, and stumbled into her room, the door closing loudly behind her. Falling out of her heavy coat, she lay down on the bed and sobbed deeply into the rich bedspread, letting fourteen months of emotion escape.

Nineteen

RICHARD PHILLIPS LAY silently on his back in the four-poster bed at the five-star hotel in Philadelphia, a stunning twenty-something graduate school Psychology major asleep to his left. Thinking whether he wanted to wake her for another go at what had been pretty good sex, he was startled by the ring of his cell phone at his side. Glancing at the large clock next to the bed, he was surprised that it was almost 2:00 p.m.

"Richard Phillips."

"She's awake."

"No kidding. Is she going to be all right?"

"Yes. Full recovery expected. The media is already starting to converge."

"Thanks. You'll have your money when I get there."

Richard reached past the clock and lifted the half-empty glass of Scotch to his lips, finishing the drink with one gulp. He pushed the sleeping student and told her to get dressed and get out.

The lives of many had changed when Dawn jumped four stories to her near-death, with three former Fair Shore residents more impacted than most. Richard Phillips blessed Dawn on every one of the over 400 days since, for her decision to jump. He'd grabbed the opportunity to tell the world of her courage and how he had helped her in her crusade against Fair Shore's establishment. He had convinced her boyfriend Tripper to quit school and join him in his company, increasing Richard's credibility when he spoke about his role in Dawn's life. Tripper had made and spent more money than he had ever thought that he would see. Richard's articles and speeches, created either alone or in conjunction with Tripper—about taking a stand and fighting for what is right—had earned him over a million dollars since that November evening, putting him onto the A-list of public speakers at the Altamont Speakers Bureau. The young woman that Richard kicked out of his hotel room had heard him speak at the University of Pennsylvania the evening before Dawn had woken up, and had approached him after his speech with a desire to get to know the mentor of one of her heroes.

Joseph Bruschi slept well, content with his growing reputation as a serious writer, having written a best-seller that won multiple prizes about Dawn's fight against the Connecticut town's male-dominated sports franchise. Completed within two months of her plunge and rushed to press, his account had become the official version of what had really happened. His reporting for *The Fair Shore Quill* for ten years had given him an inside track to all the details of what had transpired, and he aggressively used them to pull together his best seller. The town had not appreciated his coverage, the paper firing him one month after Dawn's plunge. It turned out for the better when the prestigious *Hartford Courant* hired him to write the story. With a television movie planned and a follow-up book in the works, he had grown wealthier than he had ever expected.

Twenty

ERICA AWOKE ON the hotel bed where she had fallen asleep. Glancing at the clock, she gasped, realizing that she had left her daughter alone for five hours. Jumping out of bed, she rushed into the bathroom to splash water on her face, threw off her wrinkled clothes and put on another outfit, put on some lipstick, gathered her purse, and headed out the door and down to the lobby. Stepping off of the elevator, she noticed a larger-than-average number of people in the hotel; she thought it strange that there would be this type of influx on a Tuesday evening. At the exit, she was startled to hear her name shouted from someone to her left. Looking over, she noticed a group of reporters and camera operators, lights suddenly on, surging toward her.

"Erica, what does it feel like to have your daughter gain consciousness?"

"Erica, what did your daughter say?"

"Mrs. Mortenson, is Dawn's father going to be here?"

"Erica, is Dawn going to be able to talk to us today?"

"Is it true that Dawn has brain damage?"

"Richard Phillips has released a statement saying that she will be fine. What is his relationship with you and your daughter?"

As Erica stopped and turned to face the crowd, she saw faces that had become familiar to her, reporters who had come to the hospital and hotel over the months to hear updates about her celebrity daughter's condition.

"Thanks so much for your interest. I really don't have answers to your questions. My daughter woke a few hours ago and we only had a chance to talk for a few minutes before the medical staff took over, and then she went back to sleep. It is my understanding that she is going to be fine, that she has not had any lessening of her mental faculties, and that it will be a while before she is fully reoriented to her situation. Right now she needs rest and quiet so that she can begin the long process of rehabilitation.

"Janet, to your question, Richard Phillips has no relationship with my daughter or me, although he'd like everyone to think the opposite, so he can sell more articles and memberships to the various entities he has created around my daughter's tragedy. That's all I can say now; I really need to get back to see her. I will let her know of your interest and I'm sure we will have more to say over the next few days."

Erica turned, pushed past a handful of reporters who tried to block her path, and rushed out the door and across the street. Thankful that there wasn't a herd of reporters at the hospital, she explained to the few who had gathered there that her daughter would be fine. Striding through the lobby, Erica then said hello to the security staff that she had come to know so well.

As Erica got off the elevator and onto her daughter's floor, she was startled to hear a deep familiar voice say, "Hello, Erica." She turned toward the tall man who greeted her, while she walked toward her daughter's room. Pausing, she involuntarily started and then moved back, catching herself as she bumped into a chair.

Turning crimson, she stood completely still as he stepped forward to embrace her. Moving her purse from her right hand to her left, she slapped him as hard as she could across his left cheek.

"You opportunistic bastard, how dare you show up here within hours of my getting my daughter back. Did you bring your own photographer to make sure to capture the pivotal moment when you emerged from your celebrity to help your former student get her life back together?" As she readied herself to hit him again, a flash went off to her right, followed by two other quick bursts as she shielded her eyes from the light.

Richard motioned the photographer away as he felt his face. Erica, seeing the gesture, swung around and charged the photographer, who stumbled over a table and fell to the floor, his camera jolted out of reach. Erica jumped to the camera and smashed it repeatedly on the concrete floor, taking a moment to remove the memory card from the pieces lying on the floor.

Richard took two steps toward her and then stopped, Erica turning to face him, the memory card safely in her pocketbook, which she held firmly by its strap against her left side.

"You are a lowlife, Richard Phillips, using my daughter's celebrity to promote yourself. I was physically ill the first time I saw you refer to her as your best friend, with Tripper by your side in one of your infomercials for your Institute for Personal Change."

Pivoting around to see where the photographer was and noticing him slinking away, Erica turned back to Richard. "I suggest that you get your sickening presence out of my sight and never come in contact with us again."

As Richard tried to speak, Erica took two steps forward so she was in his face.

"I am deadly serious, Richard. If you try to get in touch with my daughter or come within sight of me again, I swear I will destroy the business you've created around my daughter by going on every media outlet in this country and telling them of your duplicity. I've waited fourteen months to get my baby back and *I will not let someone like you hurt her in any way*."

Richard's mind was churning as he tried his best to figure out what to do or say. He had not expected this response, knowing that Erica had at one time been attracted to him, as most women had been throughout his life.

Deciding to do nothing, he turned and walked slowly away with the photographer, looking back to see Erica take off down the hall in the opposite direction.

Twenty-One

DAWN FELL INTO an overstuffed chair in the corner of the large living room they had entered, dropping her backpack by her side. Erica followed her into her former college roommate's cottage in the woods.

Dawn's recovery once she regained consciousness was like nothing the hospital staff had ever seen. Erica had gotten clearance to let her out of the hospital after only three weeks of recuperation and in-hospital therapy. They had chosen not to mention her departure to anybody except the key hospital staff, but somehow the media had found out and amassed around the car that Dawn and Erica were going to use to get to their country hideaway in the Catskill Mountains. Seeing the crowd, Erica and Dawn retreated back into the hospital, where Erica spent three hours with friends creating an escape plan. It included four limousines with tinted glass entering the hospital's underground parking area, and then leaving at different times and going in four directions. Erica felt pretty certain that they had eluded the media, and very certain that nobody knew where they were headed, since she hadn't told a soul about her close-lipped friend's cabin in the woods, a place they could use for as long as they desired.

"You want to go for a short walk down by the lake, or would you rather rest?" Erica asked her daughter.

"I'd love to get out for a short walk. It's beautiful outside, with the light snowfall on the ground and the sun shining like it is. Just don't expect me to hike twenty miles, at least not today."

Erica put her arm around her daughter's shoulders as they began their walk, Dawn moving into her mother's embrace. Walking slowly, they talked only about what they were seeing, which for Dawn was almost overwhelming after her extended coma. As they lingered along the lake, Dawn looked at her mother and said, "I know you were told to limit our discussion of Fair Shore until I had recovered more fully. I think that time is now."

Erica reluctantly nodded her head in agreement, waiting for the questions.

"What happened to all the Fair Shore friends we made? You have talked cryptically about Richard and Tripper profiting from what I did, but I don't really know what that means. And how about other friends: Tripper's parents and my friends on the field-hockey team, and the other members of Max Lunatic? What's everyone doing?"

On the one hand, Erica had feared this question, knowing it would be coming and unsure about how much detail she should give, especially since Dawn's feelings were so intertwined with the actions of the Fair Shore citizenry. On the other hand, she wanted her intelligent and strong daughter to know everything, so that Dawn could begin the psychological healing process with the same certainty that she had about what she needed to do to fix her body.

"That's a long answer, one that will probably continue throughout our time here. I'll start with Tripper and his family, since you have already heard some of my negative thoughts about Richard and positive thoughts about Joseph.

"Tripper's mother was devastated by what happened to you, possibly the most depressed of anyone in Fair Shore. I don't think she has recovered, to be honest with you, with it happening in the town where she was raised, by people she knows, to someone she loves. But what has really cemented her ongoing depression is the reaction of her son. Richard approached Tripper soon after you entered the hospital, with the idea of the two of them touring the country, telling the story of how brave you were. And he convinced Tripper that it would be a noble and lucrative thing to do. It has been lucrative, with both Richard and Tripper making a lot of money telling their version of your story. His parents are very upset with his choice—as am I and many of his friends. I would think that you'll have a chance to decide for yourself about him at some point when you see him. That's really all I have about him.

"Johnny took your plunge and the ensuing press coverage as an opportunity to go on the road with a band he formed soon after your hospitalization. You might remember that Johnny had been reverting to some of his rock-and-roll celebrity behavior in the months leading to your injury, hitting the booze and talking more and more about the good old days. Well, the spotlight that was shone on Fair Shore obviously fell to some degree on him, and as he did interviews about what happened to you, he also got questions about what he was up to and whether he missed the road. After he'd been asked that for the fiftieth time, he finally said, 'Ya know, I do miss it, and I've started to put together a band and we'll be doing some touring around some songs I've written. We'll do a mix of the old and the new and see what people think.'

"Honey, he hadn't written a word in years, but the response to that announcement was larger than any of us could have imagined, and all of a sudden, he not only saw that there was still an interest in him, but that he damn well better deliver new songs and a new band. So he did. He holed himself up in their basement for a few weeks, wrote some really good music, called some old friends he hadn't seen in years, practiced at one of their old haunts in New York City, and began to play at some small venues, working up to bigger places as his confidence and the audiences grew. And I guess he got what he wanted, because the questions about you lessened and the questions about him increased."

Erica paused, running her hand through her now long red hair. Picking up a stone and throwing it into the lake, she thought for a few more moments and then said, "Johnny wasn't there for Melissa. He went off looking to rekindle his celebrity and she stayed home, trying to make some sense of what had happened to you. As I said earlier, she is still struggling with that question.

"About five months into his touring, Melissa sat him down and told him that he had to choose between her or his former life, because she had moved past those drunken days and she had expected him to as well. So he stopped touring and they are back together doing good things in Fair Shore."

Dawn, a tense and drawn look on her face, stopped walking to listen to her mother. Erica, noticing the look, paused as well, saying, "Why don't we stop with this conversation and get back to the cabin and warm up? You've probably heard enough for one walk by the lake." Dawn did not argue and they started back. As Erica walked up the stairs to the cabin, Dawn stood quietly, looking out at the lake, turning over a stone she had been holding. Seeing her standing alone, Erica paused and then opened the door to the cabin.

Dawn and Erica stayed for two weeks in the cabin, resting and strategizing about their next steps. Erica, Dawn, and Ernestine called a press conference in New York City for the day after they left the cabin, before heading back to the hospital for a full medical check-up. At the start of the press conference, Erica explained to the large group of reporters that this would be the only chance for the press to ask any and all questions, because following that afternoon they would be talking no further with them, focusing instead on getting their lives back together.

The meeting lasted a little over two hours. Erica asked at the two-hour mark if there were any more questions before they went back to being regular citizens. After three more questions, one of the reporters stood and thanked the three for their time and honesty; those who remained applauded them. Most of those in the audience seemed truly appreciative of the effort that the three had made to answer their questions, and came up to shake their hands and wish them well.

As they drove away from the hospital toward Fair Shore after Dawn's thorough and positive checkup, Dawn and Erica both expressed anxiety about returning to the home where Dawn had been kidnapped. It turned out to be an easier re-entry point than they had both expected.

In the living room after settling in, Erica said, "I do like this house and yet I'm not tied to it in any special way. If you decide that we need to move after you've gotten a better sense of the atmosphere in town, then we're out of here. Our conversation at the cabin about moving to the West Coast sounded good to me. My boss has been very clear that the firm will be able to make whatever arrangements are necessary to keep me, so I have total flexibility work-wise. Andre has shown that he means what he says, letting me work from the hotel and your hospital room during your recovery. There have been no double messages from him on that account. He said you were the first priority and that if you decided that we needed to leave this area, it would happen—no questions asked. He's a good guy; you'd like him."

Erica turned to Dawn and asked, "So, what do you see yourself doing now that we are back in town, out of the limelight, and with you getting such a positive report from the doctors? I've deliberately not asked you that question until now, so that you'd have some time to get healthy again."

"That's the question that has been with me front and center since we knew we'd be coming back here. I'd really rather not go back to Fair Shore High to get my degree. My best friends have graduated and there is nothing for me there but aggravation, if my first couple of months were any indication.

"If it were possible to get a tutor or home-school my final credits that would be great. I could really blitz the schoolwork being on my own and I could probably graduate in June or July and go from there. I know I'm behind on college applications, but maybe some schools would let me apply late because of my situation. What do you think?"

Erica shifted in her seat to face her daughter. "What you said is my strong preference, as well. I didn't want to influence your decision, but I don't see any advantage to your being back at Fair Shore High. You are disciplined enough to do well with home study and your grades are good enough that I doubt there would be any issue from the state with that plan. I guess we always have to consider that our friend the principal might try and throw something in our way, but I'm hoping that he realizes it's to his best advantage to let you graduate and be on your way, and out of the small amount of hair he has left."

Dawn laughed, saying, "Let's hope you are right."

Twenty-Two

"HI, COACH." DAWN'S first stop after she had gotten a visitor's pass at the Fair Shore High School office the next Monday afternoon was at the office of Pat Roberts, her former field-hockey coach.

"Dawn!" Sitting behind her desk, looking at the contents of a manila envelope, the young coach jumped up and its contents spilled onto the floor. Sprinting around her desk, she threw her arms around her former star field-hockey goalie, rocking her side to side before catching herself and stepping back. "Damn, that's stupid. Are you all right?"

"Coach, I'm fine, and I really appreciate your reaction to my being here. Not everyone has had the same response. Do you have any time to catch up, or do you need to get out to the gym?"

"Sure, I have a few minutes. What's on your mind?"

"I had a chance to see Ernestine in New York City when we gave our one and only press conference. She seemed alright, but that was just a snapshot. You've seen her work her way through this whole process. Is she all right?"

Pat did not hesitate. "She is fine; she really is. You don't have to worry about her. Others, yes, but not Ernestine. As you can imagine, she had no idea what to do with her anger at what happened to you. Since she had never been touched by Buddy, she was able to get on with her own life pretty quickly. But the fact that you were in the hospital and might not live left her with so much anger she couldn't put anywhere, so she went through months of meltdowns and screaming matches and thrown chairs and battered locker doors and smashed windows. She was a mess. I really think that sports got her through it, and I don't mean to be self-serving. She put all that anger into the remainder of the field- hockey season, basketball, and softball, and she was unbelievable.

"You could not stop her—nobody could. She would be triple-teamed in field hockey or basketball and she'd score. She'd be batting in a softball game, get hit by a pitch, and refuse to go to first base, telling the umpire that she was fine and wanted to hit. They had to look in the rule book to see if that was legal. And in fact it was,

123

in Connecticut—a rule that has since been changed.

"She scored the game winner in every field-hockey game we played after your fall, and we did not lose a game; we went all the way and won the state championship and she willed it to happen. She would not allow us to lose. Same thing in basketball. She averaged 37 points a game and when we were down she would get the team in a huddle and tell them that they were not allowed to lose, that she would not let it happen, and then go and score 15 points in a row and shut down our opponent's top player. We were getting creamed by Wood Ridge midway through the first half. Their 6'5" All-American center was killing us. She told me in a huddle that she was going to take her on one-to-one and stop her. I mean, come on, she's good, but you don't defend someone 15 inches taller than you. That just doesn't happen.

"You should have seen the look on their team's face when Ernestine came out and stood next to their star. They were laughing and pointing and taunting her as the play began. Their center scored the next two times they came down the court, and then only scored three points the rest of the game. Ernestine got so into her head that she couldn't *buy* a basket. Ernestine blocked three of her shots, stripped her of the ball a dozen times, and the crowd went berserk. I have never seen anything like it in all the sports I've watched or played. Michael Jordan, Mia Hamm, Diana Taurisi—I've never seen anyone play to that level, at any time in all my years in sports. Never. She was in a zone that few ever approach and I think that pulled her through. She'd play the game, shower, and head to the hospital to sit by your bedside and talk with you for hours. She'd say 'I know she can hear me and I want her to know I'm here and we are going to get through this together.' I committed to myself that you would hear that story first-hand, and there you have it. She is an amazing person and an even more powerful friend."

Pat stood up quickly and left the room to get a box of tissues that she put on the table between her and Dawn, who was also crying. Sitting quietly for a few minutes, they gathered their thoughts.

"So that was Ernestine. She got through it and when she said that she wasn't going to college until you were better, I hired her to be my assistant and she has been an awesome inspiration for the girls who are still here. She and a few other key people, students and teachers, have really helped, including a number of the football players; and that has been huge. That being said, I need to start practice."

As Dawn walked out of Coach Roberts' office, she turned into the hallway and ran into Nat Brandon.

"Dawn, I heard you were back. How the hell are you?"

Stepping back and creating space between herself and the popular football player, Dawn smiled and said, "I'm all good, Nat. The doctors say that my recovery is way ahead of schedule and that I'm gaining strength every day. How are you doing? Last time I saw you was when you defended Ingrid against Bart. You'll always be one of the good guys on my list after that one."

Furrowing his brow, Nat replied, "Jesus, what a nightmare. Who would have thought that anyone would want to do what they tried to do to you and Ernestine." Pausing to take a deep breath, the muscular athlete continued, "But to answer your question, I'm actually doing very well. Grades are good, the team came together this year in a way that nobody could have imagined, and I've become a peer counselor, trying to help people work through the aftermath of the scandal.

"I've got to run, but do you want to get together later and catch up? I don't know how much you want to reconnect with the town, but you have an open invite to come to our house for dinner. It's your call."

Dawn paused, finding herself ill-prepared to handle such a sincere and positive invitation from a member of the football team that she had challenged so strongly and successfully over a year ago.

"Nat, that is really nice of you; and to answer your question, I don't have a clue what I want to do now that I'm back. But dinner sounds great. How about next Monday night?"

"You are on; we usually eat around eight o'clock, so why don't you come over at seven-thirty so the family can see you before we jump into the food. Your mom can come too, obviously."

"I know she has a meeting that night, which is why I suggested it."

"Great, we will see you then."

Thinking to herself that talking with Nat and her former coach had been a good beginning for easing herself back into the town, Dawn decided not to push her luck. She turned and headed toward the nearest exit, happy to be going home.

Twenty-Three

"GOOD MORNING AND welcome to *What's Happening*. I am your host, Shannon Trevalian, and my guest for our half hour together is Dawn Mortenson, the teenager who challenged the status quo in Fair Shore, Connecticut and won, losing fourteen months of her life in the process. You must have lived under a rock for the past year and a half if you have not heard about that situation, where the effort led by Dawn to gain real and not just legal equality for the female sports teams in Fair Shore led to the kidnapping and attempted rape of Dawn and her best friend Ernestine, a plan that was foiled when Dawn jumped out of a fourth-floor window and into a hospital bed for fourteen months, only to fully recover and return to Fair Shore.

"Dawn, it's great to have you on the show."

"I'm glad to be here, Shannon."

"Which is actually surprising to me, since at your press conference on March 13th you were very clear with the press that you did not want to spend any more public time talking about what happened to you last year?"

"Yes, and I want to thank the press, at least the responsible ones, for respecting our wishes."

"So why agree to come on our show?"

"First of all, our family has been big-time supporters of public radio from before I was born. Second, my mother has listened to your show for the three years you've been on and knows you to be a fair interviewer."

As Dawn sat in the NPR studio, she thought back quickly to the conversation with her mother about coming on the show. They had discussed whether she should bring up her concerns about what she had heard from girls all over the country since she had been out of the hospital.

"And the third and major reason is that, since I got out of the hospital, I have been inundated with emails and letters from all over the country about terrible things that are being done to young men and women, and I wanted to share that information with you and your educated audience."

The experienced interviewer leaned forward as Dawn made her third point, not having been told of this reason for being on the show.

"So why don't we start on point number three. What have you heard that disturbed you?"

Dawn took a sip from the water glass to her right before responding.

"As I said, I heard from many people from all over the country. I've talked to or received specific information from a lot of them.

"I have received dozens of stories about teenage girls and boys *and younger* who have been sexually abused and raped once or multiple times. *Multiple times.* Often by family members, relatives, or friends of the family. Think about how many hundreds of thousands of young girls and boys and young women and men must have been through that type of degradation and violation every year, if I have heard about only dozens in the couple of months since I have been out of the hospital. This is an epidemic and needs to be addressed."

Shannon Trevalian leaned closer to Dawn as she was telling the story, choosing not to jot down any notes, and feeling her heart racing. Looking past Dawn toward her producer, she saw that she was motioning her to keep Dawn talking. She didn't need to be told.

Dawn had been in another place as she was talking, not making eye contact with her interviewer as she recounted what had been told to her. She now shifted in her chair and looked directly at Shannon, asking, "What kind of people would do that at all, much less *repeatedly?*

"And I didn't go seeking this information; people who heard that I stood up against sexual abuse and bullying reached out to me. I choose to mention it on national radio in order to raise consciousness about how the lives of many young men and women are being impacted by this abuse. That fact—and it is a fact—makes me crazy, and I get very angry about the complacency that exists in our society around this issue. I thought you might be receptive to hearing about what I have heard."

"I'm glad that we are having a chance to talk this freely," Shannon responded. "We are going to take a short break and come back to continue this important and timely conversation."

The Mortensons' answering machine was full when they got back home, its red light blinking evenly as they walked through their front door. Three were from friends in town congratulating Dawn on her interview. Eight were from Fair Shore residents, angry about how she had once again brought their town to the attention of the media in a negative way.

The final message caused Dawn and Erica to replay it multiple times. "Dawn, I'm sure you have a number of messages on your machine so I will keep this brief. My name is Nathan Pomerantz and I am what many people call a social change activist. I can help you if you are deciding to help people who are getting hurt in our society. I'm out-of-my-mind, got three PhDs before I was twenty-one, and I don't like where our society is going. We've lost too many young people to the kind of behavior that you described during your interview on NPR. I want that to stop. I've created an organization headquartered in New Haven, Connecticut called The Information Is Power Consortium that fights against that kind of behavior. Hope to hear from you after you check us out at www.ipc.org."

After listening to the message for the third time, Dawn looked at her mother. "What do you think? Sounds like just the kind of guy we need to add to our small circle of friends. Another lunatic genius. Let's call him."

Dawn dialed the number he had left, while her mother listened on the other line. A youngish-sounding man answered on the first ring.

"I'm so glad you called, Dawn. I was entranced by your interview and quite honestly I am concerned for your safety and—sincerely—want to help."

"Hello Nathan, this is Dawn's mother Erica. Just wanted you to know I am also on the line."

"That doesn't surprise me and is actually comforting. Your daughter can be somewhat impetuous and there are a lot of people who don't want the kind of change to happen in our country that you and your daughter represent. And I know you are very smart and a persuasive consultant so I am excited we are all talking together."

"Nathan, we would like to meet you and talk about your ideas in person. New Haven is not far from us, as you know," Dawn chimed in.

"Well hello there. At least my impetuous observation was spot-on. I teach at Yale and live in New Haven. I have flexibility this weekend if you'd like me to come down to Fair Shore or you can come up here."

"Hey Mom, want to get out of town and hang out with the lunatic fringe in New Haven?"

Smiling, Erica replied, "Sounds good to me. Nathan, are you free to get together Sunday afternoon around three o'clock in New Haven?"

"Sold. The Consortium is located at 1200 Cedar Run Road, three minutes off of Exit 56, which is Cedar Run Road. Cedar Run is one way and we're at the corner of Cedar Run and Conservation Place. Can't miss it—we're next to a large brick building with an O'Brian's Pub sign and a huge hanging leprechaun standing over the entrance. When you arrive, ask for me and I will come down and get you. Ladies, it was a pleasure conversing with you, and I will see you on Sunday."

"Well, he was right about not being able to miss it. That building does stand out; and look at that leprechaun." As Erica finished her sentence, she saw a parking spot at the beginning of a line of cars directly across from the entrance to the bar. Pulling the keys out of the ignition, she turned to her daughter. "I'm kind of interested to hear what Nathan has to say."

"So am I. He can't be any more dangerous than some of the other characters we've run into over the last two years."

Erica frowned slightly at her daughter's comment and reached over to touch her cheek. "Unfortunately you are probably right, my dear. You're probably right."

As each turned to open their respective doors, they were thrown forward with the car as it was hit by a large, jacked up pickup truck that jammed them into the car in front of them. Erica's head snapped hard against the steering wheel while Dawn's head twisted forward. As quickly as the truck plowed into them, it backed up, swerved down the street, and made a sharp turn onto Cedar Run and disappeared.

The patrons in O'Brian's and security personnel at 1200 Cedar Run saw the collision and ran out into the street, a retired policeman the first to reach the car. He jerked the driver's side door open and Erica spilled out, the policeman catching her before she hit the street. A Yale student ran to Dawn's side of the car, opening the door and yelling to the policeman that she was conscious. The officer told the student not to let her move.

When she awoke, Erica was lying on a couch in a room located in the back of the bar, the location closest to their car.

Dawn was kneeling by her side, stroking her hair.

"You're all right?"

"Yes, Mom, I'm OK. You've been passed out for about fifteen minutes and you'll be all right as well. We were creamed by a hit-and-run driver. This is Dr. Margolis."

Erica turned to the person that her daughter had motioned toward.

"Hi Erica, I'm Frieda Margolis. My office is a few doors down from the bar so I was able to come right over and look at you both. Your daughter is fine, just a little shaken. Your head hit the steering wheel and you have a nasty welt on your forehead. I just want to do a couple of tests with you for a few moments to make sure you are also all right. Dawn, would you mind waiting in the next room with Nathan?"

Dawn reluctantly returned to sit by Nathan Pomerantz, who had introduced himself to her after the crowd had thinned.

"I'm sorry, Nathan, I can't believe that this hit-and-run was planned as a way to silence me and my mother. That just sounds surreal."

"Welcome to the real surreal world, baby. This stuff happens all the time when people start to try and inform the public about how they are being manipulated. All the time. It happens all the time."

Nathan looked distractedly over her shoulder toward the door as if he expected someone to come in and sweep them up and out of sight.

"I'm just really glad you decided to come up and see us since I know you started the fight on your own."

"What do you mean we've already started the fight?"

"Dawn, my dear, I followed every moment of what you did in Fair Shore, every moment of your successful attempt to get people to wake up to the sexist crap that was going on there. You paid the price, God knows, and lost fourteen months and ten days of your life to the bastards, but you won. Fair Shore is now under a microscope and has to, at least on the surface, change its attitude toward how young women are treated. My colleagues and I follow all of the attempts in this country to help regular people to be treated with respect. Doesn't matter where it is or on what level—community, state, federal, private, public—it doesn't matter.

"Which is why I called you after I heard your interview on NPR. I knew you were well and willing to continue to fight. I had planned on approaching you at some point after you had healed, to congratulate you on your triumph in Fair Shore; and when I heard you on Shannon's show I knew that now was the time to reach out."

Dawn's gaze hadn't left the face of the intense thirty-something sitting next to her. Round-faced and soft-skinned, he looked like he could have been in his teens except for the two scars—one on his chin and the other across his forehead—and the deep laugh lines extending outward from both eyes. *He laughs loud and plays hard*, she thought, as she observed him.

"Where'd you go, baby? Where you at?"

Caught in her thoughts about him, she blushed as he confronted her.

"You must have been thinking about me, or the crimson wouldn't be creeping up your long neck."

"I was, actually, trying to figure you out is all."

"That is not very hard to do. What you see is what you get: a dumpy, hyper-intelligent nerd who got crapped upon most of his youth. I was raised by a father, whose patents to improve the efficiency of manufacturing processes that made it cheaper to make, and therefore buy stuff, made him a ton of money—which he gave away to groups that try to make this country a better place. My need to be for the underdog is unhealthy, carrying over to the sports teams I support, the people I like, the music I listen to...that need has impacted my whole life.

"I will never lie to you, will answer any question with the unvarnished truth, and will be extremely loyal once I am convinced you are on my side. If you are the enemy I will do everything I can to discredit you and make your life a living hell.

"My paranoia does not seem to be coming from some kind of clinical deficit; it seems grounded in a significant amount of reality, as three of my closest colleagues have disappeared in the last two years.

"My evaluation of my abilities does not seem to be over-exaggerated, having scored through the roof on every test I've ever taken, completing my triple Doctorate in Marketing, Computer Intelligence, and Global Affairs from Yale when I was twenty.

"People either love me or hate me, often within seconds. There is absolutely no middle ground in how I am perceived. That bothers me quite a bit, actually. I know there are some terrific people who could have helped the struggle, who have said that they will have nothing to do with me even though they think what I am doing is absolutely the right thing to do. In those situations, I have done everything I could to connect those people with others, from whom they might learn and succeed, with mixed results.

"I love women and have had mostly disastrous relationships with them, for reasons that should be pretty obvious from our first ten minutes together. My honesty and passion and loyalty to them is usually overcome by my unwavering certainty that I am right and my inability to focus on the small things they need, which would show that I really do care. At the end of the day my energy cannot really be shared between a woman I love and the struggle with which I am involved. Knowing that I might disappear or be killed at any time forces me to keep the struggle as the centerpiece of all I do, and most intelligent, self-respecting women think there is more to life than my worldview will allow. It's probably better this way, but things can get lonely. I am blessed to have one daughter from my only marriage and she lives with my former wife, with whom I have a great relationship, now that we are not married and living together. Much of the focus of what I do is with my concern about my daughter's future at the forefront of my mind."

As Nathan paused to take a gulp of his beer, Dawn said, "I really want to hear more, but need to see how my mother is doing."

"I completely understand. I'm not going anywhere."

Dr. Margolis was just finishing her neurological examination as Dawn entered the back room.

"Your mother is fine. A little blurred vision that won't allow her to drive home, assuming your car is drivable; but basically feeling banged up, just as you are. I would recommend no alcohol and getting home as quickly as you can and into bed. You should both be back to normal in a day or two. If headaches or blurred vision are present for either of you tomorrow, you should go see your doctor."

Erica and Dawn walked slowly into the bar from the back room in which she had been examined. Erica asked Dr. Margolis, "How do you prefer to be paid, by credit card or check?"

"Don't be silly. I understand you were coming here to see Nathan. That's all the payment I need."

Smiling broadly as if anticipating Erica's need to argue, the skilled doctor said, "Erica, I will not hear anything more about this. Nathan is a good friend and if you are at all linked with what he is doing, I will always refuse any payment from you. End of story. Here is my card if we need to talk further *about anything*." They thanked her in unison and watched her walk briskly toward the door.

"Well now we have to find out whose car we were pushed into so we can pay for the damages."

"No worries, ladies. That's my old wreck and a few more dents will only make it look more exotic. Might even help me with the babes."

Dawn and Erica looked over toward the bar and the man who had just responded.

"Are you sure? You must have quite a bit more than a few dents."

"I've already checked it out and she runs fine. So does yours, actually. I took the liberty to take your car around the block and she is OK, just a little shimmy that will need to be looked at when you take it to your mechanic. As long as you don't take it up over sixty you'll be fine. As Doc said, if you are a friend of Nathan's, we are all squared away."

Before she could reply, the stranger had turned back to the bar and was in conversation with one of the bartenders. Erica looked at her daughter and mumbled, "Nice people."

"You ain't seen nothin' yet. Let's go get Nathan."

Nathan leaned against the door leading into the back room where Erica had been taken. Smiling literally from ear to ear, he moved forward and offered his hand to Erica. "I'm Nathan and I'm so sorry that you had to receive such a harsh greeting."

Before Erica could respond, Dawn said, "Mother, it is a long story and Nathan has briefed me on what he means. I can fill you in later. He wants to tell us about what he is doing and why he called."

"And I promise to keep it as short as I am able to, before your drive home to get that rest that Frieda insisted that you need."

"I don't think there is a need to keep it short, I'm..." Erica winced as she reached out to Dawn for support.

"My point exactly. You are both very strong women and you've been traumatized. Let's keep this short and we can always talk again if what I say interests you. Before I start, do you want some water or soda or juice or food?"

"The soup I saw someone eating at the bar looked good; may I have that and a seltzer, please?" Dawn asked.

"I probably shouldn't have anything to eat, but a seltzer would be great."

"Jessie, could we have two seltzers, one soup, and another beer? We will be in the RFK room. Thanks."

The waitress who had been standing on the other side of the door smiled and hurried behind the bar to fill the order.

Nathan motioned toward a large door at his right. He opened it and they entered a high-ceilinged lobby that had a marble-topped reception area facing the doors that were the main entrance from the street. Nathan explained to the three security guards who were positioned behind the desk that Erica and Dawn were with him. He pulled an ID from his pants pocket and opened a door to the left of the security station, holding it as Dawn and Erica caught up with him and entered the room. They were in a medium-sized conference room with a mahogany table surrounded by ten chairs.

"Let's get comfortable here and your food will arrive in a few minutes."

He looked at both women and said, "First of all, you need to know that I am serious about your need to get home. So I am going to give you the abbreviated version of why I called you, hopefully to be continued at a later date.

"I am a member of a loose-knit group of individuals from all walks of life who believe that the power structure of the US is heavily biased toward the extremely wealthy, to the detriment of everyone else. No huge 'aha' there; been talked about forever.

"What is different at this point in our wonderful country's existence is the very intentional way that the elite are positioning themselves to stay in power. The primary vehicle for this strategy is the elites' access to the most sophisticated accumulation of personal information in the history of the world, through access—legal and otherwise—to information about each and every one of us that allows them to target us in the most personalized way possible. Erica, they know the brand of soap you use and the size and brand of shoes that you wear. Dawn, they know how you choose to control whether you have a baby or not."

Dawn's eyes narrowed and she sat up straighter in her seat, looking directly into Nathan's deep-set, dark eyes.

"I am not trying to insult you, only to demonstrate the power that anyone who knows what they are doing has over normal people. I also know that the anger you are feeling toward me right now is similar to what you felt when your friend Lou Malone told you information about yourself when he met you, which you thought had invaded your privacy. His mother, by the way, is a member of our team. The information about what individual citizens do and how they act is out there; one just has to be motivated to find it and have the tools to then make it happen. It is not only who you refer to as our enemies, it is anyone with the right tools or enough money. The worst offenders are the tobacco companies, who literally get away with murder. They are the single industry that the Consortium has targeted specifically, because both of my parents died from cigarettes and I will do everything I can to make them unprofitable and therefore less effective at killing good people.

"Arms used to be the currency of power. Now it is information and it is held by a very small group of people, most of whom use it to disadvantage others for their benefit.

"The good news is that there are a lot of really great companies, a very large majority I believe, who are doing the right thing for their customers and the right thing for our planet. Hundreds of those companies support our efforts. Unfortunately, those who are abusing their power are hurting a lot of people.

"The thing that really kills me—and which energizes my every waking moment—is the fact that this master plan is going to absolutely screw our children out of a future that holds any hope for them. That is unacceptable to me and it should be to anybody with half a brain.

"This brings me to the makeup of our country. There are four groups of people out there right now. There are the enemies who are acting in the way I've described. They do not care about the future of the country as long as the immediate profits will make them and those they love rich for life. There are those who are totally oblivious to any of this and will remain so no matter what happens. There are those who have an idea that something bad is happening to them and their country, but they either can't mobilize themselves to look into it or have no clue where to start. Finally, there are people like myself and my colleagues who know what is going on and are motivated and knowledgeable enough to do something about it. We are supported in our efforts by the ethical companies I mentioned a moment ago.

"When I heard you speak on NPR I realized that you get it and are starting to act on it. You are using your celebrity and the media to get out the message, and that is a powerful combination that I can guarantee you has the enemy worried."

Nathan paused to take a long sip from the beer bottle that he had carried in from the bar.

"So that is who I am, what I am doing, and why I reached out to you. I would love to have both of you on our side and teach you the where, when, and how, but I need to know your reaction to all I've said."

Erica and Dawn both reached for the drinks that had been brought in while Nathan had been talking. Neither moved to speak. Nathan leaned toward them as the silence built. Dawn reached for her soup and took a taste.

"Can I assume the brilliance of my logic has left you speechless and that you just can't formulate how appreciative you are to be offered a chance to partner with someone as attractive as myself?" As he completed his question, he leaned back and spread his arms in an exaggerated display of his reaction to their hero worship.

Erica laughed while Dawn had more of her soup, watching Nathan closely. Erica put down her seltzer and said, "There is not anything that you have said that surprises me. Yes, we are in the group that realizes that something very, very wrong is happening to our country. I personally am not sure exactly what to do about it, so your ideas and invitation are of interest. Dawn, do you agree?"

Dawn stopped looking at Nathan and turned first to her mother, nodding in agreement, and then to her questioner.

"I am really interested in what you have to say and, at the same time, I need to take the time to find out more about what you do. I am also worried about my mother and feel a real need to get home. I promise we will get back to you, very soon."

Dawn walked over and offered her hand, Nathan taking it with both of his as he stood.

"I have really enjoyed meeting you and knew I would. Do you have a copy of Green Day's *American Idiot*?"

Looking intently at her questioner while continuing to hold his hand, Dawn replied, "No I don't. The songs I've heard, I like. Very different from what they did before."

"Then please take this copy. I think you'll like it. Listen particularly to track number eight."

Nathan disengaged from his handshake, reached into his backpack, and pulled out a CD, which he offered to Dawn.

"Thanks, I appreciate it." Looking at the song list on the CD, she smiled when she saw that *She's a Rebel* was track eight.

Turning slowly, Dawn moved toward the door, side by side with her mother, who thanked Nathan before they left.

Dawn and Erica got into the battered car and fastened their seatbelts. Dawn turned to her mother and asked, "Are you all right? You look drained."

"I'm fine. I just need to get home."

"You got up even earlier than usual."

"I had a hard time sleeping. Our meeting with Nathan Pomerantz got me thinking. I finally decided to get out of bed at four-thirty or so. Not sure, somewhere around there."

"Yes, he is an interesting guy. I like him and I think I trust him, although your point to him about needing to check him out makes a lot of sense. He's obviously smart enough, even without him telling us as much. I don't know; the way Dr. Margolis and the guy at the bar said 'if you're a friend of Nathan's there is no charge' was pretty interesting. I understand that cults of personality also act that way, but Dr. Margolis certainly didn't seem like someone who would be swayed by a cult figure and Nathan doesn't seem like that type of guy. He has a vision that he's rallied people around, but it doesn't seem to be about *him*; it seems to be about a sincere belief that this country is in deep yogurt and that he is going to do everything he can to get the right information to people so they can know how they're being manipulated and then make their decision about what they want to do about it.

"Bottom line, I like him and would go back and spend more time with him— although I don't know when that's going to happen. I've got a few brutal weeks ahead at work that I am going to need to push on pretty much seven days a week, until we get the project wrapped."

"Were you planning on going back to see him?"

"I'm thinking about it. He mentioned Lou Malone's mother being involved with them. I'd like to reconnect with Lou and the other members of Max Lunatic anyway, and when I do, I'll see if he minds my talking to his mother. If she says he's all right, then I'll probably give Nathan a call."

"Sounds like you've thought this out. I'll give Dr. Margolis a call to let her know that we're healthy, and talk with her about her impressions of Nathan and what he is doing. Let me know what you find out about him and I'll do the same. Although I won't be able to join you short-term, I'm obviously very interested in how this turns out."

Twenty-Four

DAWN PARKED HER car in the same spot outside O'Brian's where she and her mother had been hit the week before. Her palms were sweaty and she was nervous about meeting Nathan Pomerantz again. She had talked on the phone with Lou Malone and, after catching up, he had been able to tell her all about Nathan and the Consortium from what his mother had told him. It was all very positive. Erica had told Dawn exactly the same from her brief discussion with Dr. Margolis—that Nathan was eccentric, brilliant, and totally honest in what he and his team were doing: providing ordinary people with enough information so that they could make informed decisions, and funding and supporting organizations that promoted the rights of regular citizens. They both also mentioned the Consortium's strong focus on weakening Big Tobacco. She sat for a few minutes, breathing deeply and organizing her thoughts before she opened and then locked her door, looking both ways before she crossed the street.

She walked into the large brick building and up to the security station.

"Welcome back, Dawn. How's your mother feeling?" Caught by surprise, she muttered, "Fine, thanks, um, what's your name?"

"I'm Bernard. I was one of the guys who saw you get hit by that large truck. Nathan is looking forward to seeing you. I'll let him know you are here and then take your picture for your security badge."

Nathan came through a door to the right of the security station moments after Dawn's picture was taken and her badge created. He welcomed her and invited her to follow him. He inserted a key card attached by a cord to a unit on his belt into the locking device of four different doors on two different floors. As he unlocked the fourth door, they walked into a huge room with thirty-foot ceilings and multiple video screens that dominated the room, covering two of the four walls. Half a dozen young men and women in jeans and T-shirts sat either at desks or in chairs scattered around the room, working at keyboards and reading spreadsheets, books, or other documents that spilled onto the floor. The primary noise came from the whirring of the different machines in the room, which muted conversation.

Nathan bent close to Dawn and whispered into her right ear, "This is one of the nerve centers of our operation. This is where we research what is going on around the world. We have gotten significant funding—much of it very confidential—from many individual members of the corporate community who believe that what we are doing is critical, even if it might impact the short-term profitability of their employer. I can explain that paradox at some point if you are interested. Let's leave these folks alone and go down the hall."

He motioned Dawn out of the room, moved slowly down a long corridor, and turned right into another key-card access room. As Dawn followed, she gasped at the sight of the wall directly in front of her. The thirty-foot-high and sixty-foot-long wall was covered with a screen that, in turn, was covered with an illuminated, computerized map of the world—six continents containing steady or blinking lights of different colors. The lower third of the screen had names and locations in columns, with comments like "active" or "ready—on hold" or "organizing" next to them. A dozen men and women, mostly older than those in the previous room, were focused on both the large screen and the computer terminals that they sat behind.

Dawn stood rooted in her spot, looking open-mouthed at the multi-colored display. Nathan stood to the side, smiling as he watched her reaction, choosing not to say anything.

After a few moments, Dawn turned to him. "I have never seen anything like this. What is it?"

"Rather than bother these folks, let's go to my office and I will answer all your questions."

"So I know you checked me out. You weren't deterred by the hundreds of horrible things you heard?"

Nathan sat on one end of a beat-up couch in a room that also contained a large desk with orderly stacks of material surrounding a large computer screen. Bookshelves adorned three walls; the fourth wall contained the door through which they had just entered, and also a number of posters and paintings.

Dressed in jeans, red Converse sneakers, and a brown and green plaid shirt, he could have passed for a college student rather than a tenured university professor and leader of a large global organization.

"What I heard was pretty much what you laid out when I was here last week with my mother. If you're with him, it can be a wild and productive ride with many unexpected and often interesting twists and turns. If you're against him, he can be a royal pain-in-the-ass."

"Sounds about right to me. I'm glad you came for the reasons I mentioned when I met you and your mother last week. How is she feeling?" He squinted when he asked the question, intent on hearing her answer.

"She is fine. We both were a little sore from the accident but we're OK now. She sends her regards, and asked me to tell you that she hopes to see you again soon."

"Excellent. She is an impressive lady who will be able to help us a lot, particularly with her understanding of the inner workings of large corporations."

"She would never…"

Before Dawn could finish, Nathan interrupted.

"Dawn, don't worry; nothing we do here is illegal. I would never ask her to provide confidential information about any of her clients. Never. All I was saying was that she knows how corporations work, which will help us with our strategizing."

Dawn changed her mind, from frustration at being interrupted to feeling impressed with the fact that Nathan had inferred exactly what she was going to say.

"Now, I imagine you have a ton of questions after being surprised by the reality of our security measures. Would you like to ask questions first, or have me provide some of the history and context about what we are doing? Whichever works for you."

Being one who would naturally jump into a questioning mode, Dawn said that he could continue, anticipating that he probably would have guessed most of her questions anyway.

"Thanks."

Nathan took a sip from a water glass he had by his side. Dawn did the same with the glass he had offered her when they had entered his office.

"First of all, I'm assuming that because you are here after talking with Lou and Frieda Margolis and probably others, you have at least a curiosity about what we're doing. Duh. Although I'm hoping that you will decide to work with us that is still a decision you need to make. If you decide to bail at any time after today, just let me know and we will part as friends, I hope, and move on. This is not a cult or a paramilitary operation that demands blind adherence to our mission. We can look at it that way because of the fact that we are, as I mentioned a moment ago, doing nothing illegal.

"We are normal people who love this country and think that it is going in a direction that will leave my generation, your generation, and my children's generation totally screwed as we get older.

"We are committed to providing information to our citizenry about what is being done to them so that they can make informed decisions about how to act. We are also providing funding and sophisticated support to social activist groups and nonprofit and community organizations that are trying to make positive change occur around the globe. We are hoping and praying that we are moving toward a tipping point where enough citizens not only get it, but decide to act on what is being done to them in a way that fundamentally changes the structure of our country, and takes power away from the advantaged and distributes it among the normal citizenry, so that all of us can be living healthier lives. If we are wrong and the divide between the haves and have-nots continues to expand, and everyone continues to consume more than our planet can handle, then we will probably decide to go somewhere where we are as safe as possible from what that implies. But we are in this for the long haul and we are pretty certain that we can prevail.

"What we are *not* advocating is armed insurrection or *any type of force* to get what we want. We believe that information rules and that if we can get the right information to everyone, they will begin to act in a way that will save us all.

"Now, that is the philosophy, the general idea. Here's how we are doing this, which ties into our two command centers you just saw."

Nathan took another sip of water, Dawn sitting quietly and processing all that Nathan was laying out.

"What you saw in those two rooms is the heart of what we do. We have the ability to monitor thousands of information sources and distill down and manage the information so that we have a very good understanding of the groups that are trying to help normal citizens live the happiest and most fulfilled lives possible.

"The two primary ways we do this is by helping people understand how they are being influenced by organizations that don't have their best interests in mind, while providing funding and support to groups whose mission it is to help people help themselves. To put it another way, we are working to get people to become aware that they are being manipulated to act in a way that is to their disadvantage.

"So we monitor published and unpublished sources of information to identify those who think like we do and approach them to offer our assistance. Some agree and some decide to continue to go it alone. That's fine if it is an informed choice. We also learn from the very committed and sophisticated allies that we have, and add what they are doing to our database and the techniques we support.

"We monitor all the information used by the enemy to manipulate people—their websites, their advertisements, their actions—and then alert and/or try to legally subvert what they are doing. Again, there are many activists out there who are supporting us and whom we are learning from. The folks who publish *Adbusters* magazine include some of the most sophisticated media professionals in the business, doing great work to show people how they are being motivated to buy stuff they will never use. We don't try to replicate what they do; we promote it and pass it on. The team at thetruth.com are creating very effective media messages for young people about how tobacco companies are trying to manipulate them—and they have had great success. There is no way we could replicate what they are doing and we would never try; we just support them in any way we can.

"Now, let me apply those central points to the reason I contacted you last week. You have chosen in a local and national way to try to help people understand how they are being manipulated. Locally, you helped Fair Shore residents understand how young women were being disenfranchised and worse. You have also decided, through your NPR interview, to go national regarding what you have heard about men and women being sexually assaulted around the country.

"We identified that you are one of us and now we're trying to recruit you to be even more effective at what you are doing, by learning about and using our resources.

"Here is how those two rooms we walked through help with our efforts. The first room is the information-gathering center, where we do the monitoring that I mentioned. The second room, with the large map of the world, is where we coordinate our strategizing with groups all over the world. The folks in there are communicating with the thousands of activist groups who are working to support the core principles that I have enumerated. They are shaping and sharing the information that the first group gathers. That is why they are older. Many of them have been in the field and know first-hand what those folks are dealing with as they fight very sophisticated organizations.

"I started the Consortium as a US-focused organization. We became so successful so quickly that we attracted global partners who have allowed us to now help people on six continents.

"So that's the overview. What questions do you have?"

Dawn leaned back and took a sip of her water, multiple thoughts going through her head.

"Well first, I want to thank you for giving me Green Day's *American Idiot* CD. Great songs, with track eight being a nice compliment, I think. And so I wanted to reciprocate."

Dawn reached into her purse and pulled out Kris Kristofferson's *Third World Warrior* and Steve Earle's *The Revolution Starts Now*. "You into Kris Kristofferson and Steve Earle?"

"I know they're great lyricists but I haven't listened to either of them very much. I love music that has a message, and it certainly sounds like these two CDs are trying to say something."

"Yes, both CDs are about the difficulty of having freedom and dignity in this crazy world of ours, and both Steve and Kris have been active in human rights causes."

"I appreciate this, Dawn, and I'll make sure to take a listen when I have time. The fact that another Kristofferson song is titled *Don't Let the Bastards Get You Down* certainly motivates me to listen to them sooner rather than later.

"So what questions do you have?"

Dawn leaned back in her chair, crossed her legs and asked, "Why such heavy security if you aren't doing anything illegal?"

"Because our enemies hate us." Nathan got up from his chair and moved toward the window.

"If we are doing our job well, it will make it much harder for our enemies to continue to disenfranchise the majority of our citizens. We will be bringing information to American citizens that will help them make voting decisions that will support the regular citizens versus the amoral and their lobbyists. The power structure in Washington DC and K Street, and the tobacco companies who are the major industry target of ours because of how effective they are at murdering people, do not like us doing that and would love to disrupt our information-dissemination operation. If they can break into it by either physical force or electronic means and slow us down, they will keep us from our mission. Very tight security reduces the likelihood of their doing that. It would take even the most well-equipped people a few minutes to physically breach our security here, and that would allow us time to send our information to off-site facilities and shut down the system so they would get zilch, zippo, nada—nothing at all."

Dawn and Nathan spent half an hour talking about the Consortium's actions around the world.

"So who created this? I mean, this is a sophisticated global operation that would need finance and human resources and other departments. Are they all housed here in some other part of this building? How do people know to want to work for you? I'm guessing you don't run ads in *The New York Times*."

"The answer is me; this is my baby and I have some very powerful friends who have helped make this possible. Where everyone is located is confidential, and the people who work here are either approached by us —as I reached out to you—or know about us from their network and reach out through that network."

Nathan looked at his watch, stepped away from the wall against which he had been leaning and returned to his seat.

"I hope you have enjoyed this chat, but we are going to have to cut it short because there is a meeting I am leading that I cannot be late for.

"Dawn, here's the deal." Nathan leaned forward in his seat, tapping his left foot on the carpeted floor as he raised his right hand above his head with his index finger extended.

"I am the primary person at the top of this large organization that everyone identifies with as representative of our mission to support, through the dissemination of information and money, organizations that are fighting to generate change, which helps regular citizens, versus the well-to-do elites that control our world." Raising his left hand up by his right, he drew a circle in the air around himself with both hands.

"I am surrounded by technical geniuses—engineers, computer scientists, professors from the most prestigious universities, triple PhDs in subjects I will never understand—individuals who have built this infrastructure and made it work. Unfortunately, almost all of them are more comfortable behind the scenes than out in the world telling people about what we are doing; they are technical geniuses, not super communicators who can sell the public on what we do. That has not been such a big deal up to this point, because the organizations we support have a lot of those types of communicators who are getting their individual organization's message out to their constituencies in a very effective way, as you heard in my presentation this morning.

"Now, however, we have our infrastructure pretty much in place and we're ready to become more visible in our own right so that we can attract more funding. I would like you to be part of the small team that goes out and does interviews, speeches, and whatever it takes to get our message out to those who could support us in significant ways.

"To be very direct, you have not only the communication skills and interpersonal strengths necessary to develop these key connections, but you also have the celebrity that will allow us to access the media attention we need. It hit me when I was listening to you being interviewed on NPR. You have passion that people from all levels of society will listen to, because of the success you had fighting the status quo in Fair Shore and the price you paid for your insolence and strength. You would be the perfect person to help get our message across to a variety of constituencies in our country and abroad."

Nathan was leaning closer to Dawn as he moved his hands around in circles, supporting his words. He did not notice Dawn moving her seat back from him or the deep furrow that was forming above the space between her tightening eyes.

As he took a breath to continue, Dawn pushed her chair back, bumping into the chair behind her, while putting both hands out in front of her, palms flattened toward Nathan's face.

"Nathan, stop," she insisted. "Please stop."

Startled, he jerked back in his own chair, looking sideways at the hands that appeared a few feet in front of his face.

Softening her voice, Dawn said, "Nathan, it is very nice that you think I have the abilities that you just described. Believe me, coming from someone like you that is a real compliment."

Recovering from his surprise at Dawn's reaction, Nathan said, "And I hear a big *but* coming up."

"Yes, you do. But, I cannot possibly get involved in the way you described, at least not at this point in time. I am still recovering physically and emotionally from my year in the hospital and I need to get re-oriented to what has happened to me and the people in my life before I get involved in another fight like the one you describe. I have to get my life back, get my high-school diploma, apply to colleges, and then figure out what I am going to do. Working with you would be exciting and worthwhile and it's something I will definitely consider, but I have to wait and see how the next few months turn out. I thought I had my act together when I first arrived in Fair Shore, but what I did the first couple days I was at Fair Shore High proved to me that this wasn't true.. The psychologist I have been seeing for the past five years to help me deal with some bad stuff that happened back then has helped me get back on track, but right now I need to get centered and focused on completing my senior year and get going on my college applications, which I have not even started."

Leaning forward again, Nathan began to respond, "But Dawn, you look and sound great and…"

"Nathan, I don't want to talk about this anymore." Dawn stood up, accidently banging her knee on the table in her haste to end the conversation. Wincing, she said in a more urgent and forced tone, "Please respect that the fact that whatever I look like is in no way how I feel. I can put up a good façade with the best of them, but I need a lot of quiet time to put the pieces back together. I need you to respect that."

Nathan began to speak and then caught himself, standing to look at Dawn's face.

"I hear you; I do. I just know you would be perfect for the type of role I outlined. This is a real offer, Dawn, one that a lot of people would kill for. And it will still be available when you have taken the time you say you need, since I control the hiring here."

"Thanks, I promise to seriously consider it when I am at that point." Pausing, she said, "I do have one more question before we head out."

"Fire away."

144

"I heard that Richard Phillips does some work for your organization. What is his role in what you are doing?"

"I have known about Richard based on the protest leadership he demonstrated at Columbia in the sixties. As I was looking to recruit like-minded people to our cause, I spoke with him and brought him in as an associate member, someone who can attend our briefings and be on our mailing list, but not function as a full-time employee. I am considering him for the type of role we just discussed. He is great in front of a group and can be quite charismatic when he is on the wagon. Plus, I know that he helped you and your team in the Fair Shore struggle, which is recommendation enough for me."

"Yeah, well there is a dirt-bag side of him that you may want to factor into your decision. I feel like he has lied over and over again about how he was connected with what we did in Fair Shore to sell himself—and my mother and I don't appreciate it. I am still putting together the pieces of that puzzle, but so far I don't like what I've found out about what he's been saying and doing. And he is a nasty drunk who can't be trusted. But I don't want to waste one more minute of our time on him. He's not worth it."

"Alrighty then, enough said."

Nathan guided Dawn down two more flights of stairs and out into the lobby through which she had entered, passing two more yellow-shirted security guards on the way.

"One final thing." Nathan put his hand on Dawn's arm to keep her from heading toward the door. "I can guarantee that the august intelligence services of our great country have files on you because of your involvement in Fair Shore and now your interview on NPR. That is a fact that I hope you will believe. So what does that mean? It means that you need to at least consider what you say on the phone or put in an email to friends and colleagues. Simply use the old guideline that I am sure your mother has used in her consulting: What would it matter to you and your friends if what you said or wrote to them was on the front page of *The New York Times?*"

Noticing Dawn's tightened face, he continued, "Dawn, I am not asking you to trust me on this one. I can send you dozens of examples of how information that people have shared in private has been made public in an attempt to embarrass them. There are reactionary forces out there that look at any type of challenge to the status quo as unpatriotic or worse. And they have the means to find out what you are saying if they identify you as someone they want to discredit. Just let me know and I will send the proof, otherwise I will leave you alone, out of respect for what you say you need to do to get your life back to…"

"Code Three, Code Three, shut down, shut down."

Nathan grabbed Dawn and threw her behind the security desk, as metal sheets descended from the ceiling, covering the walls facing the street in front of the building. The sound of gunfire that accompanied the loud announcement was muffled by the sealing of the room.

The metal walls that had just been created broke open near what had been the front entrance, as an explosion was followed by a scar of flame that surged into the room, engulfing the two security guards closest to where the door had been. Nathan ran toward one of the burning bodies screaming and rolling on the floor, and blasted him with a fire extinguisher he pulled from the wall behind the security desk. Dawn, stunned by the force of the explosion, stood slowly and, seeing what was happening, grabbed a second fire extinguisher from the wall and ran toward the flames that were covering another one of the employees. As she extinguished the flames on the body writhing in pain, the fire sprinkler system activated and sent water pouring down on the small group of people in the lobby, extinguishing the rest of the flames.

Nathan crouched by the bodies he and Dawn had kept from burning, yelling, "Paul, Tonga, help us move Bill and Sven out of the room, now!"

The two employees who had just run into the room did as instructed, with Nathan grabbing the arm of one of the guards and helping Paul pull Sven out of the room, while Dawn did the same with Bill, assisting Tonga as he dragged him to safety.

Taking the key card from his belt, Nathan opened a door to the left of the security desk, bumping into other employees who were rushing in. He yelled, "Get Bill and Sven into the medical office, now!" He waited for someone to take his place and then retreated from the door, scanning the half dozen individuals standing in the doorway.

"Patricia, get up to the command center and tell Sandy there has been an explosion at the front door and gunfire. He should know already, but I want to make sure. He will know what to do. Move it, go, go, go. The rest of you get back to your locations; we have enough people down here. Follow Code Three protocols. Move it.

"Dawn, come with me."

Grabbing Dawn's hand, he pulled her around a corner, accessing another door with his key card and slowing as they approached a narrow corridor. Turning a corner, they spilled into a large room with thirty people scattered in various positions, large video monitors hanging from the far wall. Dawn noticed around ten yellow shirts in the crowd, most with guns drawn. Stopping, Nathan turned to his left, and yelled to a tall blonde-haired man in jeans and a blue shirt who was sitting behind a console, "Sandy, what do you have?"

"It looks like a truck rammed entrance A, and exploded. Bernard and Sam opened fire and were not able to stop it. There is no other movement at any other observation points, only the truck. All systems are in lock down and there does not seem to have been an attempt to breach data security, at least that I can tell at this point."

With quick steps toward where Sandy was sitting, Nathan said, "Patch me into the system-wide communications link."

Nathan grabbed a phone from the console, waiting for a sign from Sandy. When he flicked a switch and said, "You're hot, boss," Nathan spoke into the receiver.

"This is Nathan Pomerantz. There has been a breach by a truck that ran through our entrance. That area has been contained and I am asking all of you to follow Code Three protocol. I repeat, follow Code Three protocol. Security personnel disperse to assigned locations and report back to the command center as required. We will let you know more when we have confirmed more data. Keep your heads about you, people; we have trained for this and you know what to do. Nathan out."

Handing the receiver back to Sandy, Nathan looked at Dawn.

"Are you all right?"

"Yes, I don't feel anything wrong."

Nathan looked her up and down, turned her around, and then said, "You look fine. I don't see any wounds from the blast. Sandy, this is Dawn Mortenson. She is an honored guest who can be trusted completely. When things slow down, make sure she gets what she needs. She saved one of our people just now. Dawn, please find a seat and stay out of the way. I will be back to see you later."

"Nathan, is Bernard all right?"

Stopping abruptly, he turned and looked at her, his head sideways as if she were out of focus. Trying to answer, he caught himself, looked away for a moment, and then replied, "We don't know, Dawn. It doesn't look good. He would have been right in the middle of the blast."

Not waiting for a response, Nathan ran out through another door beneath the video screens on the far wall while Dawn took an empty seat to the left of the console, Sandy turning back to the monitors in front of him.

"If I could have everybody's attention please?"

Nathan, speaking in a subdued voice, leaned against the podium in a large auditorium.

"From what we have been able to tell, in conjunction with the New Haven police and the FBI, we were attacked by a remote-controlled SUV loaded with dynamite. Apparently there was enough explosive in the vehicle to bring down this entire building. From what we know, Bernard Ippolito and Samuel Phillips were able to slow the vehicle by shooting out the tires. There was only a minor explosion versus what might have happened if they had made it into the building and set off their payload. Between slowing the truck and warning us in time to secure the building, the damage was confined to the entrance area."

Pausing, Nathan pulled a handkerchief from his jeans pocket and wiped his face, still smeared with the dirt and dust from the explosion.

"They were both killed while saving our lives, oh Jesus."

Not able to control himself, Nathan leaned against the podium, tears running down his face. Half a dozen of his closest friends jumped up and surrounded him, holding him among them. Those seated did not know how to react, some of them having known Nathan for over fifteen years, and all of them never having seen him cry. Dawn rummaged in her pocket for a tissue, joining many of the others in the audience who were crying as they digested the information and watched their leader.

After a few minutes, Nathan emerged from the group and took a few long drinks from the glass of water on the podium. With a single deep breath, he moved to the side of the stage, and speaking in an almost inaudible tone, he said, "They were good men and both had been with us a long time. They really believed in what we are doing and they showed that in their actions. We will be creating a memorial fund for Bernard's wife Charlotte and for Samuel's wife Shiquanda and their two young children. They will not be forgotten."

Taking another long drink of water, he looked out at the staff who had filled the room.

"We have prepared for this day, with many of you thinking we were being paranoid because of all the resources and plans we put into place to repel an overt or covert attack. Unfortunately we were right; our efforts have obviously gotten the attention of the folks we are fighting and they have tried to shut us down."

Suddenly slamming his fist against the podium, he said in very measured words, "They...will...not...defeat us. This organization is filled with individuals like Bernard and Samuel who will not let that happen."

Taking another sip of water, he continued, "We will be getting more information to you as it comes in. The FBI is being very cooperative and understands our need for strong security measures to protect the confidentiality of what we are doing. Keep your eyes open, people, and report anything suspicious to your supervisor or security team. You know who they are."

"Bernard was a good guy. I could tell by how he greeted me today. That was very moving what you said about him and his partner."

Distracted, Nathan nodded his head, acknowledging Dawn's compliment. As if talking to himself, he mumbled, "This building is filled with very good people— amazing human beings who really want to help our country be as wonderful a place as it has the potential to be. They don't deserve this risk in their lives. Many of them have children whom they love very much, kids who depend on them to come home safe and whole."

Dawn, watching Nathan closely, decided not to interrupt his discussion with himself.

"We've got to do something; we've got to."

Suddenly rousing himself, Nathan looked over at Dawn. "Thanks for listening and for all your help today. I am really sorry that you had to be interviewed by the FBI, but the fact that you were at the blast site made that interview a necessity."

"I completely understand."

"Now I need to get you out of here safely this time."

Neither spoke as they retraced the steps they had taken earlier in the day, making their way to the room where she had sat with Sandy, who was giving orders to the staff in the damaged entrance area.

"Take care, Dawn. Hope to see you again." Before Dawn could reply, Nathan told the security team to let her leave as he touched her shoulder and turned away, leaving her to walk, through the security personnel who were standing in front of the exit, and out into the cold, where she was confronted with blazing lights and dozens of reporters gathering to find out what had happened.

Twenty-Five

DAWN HAD CALLED her mother soon after the attack to explain the situation and assure her that she was all right. After running the gauntlet of reporters at the Consortium, she called her again from the quiet of her car and explained that she would probably be on television. Erica said she had in fact been shown on the news leaving the building and that news trucks were lining up outside their home in Fair Shore. As Dawn drove slowly home on the Merritt Parkway, she thought back to all she had learned about Nathan and his group and the work they were doing, weighing the pros and cons of working with him. Although she was excited about making a contribution with such a powerful group of people, she concluded that what she had said to Nathan about needing time to get her own life back together had been absolutely the right decision. Seeing the television trucks and news vehicles stacked up outside her house simply confirmed that decision. Slowing, she called her mother on her cell and told her she would be pulling into their driveway momentarily.

Experienced with the media, she felt comfortable handling the press by stating the simple fact that she had been visiting the Information Is Power Consortium when it had been bombed. She had to stop a couple of times to keep from hitting photographers who jumped in front of her car.

When she couldn't move any further, she stopped the car, put it in park, and pushed her door open, standing next to the car and yelling to the crowd, "Please let me get my car into my driveway and I will let you take all the pictures you want; just please move out of the way."

She got back in the car and the crowd did not part for her, so she just sat where she was, waiting for a path to clear. A police officer finally made room for her to get onto her property. She got out of the car and closed the door, turning to face the cameras.

"Hello everyone. Good to see you all. Hi Janet. Nice to see you, Phyllis. Hey Randy, how are you? What can I do for you all?"

"What is your relationship with the communist anarchist Nathan Pomerantz?"

"I didn't know that he was either of those things, but I do know that he loves this country and is supporting groups who are trying to re-create a balance between those with all the money who have taken over our country and everyone else, an agenda I support. Hi Judith, what's your question?"

Feeling a hand on her arm, she turned, and her mother put her arm around her shoulders.

"Hey Mom, some of our old friends are back."

Judith Snyder, a reporter for the *Hartford Courant*, who had been supportive of Dawn's previous efforts, asked, "It is our understanding that you were standing near the point of the explosion with Nathan Pomerantz. Is that accurate?"

"Yes, it is. Nathan was walking me to the door after he had given me a tour of his facilities. The explosion happened as I was getting ready to walk out the door."

"Were you or Nathan hurt?"

"We were both shaken but not physically hurt, no."

"There are reports that two security guards were killed. Is that accurate?"

"Judith, you will need to get that information from Nathan and his team. I cannot confirm any of the specifics since I was just a visitor and not a member of his organization."

A reporter that Dawn did not know pushed to the front of the crowd and asked, "Do you see yourself as a terrorist since all you seem to do is to be connected to violence and trouble?"

"I totally resent being called a terrorist and I don't look for trouble. I just happened to be visiting this organization when it was bombed; there is no other connection except for being in the wrong place at the wrong time."

Dawn stood with her mother and answered all the questions that the group had to ask, their numbers dwindling as she did. After what seemed to be the last question, and with everyone moving away and packing up their equipment, she and her mother turned to go inside.

"Excuse me, Dawn. One more question?"

Dawn saw that Judith Snyder turned back and was standing alone at the bottom of their driveway.

"Sure, Judith. What else is on your mind?"

"How are you doing? You haven't been out of the hospital that long and now you are thrown into this situation. I was wondering how you are holding up?"

Dawn smiled slightly and replied in a low, husky voice, "I don't know, quite honestly. I think I am all right but I've got to tell you, the problems in this country are huge and it is actually kind of draining to see that not much seems to be happening to solve them. Does that answer your question?"

"Yes, thanks, and good luck."

Twenty-Six

THE DAY AFTER the bombing at the Consortium Dawn spent the afternoon in the Fair Shore library doing additional research on Nathan and his organization, coming to the conclusion that what he had been saying to her seemed to be right—that he is a lunatic and they are an above-board organization.

Dawn felt the same energy she experienced when she came home from New Haven and her second encounter with Nathan. Her positive feeling about the possibilities that Nathan's offer seemed to open up for her grew as she thought about all the really cool facts she had uncovered about his crusade.

Energized and looking forward to talking further with her mother about the possibility, and hoping she was home from her evening's work, she entered the house whistling from the CD, *American Idiot*. She locked the front door, turned, and was stunned to see Richard Phillips sitting in her favorite chair by the lit fire, glass of white wine in hand.

Dropping her book bag, she snorted, "What are you doing here?" only to be interrupted by her mother's entrance from the kitchen.

"Richard called me to say he wanted to try and mend fences, and I invited him over for a drink to discuss what he had on his mind."

Dawn stood where she dropped her bag, both hands on the jacket she was in the process of removing. She unzipped it and hung it in the closet to the right of where Richard and Erica were now sitting.

"I know exactly what he has in mind. He is..." Dawn stopped suddenly, thinking of all the work that she and Dr. Francis had done in relation to controlling her emotions and being more centered when she reacted to difficult situations.

"You know, I really have to go to the bathroom. I'll be back to join you in a moment."

As Dawn sat in the upstairs bathroom, chosen so she could run up the stairs to burn off some frustration, she breathed deeply and focused on some of the success images that she had created with her therapist in order to get into a positive frame of mind during times of stress.

Feeling much more in control, she walked slowly down the stairs and said, "You know, I think it is a great idea that we all take a shot at getting to a place of mutual respect and understanding. So Richard, it's good to have you here and I'm looking forward to trying to make that happen. Unfortunately, I can't hang out with you all tonight because I am jammed with homework, including that paper that you assigned to us that's due tomorrow.

Dawn kissed her mother and walked up the stairs, feeling very good about how she had handled the situation. And then she couldn't go to sleep immediately, which hardly ever happened to her, because all her feelings about Richard kept cycling through her brain—drunk, liar, brilliant, troubled, guilt-ridden, horny as hell, liar, a user of others, good looking, manipulator, charismatic, liar, addictive personality, shallow, brilliant, a user, a liar. She slept fitfully once she finally dozed off.

———❧❧❧———

Dawn gave Doctor Francis a call first thing in the morning and was able to have a brief phone conversation with her the following morning. She told her about her concern about how Richard Phillips could impact her relationship with her mother and also about the offer she had received from Nathan to work at the Consortium. Her therapist helped her think through various options for dealing with both situations.

Knowing that her mother was arriving home late that night, she called Ernestine and they went out to dinner, Dawn arriving back home at nine o'clock, feeling in a very positive mood until she saw Richard's car in their driveway. Walking into their living room, she saw him sitting on the couch closest to the kitchen with a glass of wine in his hand, his left arm around her mother, who had an unusual grin on her face.

"Are you stoned?"

She looked over at Richard and giggled.

"What do you think, Richard, are we stoned?"

"I do believe we are stoned, now that you ask, Dawn." Both of them giggled while messing up each other's hair.

"Cool, you deserve to have some fun, Mother, after all the stuff you've been through."

Richard reached onto the coffee table in front of him, grabbed his glass, finished his wine, and pulled the bottle out of the ice bucket on the table. He refilled his glass and asked, "How are you doing since the bombing at the Consortium headquarters? That must have been scary as hell."

"You got that right. And I'll tell you that is an impressive operation Nathan has set up; they really handled the chaos well. He is an impressive guy, as you well know."

"He certainly is. He graduated from a tough college-prep program at a top public high school when he was fourteen and enrolled at Columbia University. He finished all the classwork for his BS and three PhDs in seven years. I know you can do the math, but he had three PhDs before his twenty-first birthday. I still know faculty there who say he is the most amazing student they have ever seen. Dazzling bandwidth; knows everything. We stayed in touch and when he came up with the idea of the Consortium, he came to me for advice and I gave it. He offered me a full-time job and I turned it down, wanting to stay at Fair Shore High. I volunteer my time there on certain projects and we hang out occasionally."

As Dawn listened to Richard, she was watching her mother and she saw that she was mesmerized, hanging on his every word. She was really into him, from Dawn's perspective, and it was freaking her out. And she felt she had to get out of the room as she watched how attached her mother seemed to be getting to someone she did not trust one damn bit.

Standing up as Richard paused, Dawn said, "I am going to leave you two kids alone because I have some reading to do and then I need to hit the sack. Richard, it was nice seeing you. Good night, pretty lady."

As Dawn walked up the stairs, she was feeling pretty proud of her performance once again. And as soon as she lay down to go to bed, the moaning started, which made taking the high road a whole lot harder for her. After listening for a few minutes, she did the most elegant thing she could do to stop the noise—she went to the bathroom, accompanied by doors opening and closing, loudly, and toilets flushing, twice. And it worked. The noise stopped and she was able to drift off quickly. The guilt kicked in early the next morning when her mother looked sheepish, an affect Dawn had rarely, if ever, seen her own.

And as they ate their cereal Dawn said, "I've been giving it a lot of thought and I have decided to go work at the Consortium. I can't get them out of my mind and so I want to take a shot at helping solve the problems of the world with a group of really bright, energized people who I am sure I am going to like working with."

Not knowing how her mother would react, she was pleasantly surprised when Erica was really positive about that as a next step. The conversation was a short one because Erica had to hurry to work. Mother and daughter hugged, and then Erica hurried out the door.

Twenty-Seven

FOR THOSE OF you who have gotten this far in my story, the rest will come directly from the audio journal I am keeping. You need to hear my voice directly as the rest of this insane story unwinds. The reason, not to be dramatic, is that I don't know if I'm going to make it to the end. For whatever reason, I have been in two situations within the last eighteen months that like, oh I don't know, could have killed me. Since I decided to go and work for Nathan, the possibility of some bad stuff happening increased. I am hoping we get to the end of this story with me heading toward college with a great big smile on my face; we'll see. Meanwhile, my digital tape recorder is now my new best friend.

Most people don't think of me as a quiet, loner type. I understand why. More than a few times in my life I've ended up in the middle of some fairly public activities. What most people don't understand is that this happens, not out of some desire to be the center of attention, but because if I feel strongly about something, I have a hard time just letting it go without trying to do something, anything. I have had the benefit of dozens of powerful insights during my five years of therapy with Dr. Francis. One is the idea that one's strength can also be one's weakness. I am a passionate person, which I think is one of my strengths, but that passion gets me into a lot of crap.

I'm thinking about this as I drive to New Haven to start working with Nathan and his team. I'm wondering if my desire to join a group that's trying to right some terrible wrongs is in fact the right thing to be doing at this time in my life. This decision has created extremely mixed emotions for me. I'm not sure, as I said before, whether I have the energy it will require.

I also realize that I am moving away from my anger at my mother— my best friend—and her decision to date Richard, who I know is a bad seed. And I'm also moving away from the fact that I'm lonely, that many people I was connected with before my hospitalization are off doing different things and might not be as connected with me as I, narcissistically, would have wanted. My therapist has helped me understand that you should always try to move toward something positive

155

versus away from something negative. Hey, I never said I've got this personal development thing right.

As I'm driving, I'm also dealing with a real fear from the fact that I am revisiting a place where I was almost killed, where I am going to be surrounded by people a hell of a lot smarter than I am, and at a time when I am still feeling unsettled about my mental and physical strength. But I'm also excited because these people are having an *impact* in the way that *I want* to have, and they should be exciting to be around. Plus, I'm intrigued by Nathan Pomerantz.

I was surprised that I got through to Nathan as quickly as I did the morning after my declaration to my mother. When he said he wanted me to come up to his office at one o'clock the next afternoon, it was a major surprise. I was also stunned when I saw concrete barriers surrounding the building, although the logic of it quickly kicked in since I had seen the recent bombing attempt, duh. There were three yellow-jacketed security people standing outside the main entrance. Two women patted me down in an entrance enclosure before they allowed me to walk into the main space where I had sat previously with Sandy Jesperson, head of security.

Sandy was standing behind the security personnel, sitting at the consoles at the main security desk in the lobby. He gave me a big smile when he saw me walking toward them and he came around to shake my hand.

"Hi Dawn, great to see you again. I am so jazzed that you're coming to work with us."

I was startled by the acknowledgement of my employee status by the head of security.

"Don't look so surprised. I need to know the status of anybody coming in for a meeting, and Nathan's email was very specific about how happy he was to have you on the team. The fact that you saved Bill's life with the fire extinguisher and whatever other stuff you have done has the top guy on your side."

I stood dumb as a stone as he smiled and continued, "And I know that Bill and Sven both want to see you at some point to thank you for helping to get them out of the blast area."

I told him I'd be happy to meet them, but I had just followed Nathan's lead.

He said, "That wasn't a bad thing to do in this place."

Sandy took my picture and created a permanent employee security badge.

"If you could wait over on the couch against the wall, I will call Bernice and she'll be your escort."

Embarrassed by Sandy's compliments, I clipped my photo ID to the lapel of my winter jacket and found space on the end of the couch, away from the entrance where I could relax while waiting. .

"Excuse me, are you Dawn Mortenson?"

I snapped out of my relaxed state to look up at a young, blonde woman wearing a loose, white blouse and faded jeans.

"Oh I am so sorry; I was daydreaming and didn't hear you."

"Not a problem. I'm Bernice Novard, a member of Nathan's team. We can go upstairs now. I apologize for the delay."

"Not a problem. I didn't mean to be rude. I really was lost in thought."

"Dawn, one of the reasons we have been successful is that this building is full of people who are lost in thought."

I thought to myself that Bernice was very skilled at putting people at ease and I found myself smiling back at her as we walked past the security desk toward a set of double doors.

"Thanks for your help, Sandy."

"Great to see you again, Dawn."

I found myself having to accelerate my pace to keep up with Bernice, who swiped her pass card, looked back at me, and said, "It's going to be a lot more chaotic than normal around here because of the attack the other day. I understand that you saved Bill's life."

"I didn't do much, really. Just grabbed a fire extinguisher and sprayed him."

"Well, I'm sorry that had to be your introduction to us. I've been here five years and that was the first time anything like that has happened. I guess we *are* getting the attention of the bad guys."

"That attack aside, you sound like you're proud to work here."

"I can't imagine working anywhere else at this point in my life, which actually is a nice lead-in to my role. Nathan has a team of five of us who work with him to make sure that we are maximizing the effort of the senior leadership. I understand from him that he wants you to join our team, which I think is great, since he respects you a lot and you are obviously very skilled from what you did at Fair Shore. You won't be able to see him for a few hours, but you will get to meet some of the members of this team and we will be orienting you to what we do so you can get up to speed as quickly as possible. Nathan hopes to have you join a group that will be having dinner in our dining room at around six-thirty. Do you have plans that would keep you from staying for dinner?"

"I just have to call my mother and tell her my plans. That would be fine."

"Awesome. You will find that the hours here are hard to figure. One day you will get out at four o'clock and the next day there will be a need for a team of us to stay until ten o'clock. I would assume that being adaptable is one of your strengths?"

"Yes, I guess it is. I'm pretty good at adjusting to whatever is thrown my way, although I know that there are a lot of very bright people here so I am hoping to keep up."

"You'll be fine; your reputation precedes you. People here are cut a lot of slack if they are obviously trying hard and they're sincerely engaged in our mission. You are a fighter and you had to work very hard to make the change happen that you did."

I was stunned for the second time that day about how much people seemed to know—or at least infer—about me. It was reaffirming on one hand because it was presented positively, but on the other hand, it was intimidating since it created an expectation I was not sure I was going to be able to meet. Before I could verbalize that thought, we pushed through another set of double doors and I recognized that we were back on the floor where the auditorium was located.

"Let's go into the room to your right." Bernice motioned toward an already-opened door a few feet ahead and I walked through it, into a small conference room with two young people sitting at their laptops, talking in low, serious tones.

"Hi guys, here's Dawn." As they both got up, I was struck by their smiles; both sincere and engaging as Bernice's had been a few minutes before.

"Hi, I'm Sal."

"And I'm Amy."

"Hi there, I'm Dawn."

It didn't take a rocket scientist to see that I was way overdressed, with Amy and Sal matching Bernice's outfit of a clean, ironed shirt and jeans.

"Am I good to wear jeans in the future, which would be great?"

Bernice, who was obviously the leader of the group, looked at me and replied, "I am not completely clear about what Nathan wants to do with you other than to have you join this group, which by the way, runs this whole place, and don't let anybody tell you differently."

The three laughed and I joined in. Sal, who was a short, slight, black man, said, "You got that right. Unfortunately the rest of the building did not get that memo."

I jumped in. "Hell, there was a front page article about your leadership ability in *The Times*. I'm really surprised everyone still doesn't know."

We all laughed again, and any of my remaining jitters dissolved within that first minute.

"But seriously," Bernice interjected, "you will probably need to have a set of nice clothes, like what you are wearing today, hung up somewhere, because my understanding is that Nathan will be wanting you to do a lot of public speaking and media stuff. He played your NPR interview for a lot of us and it sure seems like you will be able to do some great publicity for us."

"Well I hope I don't let anybody down."

"Dawn, I hear you and I understand your concern." Amy, a short, pale woman with blue hair who stood a yard to my right, continued, "But Nathan is an amazing judge of character and if he is saying you can do it, then you can do it. I'm only twenty-six but I've been around."

"Oh yeah, you have."

"Oh, bite me, Sal."

"And I have never seen anyone who has the ability to instantly size up an individual like Nathan. It's kind of spooky, actually." Looking at her watch, Amy went on, "But we need to get on task cuz there is a lot going on. Miss Bernice, do you want to lead off?"

The rest of the day moved at warp speed, with members of the team walking in and out of our meeting, telling me different things about what we would be doing together. I was struck by their lack of ego and what seemed like their sincere interest in the viability of their team and the mission of the Consortium. And there were four points at the core of what was described as the team's charge—protect Nathan's health and security, ensure that the top leadership had everything they needed to do their work, handle a number of employee-related tasks and projects, and be the top team's eyes and ears in the organization.

"There is a heavy administrative focus in what the five—I mean six —of us do, but we also see ourselves as like kinda the glue that helps hold together the top leaders, by providing them both the day-to-day materials and information about the pulse of the organization." Bernice was up at a flip chart and she was summarizing what they had just discussed. Amy and Sal had to leave an hour before.

"And what is like way cool is the fact that the organization, like, knows our role and will often take one of our team members aside to tell us something that they hope will be relayed up to Nathan and the leaders. At the same time, there doesn't seem to be a feeling that we're spying on anyone. It's not like conversation stops when one of us comes into the room. So all kidding aside about our running the place, we are seen as important, I think, even though we're all under thirty. This really is a cool-ass job."

Bernice paused to take a sip of water and looked at her watch as she did.

"Damn, I need to get you to the dinner meeting. I will explain what you can expect as we walk over."

If I thought I was nervous waiting to start work, I knew I was nervous going to this dinner, as Bernice described it. Much of the socializing was done in the facility, with the building connected by an underground passage to an Italian restaurant that was owned by the Consortium. This was going to be a dinner with Nathan and his senior team, a time when he wanted to introduce me to his colleagues. I'm friggin' eighteen years old without one hour of college and no high school diploma and I was going to be meeting with men and women with triple PhDs. Oh well, the worst that could happen was that I get fired the same day I'm hired. That has got to go into some record book somewhere.

Bernice explained as we walked underground that the Consortium agreed to the offer of the restaurant from a supporter and built the tunnel to it so that members could eat a nice meal without taking a lot of time from their work or having to get dressed to deal with the elements.

The restaurant was really nicely done, like some I had been to with my parents when we were celebrating something. This was definitely not your company cafeteria. Nathan rose as Bernice brought me toward the table where the leaders were sitting.

"Hey Dawn, it's great to have you on the team. Let me introduce you."

And then the whole friggin' table stood and applauded as Nathan and I stood side-by-side before the introductions. And I began to tear up. Damn it, here I am in front of this amazing and accomplished group of activists in my first day of employment and I have not said a word and I'm about to cry. Well it could have been worse, I guess. I could have fainted or thrown up.

"Well, I guess you need no introduction to our senior leadership. As I told you, what you did in Fair Shore had been noted by us, and then saving Bill's life during the attack on our building was icing on the cake."

I blew my nose with a Kleenex I happened to have in my pocket, then looked at the team and said, "Thank you. This is unnecessary. What you are doing means a hell of a lot more to our world than the little change I made in a small Connecticut town."

As they all sat and Nathan placed me to his right, a very tall, wire-rim-glasses kinda guy stayed standing. He said, "Quite the contrary, Dawn, what you did is the model that we are trying to push out into the mainstream. It's the kind of significant change that ordinary people can make when they identify something is wrong and needs to be changed. The fact that you have the God-given ability to talk about your convictions and passions in such an accessible manner is one of the reasons we wanted you to work here. Don't put yourself down, young lady. You have caused quite a stir and we are hoping that you continue that, with our support."

As the tall gentleman sat down, Nathan said, "That's Jurgen Schneider and he's our resident global communications expert, on loan to us from the University of Berlin. Let me quickly do the rest of the introductions. First, you need to know

160

that this is the core senior team that works with me. There are ten of us in total and we're missing Ignatius Estabol, our media champion, and Jenifer Paulser, who is our finance guru. They're in the field.

"This reprobate to your left is Eric Bandler, our field coordinator, the person who is the senior interface with the organizations we support. He is a strange dude. Be very, very careful around him."

I'd already turned to look at Eric, but I was startled when he stood abruptly, pushed his chair back, and came up behind me yelling, "That is the last time you warn another woman about me, Nathan, you bastard." He grabbed Nathan around the waist and lifted him. "I'm throwing this ingrate into the stew pot; I'll be right back." Looking around, I saw they were all in various stages of laughter. Nathan was smiling as he allowed Eric to move him toward the door before he dropped him with, "You know, I wouldn't want to do that to the stew. Our chefs would kill me."

Eric came right back to his chair with a straight face, sat down at the table, took a large sip from the beer in front of him, turned to me and said, "Nice to meet ya."

Nathan, who was still standing and still smiling, said, "Well, that's Eric. The rest of the crew is Melanie Anders, our chief statistician, Harvey Roberts to her left who is our IT Head, and Ashan Chabba who works with Harvey in our global technology function. Alvin Jackson is our operations guy and Melanie Murphy controls all our hiring and people- excellence work.

"Dawn, we invited you here this evening to meet this group because, having seen what you did in Fair Shore and having heard you on NPR talk with such conviction, I thought you could be involved in getting the message out to people about what we're doing. When you're not doing that, you'll be one of our strategists to figure out how to engage young people in the battle against the bad guys. Your third role will be as part of Bernice's team, which is the interface between the executive team and other senior leaders and the rest of the staff. Since you and I spoke about the first two roles and Bernice briefed you on the third, they shouldn't be a surprise."

"No, that's not a surprise, and I'm excited about being able to help in any way I can."

"Excellent. Then enjoy the meal. When dinner is done you can head on home and we'll continue the meeting."

As the group got back into their conversations, Jurgen asked me how I had decided to start the fight in Fair Shore and we talked for the next hour about a lot of things, some of which didn't include me.

I ate very little because my stomach kept tightening as I listened and learned the background of this brilliant group of leaders. They had all been members of activist organizations for years, with personal experiences that covered the seven continents. The number of graduate degrees was mind-numbing. As comfortable as they tried to make me feel, I was petrified, regularly asking myself some derivation of the question, ''What the hell have I gotten myself into?''

I was actually relieved when we finished our dinner since I was beginning to feel light-headed and desperately needed air. Nathan came over and asked if I had enjoyed myself. I told him I was glad the food was good because being surrounded by such stupid people was a real bore.

"Yeah, I know, I question every day why I look to them to run this organization. Well, maybe I'll get it right one of these years."

He walked me toward the door and said, "It was dumb luck that such a large percentage of the team happened to be here today and that you got a chance to meet them. They are a brave and committed crew; I trust each of them completely."

"Well I was certainly impressed. I am psyched to get back to work tomorrow morning. Thanks again for your trust in me; I really do appreciate it."

"No thanks necessary. You are one of us. I am traveling for a bit but I will see you in a couple of weeks. If you have any questions, Bernice is the go-to person. You take care."

And he was gone, poof.

Twenty-Eight

AS I WRAPPED up work the next day and headed home, having not seen my mother the previous evening when I got home from the dinner with Nathan and his team since she had an overnight in Boston, I decided to let her drive the Richard conversation from now on. If he's at our house when I get home, I will be pleasant. If he's not, and if my mother doesn't bring him up, that's probably just as well. If she does, I'll do my best to present an unemotional, factual response to whatever she asks. Oh, that sounds so logical. If only it were so.

Over one of my favorite meals, my mother asked, "So how is it going at the Consortium?"

"Well, I can tell it to you this way. I am floored by how much Nathan is asking me to do. I'm missing something here. Just yesterday he asked me to call him in Japan and he told me I would be starting the role he had discussed with us as one of the spokespeople for the firm, and that he was hoping to draw in more donors, who now know about us after all the publicity that happened when they attempted to destroy our headquarters.

"He also added another role, as part of the team that'll be thinking through how we should be spending the money that could be streaming in because of the attack. Since the explosion at our office, we received seventeen calls from legitimate donors who want to speak to us. They had no idea about the scope or sophistication of what we were doing before the attack."

"That's fantastic. We knew he respected what you had done in Fair Shore and on NPR, but this just proves it. I am *very* proud of you."

"Well, I actually pushed back on the second one. It just seems that role might be too much too soon. I'm concerned that people who have been with the Consortium for a while will resent me—or worse. He didn't buy it."

"Good for you for bringing that up. Keep your eyes open for any kind of negative reaction and you can always revisit it with him."

"That's the plan, thanks."

"We also need to come up with a plan about Richard."

"What do you mean?"

"I like him a lot; he has shown me a side of him I never thought existed as I watched him move front and center into the whole media reaction to what happened to you. He makes me feel special and that has not happened in a while, as you know. All I am asking is that you give him a chance and stay open to the possibility that he is not as bad as you believe he is. Would you do that for me?"

"Mother, I will be happy to stay open to that possibility."

"Wonderful, thanks."

"Hang on, I'm not done. I will be happy to try. But the facts as I see them are this.

"One: You are drawn to troubled men.

"Two: He lied over and over again about his relationship with us. If he's willing to lie to millions of people on TV, what would keep him from lying to you and me?

"Three: He has a big-time drinking problem that he said he would do something about and hasn't. You were both stoned the other night for God's sake, and I'm going to go out on a limb here and suggest that *you* didn't bring in the wacky weed.

"Four: From what his friends told you, he has heavy psychological issues about what he *thinks* was his role in the death of his brother and some activist students at Columbia.

"Five: He is a womanizer.

"I don't think my feelings about him are uncalled for. I really don't. That being said, you saw how I was the other night and I'll continue to act that way, watching for proof that will neutralize what I think about him. I have big doubts, Mother, but I love you more than anybody in the world and I want you to be happy, and if you want me to give him the benefit of the doubt, then I will."

And then she blew. "Where the hell do you get off judging someone you barely know? He is kind and generous and makes me feel special. He explained that all he has done since your fall was to keep what you have done alive in people's minds so that you would be remembered if you died, and appreciated if you came out of your coma. What he is giving me right now is what I need after all the craziness we have been through. And I need you to respect that, and your words and actions will have to show that, if you really love me the way you say. And right now I need to be with him and I am going to his place for the night."

She grabbed her jacket off the coat rack and her purse off the end table, and she stormed out the door and stomped down the stairs. And I was stunned, since my mother had never done anything like that—*ever*. I sat quietly thinking about what was going on, before I went up to bed. I cried myself to sleep for the first time since my parents told me they were getting divorced.

"Are you all right?"

I glanced up from the computer screen that I had probably been looking at blankly for ten minutes to see Bernice looking down at me with a concerned look on her face.

"Hey there. Yeah, I'm fine. I was just thinking of something. How are you?"

"I'm fine and you are not yourself. When did you get in?"

"Um, early. I have stuff I have to get done."

"Yes, I know that, since I assign most of it to you. What's going on?"

"Can we talk later? Maybe go over to the diner for lunch?"

"You got it. I will come get you at noon."

I really like Bernice. We've become friends in the short time I've been at the Consortium. She's a good soul, caring, great listener, smart as hell, and it's not all about her. And she gets stuff done and has huge energy that she can turn off when she's concerned about you or she needs to be listening. I haven't seen many people with the ability to really turn on the energy and then really turn on the empathy. And I trust her completely, although my guard is still up because of how certain "friends" have turned on me.

And I didn't sleep well last night. My mother and I never fight like that, like *never*. Which got me wondering if I'm right about Richard? She has a pretty well-developed crap detector and can really get an accurate read on people without a whole lot of information. And with Richard, she has tons of data points—damn, I sound like an engineer—to base her judgment on. So maybe I'm wrong about him, which has certainly happened more than once in my life, with Tripper being an all-too-recent example. I need to get other people's input at some point. I'm too emotionally involved in this. And I'd better get to work or I'm outta here.

Bernice came over right at noon.

"Come on, let's get moving and drive some guy's crazy over at the diner."

"Sounds like a plan."

You need to know about Bernice and guys. They love her. I mean can't stay away from her *love* her. She is really out there so you know she's in the room, and she has a killer body, which she doesn't flaunt. Particularly with the Consortium dress code, which is jeans and sneakers. But when she wants to dress up, the guys don't stand a chance. I only saw that once, when a number of us went out to a teen club the first week I was on the job. She changed into tight pants and a silk top and spiked heels and guys could not stay away. It was comical. The rest of us could not stop laughing watching these guys elbow each other out of the way so they could try to impress her. And it's not like the rest of us are dogs, it's just that she has a special way about her when she wants to turn it on. So when she mentions driving guy's crazy, there are notes of truth in that throwaway line.

It was a five-minute walk to the diner, which is officially called the Atlantis Diner, but everyone I know calls it "the diner." It was a pleasant walk with clear skies and no wind, a wonderful winter day. The hostess Irma, who is also a fan of Bernice's, gave her a big hug, called her darling, and brought us to a booth in the back, even though booths are supposed to be for three or more.

"Now darling, Silvio has asked me to let him be your waiter so you need to let me know if he gets inappropriate in any way, and we will deport him to some lonely destination where you will only be a fond memory, all right?"

"Yes, Irma, I promise to give you a full report."

She gave Irma a big smile and then said, "And here he is now. Hi there, handsome."

And Silvio is one handsome guy, a solid six feet with curly dark hair and huge black eyes in a sculpted Italian face.

"Hello Bernice. Hi Dawn. What visions you both are. How are you both today?"

When we responded in the affirmative he gave us our menus and then left us alone, a charming professional. After we ordered, Bernice looked across the table at me and asked, "What is going on today? I have gotten to know you pretty well over the last few weeks and you are just not yourself."

"My mother and I are very close and we had a horrible fight last night about a guy who actually has a relationship with the Consortium and she stormed out of the house and ended up staying with him. She has never ever done that before and I don't know what to do."

"All right, thanks for trusting me with that. Would it help to tell me who the guy is? Maybe I know him."

"His name is Richard Phillips and..."

"Richard Phillips? You're kidding me!"

The churning feeling in my stomach was immediate when I saw Bernice's negative reaction to the sound of his name.

"I wouldn't kid about something like this. How do you know him?"

As I watched the look on my friend's face, I got more and more concerned. She was clearly weighing what to say, and Bernice is not a think-long-and-hard-about-what-she-is-going-to-say kinda gal. But I decided to wait rather than push the issue.

Bernice busied herself with putting her napkin on her lap before she looked at me and said, "Dawn, I know Richard Phillips very well. He is like kind of a major topic among a number of the women here. I don't know how to say this since we are talking about your mother, but I am your friend and you need to hear it straight. Richard is a self-absorbed, deceitful woman-screwer who has slept with at least a dozen women in this place and misrepresented himself to every one of them. Thank goodness it seems like he hit a critical mass, so his negative reputation is so pervasive that no self-respecting woman will go out with him anymore and he seems to have moved on. It really concerns me that your mother is involved with him and I hope she has her wits about her because if she doesn't, he will use her and let her down hard. I'm sorry to have to tell you that, but you need to know."

And I was surprised by my reaction, which was almost positive in some sick kind of way. It dawned—sorry, no pun intended—on me that my reaction probably reflected vindication in some way, that I had been proven right in the horrible fight that my mother and I had gone through. That being said, I wasn't sure what to do with that information, but Bernice solved it for me.

"Dawn, I would be willing to sit down with your mother and tell her what I know, if that would help. This bastard is no good and it is the least I could do."

"Bernice, I really appreciate your honesty. I really do. And your offer means a lot to me because my mother does *not* have her wits about her and her thinking is off because of how long she's been out of the dating scene worrying about me. He is also, as you were implying, really good at what he does, as I've seen first-hand in his interactions with me. At the same time, I wouldn't want to put you in that situation, which would be awkward at the very least."

"You can stop right there. I am a big girl and he has hurt some friends of mine in a really nasty and planful way. I would have no problem talking this through with your mom if you think it would be helpful. I am absolutely serious. I would not volunteer if I weren't ready to follow through. He is a bad guy, and the fact that Nathan, who is a really good judge of people, keeps him around is a mystery to me."

"Thanks again, Bernice. I need to think this over. I'm too emotional and sleep-deprived at this point to be sure I'd be making the right decision for my mother. Let me think on it and get back to you."

"OK. Hang on a minute, though, there is another option. I have gotten to know his sister. Why don't I introduce the two of you and you can get a better sense of him from her."

"That sounds great. What a cool idea, you problem solver, you. I'll look forward to meeting her."

I felt relieved on some level and it put me in a much better mood. Bernice and I enjoyed our lunch. It was amusing to watch her and Silvio flirting openly with each other. He's doing a Master's in environmental studies at Southern Connecticut State and he plays classical guitar. When we walked back to work, she mentioned that she was thinking of taking him up on his offer to serenade her at one of the regular musical gatherings that he and his friends put together. When she asked me if I would go along, I happily nodded yes; time to get a life.

"It's nice to meet you, Dawn. I'm not sure how I can help, but I love Bernice and if she said you have a problem she thinks I can help with, I'm all ears. What's going on?"

With that opening, Lisa Phillips leaned back in the rectangular booth of the modest restaurant in Stamford, Connecticut where we met.

I had been stunned from the moment I spotted Lisa because she was a female copy of Richard, maybe a couple years younger, but mirroring his face, voice, and body to a freaky extent. Her light brown hair and light blue eyes were exactly the same except that she was missing the strands of gray that were creeping into the hair in Richard's beard and on his head. And if I wasn't mistaken, she was also very close to his height of six feet. I was literally squirming in my seat as I kept noticing traits that solidified the resemblance.

I guess Lisa noticed my discomfort because she said, "Yes I know, we look alike in a way that really gets on the nerves of some people who know us both and who don't like one or the other of us. I understand from Bernice that you fall into that category regarding my older brother."

"You heard right. And Bernice said I could be straight with you about your brother so here it is. I think your brother is a nasty drunk who took the fact that he knew me at Fair Shore High and used that to his advantage in a way that I find disgusting. The fact that he's sleeping with my mother makes me physically ill and he's caused the second biggest rift that we've ever had in what up to now has been a phenomenal mother–daughter relationship."

"What was the first?" Lisa sat back calmly, watching my face as she asked the question. When I didn't answer, she said, "My brother's story is pretty straightforward. I'm going to lay it out for you with complete candor, warts and all, and you can interrupt at any time if something is not clear. Before I start, what *is* the first big rift that influenced your relationship with your mother? That context will help me put my brother into clearer perspective for you."

168

I had no interest in talking about my father with someone I'd just met, or with anybody actually. I took a sip of water. "My father is a very bright college professor who is also an alcoholic womanizer who did some bad stuff while I was growing up, which impacted my relationship with my mother and the world in general. My mother and I have been best friends now for five or six years. He gradually moved out of the picture while they got separated and then divorced. That formally ended two years ago when we moved to Connecticut and he stayed in Boston. So my dad is at the top of the list of people who came between my mother and me, and Richard is number two and he's really trying hard to replace my father as the biggest dirt bag in the world."

I noted with satisfaction that Lisa showed some discomfort in the form of a frown and accompanying color at her throat as she listened to my brief statement about my family. She recovered quickly, which was no surprise, leaned forward and said, "Thanks for that; I was touched by your brief story because you just described *our* father. I am sorry you had to live through whatever bad stuff your father made happen.

"When I mentioned earlier that Richard's story is straightforward, I didn't mean it was without drama or nuance. I just meant that what's going on with him is pretty easy to understand. Richard is a narcissist or you could say he's self-absorbed, or as some who are clinically trained say, he's a sociopath. He only cares about himself and getting what he wants. If something gets in the way of that, he does whatever he can to get over or through the obstacle to his goal. So much of what you have seen with him is because he's jealous of all the attention you've received, so he has interjected himself into your life in a way that will allow him to share the glory.

"Richard has hurt a lot of people physically and mentally; he leaves hurt feelings, at a minimum, in his wake. As you've probably heard, he was the reason that our brother and two of his classmates at Columbia were killed.

"He and I were quite close when we were growing up, until I started to witness how he was hurting people. I confronted him about it more than once. He charmed his way out of any responsibility for whatever I brought up, and then he would do it again. My father supported everything he did, but my mom became increasingly frustrated with him. She and I began to distance ourselves from him while he was in college, and then when my younger brother died because of him, I wrote him off as did my mother and to a large extent, my father. So he is estranged at best from all of us.

"That probably does not seem to bother him too much because he's smart and engaging and charismatic and connects with very bright and influential people who have created a second family for him. Nathan, until recently, was one of those people. As you must know, they have known each other for years, and they were quite close before Nathan started to see through him. That hit home with Nathan when he figured out how Richard used you and your mother. Sociopaths are extremely adept at getting what they want through people who would not normally be fooled, which was the case with Nathan for a number of years.

"It really saddens me to have to say it, but be very careful around Richard, Dawn. My brother can be vicious and he has, as I've said, hurt a lot of people in a big way. I know you and your mother are smart and accomplished, but if you end up in his sights, he could make your life very difficult, and I am not being a drama queen here. If he is willing to physically and mentally hurt his blood relatives as he has, believe me, there is no limit to what he would do to someone who has kept him from reaching his goals. If he sees you as responsible for coming between him and Nathan, for example, that would be all he needs to decide to come after you and those close to you. You cannot underestimate him."

As Lisa was talking, I saw her literally shrink in front of me. Her shoulders sagged, her eyes tightened, and all sense of the super-confident, assured woman who had started our meeting was gone within moments. The change in her demeanor was as scary, if not more so, as the chilling words she was saying about her only sibling. I reached over and tried to hold her hand, but I seemed to startle her. It was as if she came out of a trance. She pulled her hand away and barked, "I don't want your pity. I just don't want you to go through what I have gone through at the hands of that monster."

She got up abruptly, looked down at me and said, "I have to go. I had no idea how telling that story would impact me. I thought I had gotten my head around what he has done, but I was obviously very, very wrong. I am sorry, I have to go."

She jerked her wallet from her purse and before I could say anything, placed a twenty-dollar bill on the table and lurched out the door without looking back. She almost ran down the waitress who was arriving that moment with our food.

"My friend isn't feeling well. Please leave the food here and I'll eat what I can and pay for both meals, thanks."

"Um, all right, I uh hope she feels OK."

Twenty-Nine

I ANSWERED MY cell on the first ring, seeing it was Joseph Bruschi.

"Hi Joseph, what's up?"

"Hello Dawn. I am glad I caught you. How are you?"

"Life is a bowl of cherries, my friend, a bowl of cherries."

Chuckling, he said, "Well, I have done some digging about what you uncovered in your conversations with folks inside and outside of Connecticut since you returned and not only was everything you said accurate, but there is some other very bad stuff that has gone down and it's newsworthy in a potentially major way. Here is my concern. As soon as I publish anything, they're going to ask if what I'm writing about is specific to Fair Shore. It's a legitimate question, since I live in town and of course I was a reporter here for ten years. A corollary question will almost certainly be whether what you discussed on NPR was part of my story, and that's another legitimate question, since people in this town are hyper-vigilant about the town's reputation—as you know only too well —and they are not stupid.

"I'm concerned that you might be identified as once again responsible for besmirching Fair Shore's reputation and that you'll have to deal with some of the same garbage that landed you in the hospital. As eager as I am to uncover the bad stuff you discussed with me, I am not interested in bringing a ton of grief down on you, I'm really not. There are plenty of other stories that would not in any way be connected to you, if you told me you were concerned about the direction I want to take based on what you shared with me."

"First of all, thanks for asking me. I really do appreciate your sensitivity. You're right; I'm very concerned about once again being the center of attention. And I don't want people to think I'm bringing bad publicity to Fair Shore. I am not looking to have to deal with that in the short term, my comments on NPR aside.

"That being said, I can look anyone in the eye, like you can, and tell anyone who asks that none of these situations happened in Fair Shore; they happened in towns all over the country. So go ahead and print the article, make it clear that it was in towns inside and outside of Connecticut, and we should be all right."

"That makes perfect sense, and if you sleep on the question and come up with a different answer, just let me know. Otherwise, I'm going to write these stories under the umbrella of the sexual abuse of young women and men. Thanks for the go-ahead, Dawn, and for pointing me in the right direction. And let me know if I can help you in any way."

As I got off the phone, my excitement with what Joseph was committed to do trumped in a big-time way my concern about the repercussions. I jumped up from the couch, did a little dance step that will definitely not win any awards, and shuffled toward the kitchen to grab a snack. My cell rang again and this time it was my mother, which fired me up until she said, "Richard called and I am going to meet him for dinner and then I'll probably stay at his place for the night. Anything of note going on?"

"Not a thing. Have a great time and I will see you tomorrow night."

Man, I'll tell you, if I were a dependent or destructive type, a call like that would have made it real easy to trigger some bad behavior. It would be a great excuse to go to the liquor cabinet and drink a bottle of wine out of frustration with what the person I love more than anyone in the world was doing. But I moved out of my really destructive phase a few years ago, so my biggest self-destructive move was to pour some potato chips in a bowl and scarf them up. They didn't stand a chance. And I watched some stupid show for half an hour and then said screw it and went up and went to bed, knowing I can usually fall asleep within a few minutes under any circumstance. Which worked, allowing me to feel quite rested when the alarm went off at five o'clock the next morning.

Thirty

I COULD NOT have been feeling better as I walked out of the Consortium at six-thirty the next evening. And then I saw Richard out of the corner of my eye, leaning against the wall right outside the door.

"Good evening, Dawn, nice to see you."

"Hello Richard."

"Did you have a good day?"

"It was very nice. What's up?"

"I would like to buy you a coffee and ask you a couple of questions. It should only take a few minutes and you can head home to dinner."

"I'm really beat. There's been a lot going on."

"I promise it will not last more than twenty minutes. It is really important."

"All right, the Atlantis Diner is only a couple minutes' walk from here."

"Perfect."

We made small talk as we walked across the street and over to the diner. I was really relieved when I saw Silvio standing next to Irma. When he saw me, his warm smile accompanied his hug, and he said, "Dawn, it is great to see you. Irma, I'll show them to a booth."

"You have admirers everywhere, it seems."

"Silvio's a great guy."

As we sat in the same corner booth where he had put me earlier in the week, we both ordered coffee.

"So what's so important?"

"You get right to the point, don't you?"

"We have twenty minutes; I want to make the most of them." I gave him what I hoped was one of my most engaging smiles, one that might even be called seductive. I was really hoping he would walk away from this meeting feeling less threatened by me than he had every right to be. I can be so friggin' naïve.

"You do have a beautiful smile, as I am sure you know."

When I just kept smiling he continued, "OK, I have heard from people I respect that I should try and work things out with you."

Goddamn it, Lisa must have told him what we discussed. My smile was gone, and I sat up prepared to let him do all the work and not give him anything to attack. Naïve thought number two. Damn it.

"All that I have been doing in the fourteen months since you were hospitalized, and the month before and months after, was meant to defend what you did and get the word out about your courage so that young people, who I feel so much connection with, would have you as a role model. Show them what courage looks like in the face of the bad stuff that goes on in their increasingly complicated lives. That's the truth. I don't think you should condemn or hate me for making money off those efforts. I put hundreds of hours of my time into telling your story and traveling all over the country getting your story out there and I should have gotten something in return, don't you think?"

I had mixed emotions as I listened to him. The first was that he's really smooth. He's a good talker all right, and I can see why he had been so successful telling my story. Impressive. The second was that it gave me pleasure to watch his discomfort. This smooth operator was really on the defensive and trying like hell to get me on his side. It was really, really nice to see him squirm. And the third was a heightened certainty that he is a lying dirt bag who would say and do anything to get what he wanted.

So I just looked calmly at him as he asked the question, and I actually felt no need to reply. I was going to Zen my way through this conversation. Oh yeah, that was wrong-ass thought number three.

"So I want to know what I need to do to become the friends that we started to be when you were in my class before your jump. I would really like that because I am falling in love with your mother and I would very much like your support."

Silvio arrived at that moment with our coffees, which gave me a chance to try and relax as I digested what he had just said—he was falling in love with my mother. Oh man, that was the last thing I wanted to hear. I busied myself with putting milk and sugar in my coffee and then decided not to try and take a sip since I knew my hand would be shaking and I didn't want to give him that satisfaction.

I sat back against the cushion in the booth, I looked at him, and I smiled a tight smile.

"Richard, I appreciate your making your case. I really do."

I could feel my eyes narrow as I prepared to say the next sentence.

"And unfortunately for the three of us, I don't believe a word you said. I have heard from people I trust that you are only out for yourself and you'll do anything to get what you want. I believe you're using my vulnerable mother to that end, and that has caused the most serious rift in our relationship other than what surfaced when my father and mother divorced."

"Now wait…"

"*Let me finish, Richard.*"

I sat up straight, leaned forward, and raised my right hand *and* my voice to stop him from talking.

"Nothing you can do will change those feelings. I know I am right. I will do everything I can to end your relationship with my mother and get you out of our lives."

I leaned back but kept direct eye contact with him. His glare was unwavering. In an attempt to regain his composure, he lifted his coffee cup and I was gratified to see that his hand shook. He noticed it too, and put his cup down without it reaching his mouth.

He pushed the cup and saucer to the side and leaned as close to me as he could across the large table. He had some trouble lowering his voice to say, "Listen, you bitch. You are screwing up important relationships with my family and very important friends in my life and you'd better decide to stop."

"Or what?"

"You have no idea who you are messing with."

"I am sure I do, but I'm going to make it my business to find out the complete story."

I had purposefully raised my voice so I could gain the attention of the other patrons. I saw one couple in the booth across from us turn to see what was happening. I also noticed Richard's face getting red and a couple of the veins in his neck getting enlarged. In a voice much louder than I am sure he intended, he threatened, "You might not have time, you bitch. You're dead meat!"

Silvio came running over, bless him. Standing over Richard, he asked, "Is everything all right, Dawn? He just threatened you."

I smiled and said, "Everything is fine, my friend. This man was just leaving."

Richard glared at me and snagged his coat, pushed Silvio aside, and sauntered out the door. I grabbed Silvio's arm as he was pushed aside and I pulled him away from my retreating former teacher.

"Let him go, Silvio. It's over."

"Are you sure you are all right, Dawn?"

I hesitated to respond and he quickly decided, "I am going to take a break and walk you to your car."

I didn't argue. I was drained from the encounter. "That would be very nice. I just want to sit here alone for a few minutes and sip my coffee before we go. OK with you?"

"Of course, no problem. Just let me know when you're ready to go."

I sat for a good twenty minutes, going over what Richard said, remembering especially his threat about my not having time to look into his background. Frankly, I figured he was just being a bully and a blowhard. I finished my coffee and Silvio walked me to my car without asking any questions. I gave him a hug and thanked him, buckled up, and pulled out of the parking lot. I admit, I did watch to see if Richard was anywhere in sight. He wasn't, thank God.

I drove home in the slow lane the whole way. I called my mother to explain I would be late for dinner. I was shaken. It's one thing to be brave for myself. I'm self-absorbed enough to do that well. It's a whole other thing to be brave when the person you love the most in the world is in love with a person you fear; an entirely different level of garbage.

My normal way of handling anything that I have to work through with my mother is to sit down and have it out. No bull, just an honest statement of the facts and feelings. We developed that style as she worked through her very complicated relationship with my narcissistic, lying father. We had to be honest with each other since he wasn't being honest with us. And that way of relating obviously helped as I was going through all the crap attached to helping the young women in Fair Shore High. When I had a problem that might reflect badly on me or show that I didn't have a clue, I told my mother and we discussed it. When we didn't agree, we told each other why, listened, and came to our own decision with another perspective to factor in.

That style was not operating now, and so I had no idea what I was going to say when I got home. I thought it would be best to listen more than talk and see what happened.

"It is good to see you, Dawn. I made your favorite vegetable and noodle soup."

"Richard just publicly threatened to have me hurt if I didn't stop messing in his life." So much for waiting to see how the conversation progressed.

My mother stopped what she was doing and put her left hand on the hutch next to the door into our kitchen.

"Did he touch you?"

"No, he threatened me at the diner in front of some customers and my friend Silvio."

My mother straightened and walked quickly over to me and we hugged. We separated at the same moment and sat together on the couch.

"You have to tell me exactly what he did."

"Mom, I'm all right and I'll tell you everything. I can smell the soup from here.

176

Why don't you make sure it doesn't boil over and let me get changed and I'll tell you everything, I promise."

And over a wonderful meal I told her about my conversation with Bernice, then Bernice setting up the meeting I had with Richard's sister, ending with the confrontation with Richard. She asked no questions, just listened and occasionally reached over to hold my hand.

"So that's what he said. It was loud enough for Silvio to come over and ask if everything was all right since I had just been threatened. I had met Silvio before, when I was in the diner with Bernice and the other Consortium people. At that point, Richard got up and pushed past Silvio to leave. I held Silvio back and he volunteered to walk me to my car since Richard had threatened me. I didn't argue. That's the whole story, Mother, word for word."

We sat in silence for a few minutes. We digested our food and my mother digested my words. I have learned not to interrupt my mother when her mind is in overdrive and she's working on a problem. She finally put her fork down and pushed her plate away. She looked steadily into my eyes and said, "Dawn, I have made a very serious mistake that has hurt you in multiple ways. I am so sorry for doing that to you. I obviously had no idea how my judgment was impaired by my need to be treated with what I thought was love and passion by an intelligent and attractive man."

She took another sip of water when the doorbell rang. Neither of us had heard footsteps on our porch. There was Richard standing at the door with a large bouquet of flowers in hand.

My mother looked at me and whispered, "Please don't move. I need to take care of this, and it will not take long."

She got up deliberately and walked to the door. She stepped out onto the porch and closed the door behind her. I could hear Richard start to talk, but she slapped him across the face. When he tried to continue, she slapped him again.

I overheard the whole conversation.

"Using me is one thing. As Dawn has pointed out to both of us, I seem attracted to lying dirt bags. But threatening my daughter is beyond low even for someone like you. If you ever try to approach either of us again in any way, I will call the police and make a very public scene. Take your goddamn flowers and get the hell off our property and we'd better never see you again. I know I have said this before. This time I am deadly serious because you have threatened the one thing in my life that has value to me."

Without waiting for a response, she walked back in, slammed and locked the door, and came and sat back down. When she looked past me toward the porch, he was gone.

Thirty-One

RICHARD DISAPPEARED FROM our lives. He did not call and my mother and I did not see him lurking anywhere. Gone. And my relationship with my mother got back to where it had been before he had insinuated himself between us.

We both got very busy. My mother did more traveling once she was back into her job full swing and I was studying for my high school equivalency and working at the Consortium.

"All right, Dawn, you are ready to move into the big time. You have a meeting with the *top guy* set for dinner this evening and you will soon be hitting the road, creating visibility for us, and making us proud."

It was a month after my mother booted Richard out of our lives and I had gotten a full orientation to the inner workings of the Consortium. I had been introduced to all of the key staff, and a number of the major contributors, whom the brain trust thought would want to meet a teen activist, as they were calling me. I had caught glimpses of Nathan as he scurried about and gave update meetings to the staff via satellite or in the briefing room where I had seen him talk the day of the bombing. Having dinner with him tonight would be the first face-to-face since my dinner with his leadership team. Bernice stood in my cubicle and read from her notes about how I was going to be utilized. I was smiling.

"And then in a week you head down to DC, Virginia, and Maryland with him and Ignatius, to meet with a number of national and global mucky-mucks in different organizations to discuss our vision and what we are doing to help people to thrive in this crazy world.

"You have to be very, very careful when Ignatius and Nathan get together. Two philosopher kings feeding off of each other's insanity. It is a real show. And that is the Dawn-Mortenson-is-going-to-change-the-world itinerary."

"Can we snag a conference room? I have some questions about what's coming up."

"Let's do it."

We had to go down a floor where we found a small room that was free. We called the booking folks to ask if we could have it for half an hour and got it officially reserved. Bernice sat down at the head of the table. She poured some water from the pitcher on the counter to the left of the door. I also filled a glass and sat down five feet from her on the side facing away from the one floor-to-ceiling window.

"Fire away, my friend."

"The key one is about how people here will respond as I become so visible in my role, and in my involvement with senior members of the organization. I would have to think there would be some jealousy or some 'who the hell does she think she is' thoughts going through the minds of certainly the younger folks. I mean, here I am, less than three months, and I'm going on road shows with Nathan. I mentioned it to Nathan the last time we talked on the phone and he wasn't concerned, but I am. How should I handle the ruffled feathers?"

"It's a great question and legitimate. Yes, there are a few people who have asked the 'what the hell' question right after you had dinner with the leadership team. Nobody out of the six on our immediate team, for sure. We all know that you aren't an egoist and that you were in fact brought in to play this role because of how you handled the situation in Fair Shore. Now that I think of it, one person outside our team did mention that they didn't trust you because of something their friend Richard Phillips had said to them. It seems like he was spreading some rumors about you that might have created some animosity or jealousy. Now that he's out of the picture—from what you've shared with me—and now that you'll be generating some good will for us, I don't think you need to go out of your way and do anything. Just be you and it will all blow over, I'm sure."

"What else do I need to know about Nathan or this other guy we will be traveling with? And are there any other consultants or clients I'll be interacting with that I should know about?"

"You know what you need to know about Nathan. Be your high- energy, intelligent self and you will be fine. Just don't try to fake it with him. If you don't know, tell him that, but if you try to dance your way around him, he will know it and you will lose credibility. One of the reasons his radar was turned on you in a positive way was because of how you stood up to the Fair Shore establishment and took no crap from folks who questioned your motives. The deal was sealed when you told it straight on the NPR interview. He knew you were one of us at that point. He has a strong crap detector as you have heard before, which is turned on all the time since people are always trying to get stuff from him. The only time it's turned off is with people he has known for a long time. That might be why he got it so wrong about Richard Phillips. Be completely supportive of what we are doing and completely honest with him, and you both will make a hell of a team. Question what we are doing or try to get over on him and you are toast.

"As you have heard and seen, he is a fascinating mix of contrasts. He is like brilliant and does not suffer fools gladly, but it is not all about him, it's about helping others. He can be a loner and very private and holed up in his office or at his cabin in the woods for extended periods of time and then be very social and in the middle of the action for a big party or celebration or meeting where he reveals very personal information about his concerns or weaknesses. He is funny as hell and can be loose and engaging and the next day he can be tight and argumentative if things are not working out. He inspires amazing loyalty among very bright and accomplished people, some of whom he has argued with in public, because they know, at the end of the day, it was not personal. The fight was all about getting it right and ensuring the success of the Consortium. He is a leader who has an extremely clear focus on what is wrong with our world and what can be done about it.

"Ignatius is also a trip, in some of the same ways. He is brilliant about the media and how it works and how it can help and also hinder us. He is a pretty quiet guy until he gets with Nathan and then you don't know what to expect. They have been friends since high school and trust each other completely. When Nathan has a problem or a really sticky issue to deal with, he will pull Ignatius into the conversation and they usually figure it out. You will have fun with them.

"On this junket you will gain a full picture of their vision and how they deal with clients and the media. The two speeches you are giving on your own are to friendly audiences and are short so we don't expect any drama around them. The anti-Big Tobacco speech you are doing with Nathan has the potential to be the most volatile, as you have seen from the wording of what you and Nathan will be saying. You are going to have a fascinating time."

We spent a few more minutes discussing what was coming up and then I went back to my cubicle feeling much better about how things were going.

And as it turned out, the media blitz went extremely well. My presentations were *awesome!* Sorry, I can't help myself. I got a standing ovation from a group of young leaders and the second speech to a non-profit gathering ran over because of all the questions that my comments had generated. I was buzzing and then Nathan and Ignatius both told me that it had gone beautifully from what they had heard and seen. I was so excited. And then I saw them gain agreements from three different corporations to publicly support our efforts with major grants.

The final talk was when Nathan and I spoke to a group of anti-tobacco activists in a meeting that the Consortium had pulled together, with a view toward uniting the different groups who are fighting the big tobacco companies.

I began by telling my story about how my four grandparents all died from lung cancer within five years of each other. They were all in their fifties or sixties.

In five years my entire connection to the four people who had so influenced who I am and what I do was gone, murdered by Big Tobacco. And then they murdered two of my four aunts and uncles and are going after the remaining two who are still addicted to cigarettes.

And now they are after my generation, with five of my closest friends hooked on nicotine. I am working at the Consortium because I have seen the data on how Big Tobacco has lied and done everything possible to get young people addicted. There are legitimate estimates, as you all know, based on current smoking statistics, that one billion people will die from smoking-related illnesses in the twenty-first century. I want to try to lessen the effectiveness of their killing machine and am honored to be in a room with so many who have worked so long toward the same goal.

And then Nathan gave the most compelling speech I have ever seen or heard, and here are his verbatim closing comments:

And here is the key, my friends, the fact that keeps me up at night and caused me to bring us all together here today. And unfortunately everyone in this room knows this well. The only way that Big Tobacco can continue to generate huge profits and succeed in their mission to sell as many cigarettes and tobacco products as possible that kill millions of people a year, is if they target and get our children, grandchildren, and great-grandchildren to start smoking before they are eighteen. All their research has shown that the very large majority of smokers start before they are eighteen, no matter what country they live in.

I have pulled you all together here today so that we can work on combining our resources in a way that makes them less efficient and effective at killing our loved ones. To that end, the Consortium is putting up two million dollars to sustain this effort to get all the anti-tobacco groups represented in this room collaborating as effectively as possible to make Big Tobacco unprofitable.

Because my daughter is ten years old, she is their target and I swear to you as I am standing here that I will do everything I possibly can to keep them from murdering my little girl.

I will not let them murder her or her friends. I will not let them murder the young ones you love. I will not let them murder the family and friends that you cherish. I will not let them decimate her generation as they have the generations that have preceded her, as Dawn described so movingly. Because we all know they will lie and cheat and spend hundreds of millions of dollars a year to figure out every possible way to get her to try a cigarette. I will not let this happen. I love her with all my heart and want her beautiful smile and generous being to impact thousands of others as she has impacted me.

I will not let them murder mine, I will not let them murder yours, and I will not let them go unpunished. I look forward to working closely with all of you to bring these murderers to justice. Thank you.

And the place went nuts and he received a five-minute standing ovation.

Our anti-Big Tobacco speech was the final meeting of our media blitz. All three of us were way beyond excited when we got together for our last dinner before heading home the next day.

"I want to make a toast," Nathan stood in front of Ignatius and I with his bottle of beer held over his head, "To the most powerful three-person team in the history of the social change movement!"

Ignatius and I were smiling ear-to-ear. We raised our drinks in agreement. Ignatius yelled, "Hell yeah, we are the best and we rock."

Nathan sat down and drained his beer, caught the eye of our waitress, and asked her to bring another round to the best team of consultants in the land. And Ignatius looked at her and yelled, "Hell yeah, we are the best and we rock." Nathan seemed to think this was hysterical. He put his arm around Ignatius and yelled in his ear, "Hell yeah, we are the best and we kick ass."

And we all laughed again. Now I was a little self-conscious since we were, in my mind, a little loud, but I looked around and I didn't notice anybody who seemed to be taking exception to our declarations of how good we were, so I sat back and smiled at my colleagues. Well, that was a mistake.

"Ah the beautiful damsel has finally realized how lucky she is to be out on the town with two such amazingly handsome hunks, and she has sat back in satisfaction that she has us to herself. I don't know, my friend, do you think she's getting a little smug, or maybe a wee bit cocky for her own good?"

"Good question. Let me ask her. Fair damsel, are you sitting there thinking about how lucky you are to be in our company, or is something more sinister buzzing around in that fertile mind of yours?"

"Truth be told, I am thinking that we not only kicked ass today, but we have changed the face of corporate America forever, ushering in an era of collaboration and transparency that they'll sing songs about around the campfire for years to come. So I say to the two of you, hell yeah we are the best, and we have positively changed the world forever!"

Nathan and Ignatius both jumped up and cheered, turning to the startled patrons. Both of them put their arms around me and lifted me in the air, exclaiming together, "We would like you to join us in congratulating the newest member of our team on a sensational day dedicated to changing the world for the better." And some people in the restaurant actually clapped!

I won't forget that anytime soon. Our food came and we quieted down and talked about what we had accomplished in our five days. No more declarations of greatness, just serious talk.

That weekend was relaxing. My mother and I went into New York City and did our museum thing and we spent the rest of our time catching up on our fun reading. First thing Monday morning, when I booted up my Mac at the Consortium, I saw an email from Nathan: "To all employees—we put on a concentrated media blitz in Washington DC, Virginia, and Maryland last week, and generated significant exposure about our efforts. The fact that we were successful in getting the word out is indicated by a significant number of phone and email threats against the Consortium over the weekend, threats to the organization, as well as to particular members of the organization, including the team members who were visible last week. We are taking these threats seriously and ask that all of you be particularly vigilant as you come to and from work and as you go about your normal activities. We know from the bombing that our enemies are capable of serious damage. If you have any questions, please talk to your manager or Human Resources about what precautions you should take. And thanks again for the quality of the work you are doing. If we were not making a difference, nobody would care to try and deter us. With much respect and love, Nathan."

After reading Nathan's email three times, I hustled over to Bernice's cubicle and, before I could say a word, she said, "Sandy wants to see you at ten o'clock this morning in the security office to discuss your personal safety."

"Damn, Bernice, you all are scaring me."

"That's a good thing, Dawn. These threats are serious and your name was mentioned in more than one of the messages we received this weekend. Apparently yours and Nathan's anti-Big Tobacco speeches were recorded and put on the internet and have generated much of the negative reaction. Since you're now one of the faces of the Consortium, you'll be getting more rather than less of this attention. I just don't think anyone expected you to be singled out so quickly. You need to take this really seriously and keep a low profile for a while, which is what Sandy will be discussing with you at ten o'clock."

"Morning Dawn. Thanks for coming in."

"Bernice briefed me about what's going on. I will do whatever you say, Sandy."

"Good, because you need to stay calm and focused over the next few months.

Patterns you are used to following will need to be altered, which takes concentration and discipline. Here are the most important things: you need to vary your routine, travel with others whenever possible, let us here in Security know your plans, and be guarded around new people who surface in your life. I am going to go into depth about each point and I have materials I would like you to read that flesh out what I'm saying. And here is my card with my cell and home number; you can call or text me any time that you have concerns or questions. You do not have to worry about interrupting my family. When my wife and I got engaged she knew she was marrying into a nontraditional relationship and she's used to interruptions at all hours."

Sandy spent half an hour with me, expanding on the key points I just mentioned. And I read every word and did get back with a question about how specific he wants me to be about telling him my schedule each day. His reply: "You cannot provide too much detail."

"All right then, very clear. Let me know if I am giving you what you need." And apparently I am because I didn't hear anything from Sandy or his team.

A few days after that meeting, I got a call from Ernestine, who told me I really had to be careful because she had run into Tripper and he had said that I'd made his life a living hell, that he'd heard I never wanted to see him again, and that I had poisoned his family against him so that his own mother didn't want to see him. She continued, "He also said that other good friends have turned against him because of you and if he could strangle your pretty little head he would do it. He said you were dead to him and that he had hoped that when that bomb went off at the Consortium, you would be buried under the whole damn building, crying out for help that never came. And yet you not only survived, but 'are a goddamn hero.'"

Ernestine finished the conversation on a really cheery note when she inferred that Tripper is really unhinged and he sees my rejection as the reason for all his unhappiness, that he could do something really stupid to me, and that I should be careful where I go alone.

Thirty-Two

I AM TIRED, really tired, and really scared. And truth be told I brought it on myself, damn it, and there is a pattern here; and all kidding aside, this pattern is getting old and I have to figure out what to do about it.

I was really excited about Joseph Bruschi's exposé being published on how young girls and boys are being sexually abused. He showed me the final draft of his article and I appreciated that he didn't mention Fair Shore. He wrote about interviews he had with dozens of young girls, boys, and parents inside and outside of Connecticut. So I figured that the Fair Shore citizenry wouldn't think I was tied into the exposé. Yeah, right.

Within a couple of hours of the three-page article coming out in the *Hartford Courant* I got the first call, which was short and sweet: "So you're at it again, huh, bitch? Well maybe a permanent stay in the hospital or a drainage ditch somewhere will help you learn your lesson and stop focusing people on what's going on in Fair Shore." And it was followed by other calls with a similar tone. The whole thing brought back very painful memories from two years ago.

That first night I didn't sleep well, and the next day I got a Fair Shore-related call at work; and though they've tapered off now that three weeks have passed, it's very clear that it's not because people have forgotten I'm here. Somebody put up a website a week after the article was published. They photo-shopped Joseph and me in bed together, under the headline, "In bed together, soon to be dead together."

And that one got the attention of the FBI. The agent who interviewed me was thrown off during my initial interview with him when I answered the question, "Do you have any idea who would be so angry at you that they would want you dead?"

"Well, Agent DuBois, I actually do. And it's a pretty long list."

"Seriously, a long list?"

"Unfortunately, yes."

I sat back on the couch in our living room, crossed my legs, and looked at the jacked, forty-something agent.

"We're taking this threat to you very seriously so I need to know about each of the individuals or groups that might be interested in hurting you. Please be as specific as you can."

"OK, here goes. The first person is named Jed Ostracher. He is my cousin and he tried to rape me in my father's kitchen when my mother and father were out. He was seventeen at the time; I was ten. I was able to gouge his eye enough so he was hospitalized and lost sight in it permanently. I pressed charges and he went to prison. I understand he recently got out of prison on good behavior. Oh yeah, that's Jed all right.

"The second person who…"

"Excuse me Ms. Mortenson, you said you put him in the hospital, is that right?"

"Yes, Andrew. It *is* Andrew, isn't it?"

"I prefer Agent DuBois."

"Hey, this is difficult enough to talk about. Please call me Dawn."

"All right, Dawn. Please tell me how you put a guy almost twice your age in the hospital."

"I had been taught some self-defense since I was eight years old by a karate instructor who I trained with, because my father and mother wanted me to be able to protect myself, since they thought I might grow up to be pretty like my mother and need to deal with unwanted advances. So I gouged him in one eye and hit him in his Adam's apple as I had been taught. Luckily he had leaked some of his sperm onto my pants so they had DNA evidence that put him away. Did you need any other details?"

"No, that was very clear, Dawn, thanks. I interrupted. You were going to tell me about the second person who would want to hurt you."

"Yes, that would be one of the teachers at Fair Shore High, Richard Phillips. Do you know him?"

"No I don't."

"OK, this is a long story. The really quick summary is that he threatened to kill me recently in front of some witnesses at a diner after I told him that I would do everything I could to keep him out of my mother's pants, and from making a lot of money off the story about how I jumped out of a fourth-floor window to keep my friend from getting killed. My mother stopped seeing him after I told her what he had said, and then his sister and a long-time friend got on his case for how he was acting. So he would rather that I not be around to mess up all his lies and bad behavior. What more do you need to hear about my good buddy Richard?"

"I am familiar with the Fair Shore story and your involvement in it; that got a lot of circulation."

"Tell me about it. That situation is part of this list."

"I had not heard the name 'Richard Phillips' attached to it. Please clarify his involvement for me."

"Yeah, I guess my short version was a little confusing. Richard was one of my teachers at Fair Shore High when I got involved with trying to gain equal stature for the women's sports teams. When I ended up in the hospital for over a year, he went out and gave very lucrative speeches about what I had done, portraying himself as much more of a friend and connection than he really was. When I gained consciousness, my mother told him to leave us alone, that she was quite aware of how he had misrepresented himself.

"Somehow he was able to convince my mother—who is very smart, but also someone who's attracted to brilliant bastards—that he was a good guy, and they began dating. When he heard that I was actively trying to convince my mother to dump him, and that I was also telling people close to him what he had really done, he threatened to kill me, in front of some customers and a waiter friend of mine at the Atlantis Diner in New Haven. When I told my mother what he had said, she slapped him and told him to get out of our lives. I've had conversations with his sister and other people who told me to be careful—that he's a sociopath who'll hurt anybody who gets in his way—which would be me."

"That's very helpful, Dawn. I would like the name of the waiter friend of yours at the diner and Phillips' sister, the woman you talked with."

"That's easy; the waiter is Silvio Giambara and he works at the Atlantis Diner, as I said. Richard's sister is Lisa Phillips and she lives in Greenwich."

"Superb. Who is the third person?"

"His name is Tripper Cardone. I went out with him a few times two years ago when we were both seniors at Fair Shore High. When I got all that notoriety for standing up against the sexism in that town, winding up with the jump from the window I mentioned earlier, while I was in the hospital he spent the year in a partnership with Richard Phillips, making money off of the fact that he had been my boyfriend. Tripper got pissed when he heard that I never wanted to see him again, which I had not said; and I was told by a mutual friend of ours recently that I should watch out for him—that he's unhinged and out to get me. Need anything more on him?"

"Yes, what's the name of the mutual friend who told you that this Tripper Cardone is out to get you?"

"That is Ernestine O'Malley. She lives in Fair Shore and works at the high school."

"OK, great, that is helpful. I might need to talk with her and flesh out what he said about you."

"That makes a lot of sense, Agent DuBois. And the next two either have been, or are being looked into, by the authorities. I'll give you the abbreviated version, and then you can find out from them what they've found out.

"The Fair Shore police arrested several people who were involved with planning and trying to execute the rape and murder of my friend Ernestine and myself two years ago. There are people in that town who would rather not have me around around, since they see that the work I did to equalize the support and funding for the male and female programs in Fair Shore reduced the prestige value—and therefore the real estate values—of their homes.

"A journalist, Joseph Bruschi…"

"I know Joseph well. He's a good reporter."

"Yes, he's a good man and he recently wrote an exposé about the fact that young girls and boys are being sexually abused in large numbers. The good folks in Fair Shore, knowing that he wrote a best seller about my original sports equality campaign, think *I'm* behind the story. When the exposé came out this past weekend, I received threatening calls similar to the ones I got a couple of years ago. I don't have specific names of anybody in Fair Shore who would want me hurt or dead or both, but *he* might; and if this problem continues, I could make some pretty good guesses about who's behind it. But right now, they would only be guesses."

"I will definitely talk to Joseph. I read his articles about you. He's a big fan of yours."

"He's one of the few and I trust him completely. The Fair Shore police, on the other hand, were a mixed bag. There were some wonderful and very professional members of that force. There were also a couple who were obviously not on my side. One senior member of the force took me aside and whispered, "I hope someone shuts you up for good so we can go back to doing our real work of supporting this wonderful town." I just wish I'd had a tape recorder so I could have gotten his ass fired from the force, but—fortunately or unfortunately—I haven't gotten into the habit of wearing a wire everywhere I go. Might disrupt my way cool, hyperactive social life."

"You had a Fair Shore police officer say that to you?"

"Yes I did."

"What was his name?"

"I'm really uncomfortable telling you his name. I think, when you talk with Joseph, you'll get a pretty good sense of who the good guys are and who the bad guys are in Fair Shore."

"I understand your desire to be circumspect, but it would really be helpful if I knew who said that."

"How about we leave it this way: if you don't get a sense of the senior officer on the force who is a native of the town and played middle linebacker on the Fair Shore High football team about twenty years ago that went undefeated and was the state champion and ranked number one in the country, give me a call and I might reconsider my position."

I enjoyed watching Agent DuBois smile as he took down what I said, before he replied, "I will make sure and come back to you if I can't narrow that down."

"But seriously, I'm concerned that he would figure I was involved if you start investigating him. Please be careful with how you handle the Fair Shore part of this. I don't want to have to take another four-story swan dive into the hospital."

"I understand your concern and I promise we won't do anything to alienate you from the Fair Shore police force any more than you already are. And you said there was a fifth person on your list of enemies?"

"Yes, connected to the work I do for the Information Is Power Consortium in New Haven. I've received a number of death threats related to my work there, some related to a speech that Nathan and I gave recently in Virginia against the tobacco industry. I've saved all of the voicemail messages that came in recently about that, and in the past about my previous work for female sports equality. Do you know the Consortium?"

"Yes I do, actually, and I have a lot of respect for Nathan Pomerantz. He's driving a lot of people crazy who are subverting the law, through his investigations and his publication of data that shines a light on their illegal or amoral activities. And I've been peripherally involved in the investigation of the bomb blast at their headquarters recently."

"Well, I was actually sitting in the reception area when the friggin' truck came through the front door. That is not a morning I will forget any time soon."

"You were sitting there when the explosion occurred?"

"I am just surprising the hell out of you today, aren't I, Agent DuBois? Sure wish that wasn't the case. But yes, I was sitting there when that happened. Sandy is their head of security and would be able to give you whatever information you need."

"I have met Sandy more than once. He's a real pro. You're right; I will have no problem getting what I need from him."

"So that's the whole list of folks who would like me to disappear. What else can I tell you that would help your investigation?"

"Dawn, you have been very clear and specific. I would also like to download the threatening voicemail messages you said you have. How many of them are there, do you think?"

"Over forty, if you include the ones I saved from before I ended up in the hospital."

"You have forty-plus voicemails threatening you?"

"Yes, from an assorted cast of characters, as you will hear."

After the agent listened to a few of the messages and heard very graphic details of what some of these good folk were going to do to me, he copied all of the messages onto a digital recording device and sat down with me again in the living room.

"Dawn, I'm taking this situation very seriously, as I said earlier. What I have heard today suggests that your activism has created a number of enemies who could be motivated to hurt you, which I know is stating the obvious. I'm going to suggest that we look into some protection for you."

"We already have that covered. We hired a security firm that was recommended to us a couple of years ago when we were first getting threats. Unfortunately—and naïvely, it turned out—when we thought the threat against me was gone, we told them that we didn't need them anymore, and a few days later my friend and I were kidnapped and I ended up in the hospital. Recently we asked them to come back again, so they would have information about the initial and recent threats against me. I'm being watched for the next little while until we have a better idea about how serious this is."

"I will need the name of the contact person there so I can check in on what they're doing and make sure it's sufficient."

"Here is the card for our key guy at the security company. Anything else you need?"

"That will do it. And I must say you seem pretty calm, considering what you've told me."

"Agent DuBois, I am scared to death.

"The point I was making with telling you the story of the bombing at the Consortium is that I know there are some very determined and well-financed professionals that are doing what they can to stop us. I take this very seriously.

"At the same time, I'm not going to let them ruin my life. I have good people like you, Sandy, Joseph Bruschi, and lots of others on my side and I believe I'll be all right. But you shouldn't infer that my matter-of-fact way of answering your questions means I'm not aware of what's going on. I am. And I am freaked."

"Dawn, we will do everything possible to keep you safe, which leads to my last request, and you might not like it. Since you've been kidnapped once and you're a prime suspect to be kidnapped again, I'd like you to wear this necklace. It has a GPS locator device in it that will let me know where you are. I know this might seem like overload, but you unfortunately have made a lot of enemies and until we get to the bottom of this, I'd like to be able to tell where you are in case someone tries to do something stupid. Now I..."

"You don't have to say anymore to convince me; I understand this is for my protection and I'll do it."

"Excellent; I was expecting more push back."

"As I have said, I know first-hand what people are capable of doing so this doesn't seem like overload to me."

"All right then. Hey, that looks quite nice on you. Please keep it on all the time. It is waterproof. Finally, here's my card. If we need to talk, call me any time of the day or night."

"Thanks, I really do appreciate your concern and professionalism."

With that, Agent DuBois walked down the stairs and into his unmarked car.

I was feeling really messed up. On the one hand, I did appreciate his professionalism, as I'd told him, and I was glad that he didn't seem to be disbelieving what I said because I'm a woman. I believed that he'd talk with the people he said he would, and I believed he'd do everything in his and the Bureau's power to protect me. On the other hand, the fact that an FBI agent was talking to me at all, and his reaction to my list of people who would love me gone from this world, *and* the forty-plus threatening messages on my answering machine, *and* more at the Consortium *and* in the records of the Fair Shore police department...it all left me really uptight and drained from our meeting.

I know I brought this on myself because, for whatever reason, I've decided to take on some issues that by their nature create enemies. And as I've heard more than once, "Whatever doesn't kill us makes us stronger." Oh man, I am sure glad that random thought just entered my mind because it just makes me feel so much safer.

Jesus, I've gotta get a life because I don't intend to take another damn swan dive. Been there, done that.

Thirty-Three

MY LIFE HAS been changed in a very positive way by two amazing people—although it might be hard for you to believe, based on what I've gotten myself into as this story has unfolded. First, my karate teacher in Boston. He is a former Jesuit priest and an Eastern Studies professor at Boston College. He has been a huge help since I was eight years old. And second, I would obviously not be anywhere *near* as able to do what I've done if it hadn't been for my therapist.

One of the things they both helped me understand is the pattern I follow to gain meaningful insight—what it is that best allows me to understand myself and therefore move forward with energy and focus. For me, it's to get out in nature and relax in the midst of it, alone and quiet. That pattern of being alone with my buddy Mother Nature has allowed me to observe the patterns in my life and make decisions based on those insights that have served me well. When I just charge ahead, I get stuff done because of the force of my personality, but it's often the wrong stuff or it comes at a cost, as I have already described.

And I have been charging ahead since returning from the lake after getting out of the hospital, with few exceptions. The conversation with Agent DuBois really crystallized for me how many enemies I've made, people who don't exactly want me to be hanging around our wonderful planet any longer. Hmmmm. Cause for reflection.

So I decided to go off on my own. I talked to my mother about going further up in New England for a couple of days and my reason for it; and she got it, fully on board. I explained to Bernice that I wanted to take a long weekend to recharge my batteries, that the involvement with the FBI had done a number on me; and she got it too.

So on Thursday after work, I got in our car and headed to the Berkshires in western Massachusetts, one of my favorite places on earth. I wasn't sure where I was going to stay. Just hit the road in sloppy clothes with my journal and one of my other good buddies, Henry David Thoreau, and not much else, keeping it simple.

And man, was it the right thing to do or what? Found a bed-and- breakfast in

Lenox, Massachusetts with a fireplace in my room and cookies on the bureau, no television or phone, and a comfortable mattress. I slept for twelve hours straight. The proprietor felt sorry for me when I walked down at eleven o'clock, having missed the breakfast part of bed-and-breakfast, and she scrambled up some eggs and made some whole wheat toast with homemade jam and I couldn't have felt more relaxed.

She even packed a sandwich for me and some fruit and water so I could go looking for a trail nearby, and I hiked all afternoon. I sat by a stream all by myself for a couple of hours. The music of the water on the rocks was the only sound except for the animals that came out to hang with me.

Then I hiked further into the woods and up a hill overlooking a beautiful valley. As the afternoon started crawling to a close, the music of the wind and the birds and the movement of the trees were so soothing. And then I came upon two passages in *Walden* within a few minutes of each other.

When I hear music, I fear no danger. I am invulnerable. I see no foe. I am related to the earliest times, and to the latest.

No man ever followed his genius till it misled him. Though the results were bodily weakness, yet perhaps no one can say that the consequences were to be regretted, for these were a life in conformity to higher principles. All nature is your congratulation, and you have cause momentarily to bless yourself.

And I knew exactly what I needed to do as I read those words and listened to the music of the natural beauty all around me. I needed to face my enemies one at a time and show that I care about them and want the best for them, and not be deterred from trying to make this world a better place—and see what happens.

So I put Hank back in my pack and came down from where I had been sitting at the highest point on the hill and walked slowly back to my B&B, feeling more confident and centered than at any time since I had woken up in the hospital after taking a nap for fourteen months.

I sang along with Kris Kristofferson, Green Day, and Steve Earle on my ride home. I jumped out of the car, knowing my mother was at a client conference in New York City. I turned to lock the car door and noticed a jogger approaching on the sidewalk. Nothing out of the ordinary; I've jogged past hundreds of people at night. And then a jolt to my neck and lights out.

"Well, well, the beauty awakes."

Hearing that voice made me want to keep my eyes shut, which I did, while I tried to figure out what was going on. The diamonds that were sparkling on and off behind my eyelids were interesting, and I tried to concentrate on them, but then someone shook me and I was forced to open my eyes.

And there, not two feet from my face, was Principal McMullen, my pal from Fair Shore High. And then my even better pal, Richard Phillips, pushed his face into my field of vision, so in just two moments I had a double shot of all warm and fuzzy.

I tried to move, but I realized I was tied up. My hands were bound in front of me and I couldn't move my feet either. I seemed to be in a small space and it seemed to be swaying. I tried like hell to get a better view of where I was, but the way that they had me tied didn't let me move much.

When I looked for my captors, they had both stepped away and they were now looking down on me from a standing position. They leaned over together and pulled me up from what must have been the floor and threw me roughly onto a couch. Principal McMullen arranged me so I was sitting straight against a hard cushion or backing of some sort. I decided to focus on the two of them and not my accommodations, since at the end of the day, they, and not my accommodations, were going to determine my fate. Duh.

So I looked up at both of them, smiled, and waited.

"You're smiling," Richard sneered. "As smart as you are, you really don't get it. You see, my dear, Brian and I have been planning how to get rid of you since before you took your dive. Although we both admired your pluck, we could not stand your attitude and how you were making our jobs oh so much more difficult. And then you gave us an extra year to plan while you were in the hospital and I was out making money off you, which was an added bonus."

The film had disappeared from my eyes and I was hyper-alert to what Richard was saying. I knew what I had to do: talk.

"Did you know that I talked to the FBI a couple days ago about the threats that have been made against me? And that when Agent DuBois—a really smart guy, by the way, who got degrees from Princeton and the University of Chicago—asked me who I thought would want me hurt, you two were at the top of the list. I suggested he talk with my friend Silvio at the diner who actually heard you threaten me, Richard. Principal McMullen, I suggested he talk with your assistant, Rebecca Saunders, since she really didn't like how you treated me. I understand she keeps your schedule and she's privy to many of your conversations. I wonder if she has any idea about the conversations you've had as you hatched this little plan."

I knew I probably couldn't get to Richard. They say that brilliant sociopaths are very difficult to influence since they're usually several steps ahead of everybody else when it comes to getting what they want. But McMullen is another animal, not nearly as smart as Richard, able to bluster his way through most of his life with his size and the credibility that comes, at least with men, from his having played football in the National Football League. If I could raise some doubt in him, maybe there was a chance.

"Ah yes, trying to raise doubt about the possibility of our plan's success."

You bet your ass that was what I was trying to do, and I noticed McMullen had a scowl in response to what I'd said.

"Well you see darling, there is one problem. We have a foolproof alibi: Brian and I are at an education conference in Puerto Rico; we are not even on the mainland and certainly not anywhere near where you were kidnapped. We paid cash to be brought home on a private plane and we'll be heading back the same way. No passenger manifest, no record of who we are. The Puerto Rican mafia is very efficient that way. We are miles out to sea right now in a boat supplied by our mafia friends, not a person in sight to see us dump your body overboard, tied down with enough heavy chain to ensure that you will never surface. The sharks and other fishes are going to have a ball eating your fine young body...after I'm done with it, that is."

My mind was racing. I had an idea. I realized that I didn't have to tell the truth, I just had to save my life.

"Well Richard, I'm impressed with your plan; very nicely thought out. There are, however, two problems with it. I bet you didn't know that I just talked on the phone with Tripper Cardone while I was in the Berkshires. I wanted to try and make up with him and be friends again. Now you know how infatuated he is with me, so he was really in the mood to impress me, and one of the things he was trying to impress me with was his relationship with you, and the conversations you had about how much you both hated me. And Richard, he knows about your plans, and if *he* knows, the FBI knows, because right up there with you two on the top of the list of people I told Agent DuBois to talk to was Tripper, since he'd been very vocal about how much he hates me. Whoops, a loose end."

And I knew that my guess about their relationship had scored because Richard lost his cool and hit me hard in the mouth, and as I turned to look back at him, I saw a look of fear on my old principal's face.

"And Principal McMullen, you know that Richard is smarter than you and I. Do you think he's going to let you live after this is over? You are going right over the side with me, I can guarantee that because..."

Then Richard hit me again and I went all starry nights and had a hard time refocusing. I mean, I'm the type of person who likes feedback from a guy, but this was ridiculous. When I became aware again of what was going on, I had company. McMullen was bound up next to me on the couch.

"You know, Dawn, you are too damn smart for your own good. It took you ten minutes to figure out my plan and my buddy here never had a clue. Oh well, same end result that I wanted all along: both of you out of the picture. And now…"

"*Stop the boat and everybody on the deck with your hands up. This is the US Coast Guard and the FBI and we will shoot if you do not comply.*"

We were both startled and looked over at Richard simultaneously. And man, he got this look on his face like nothing I have ever seen. He smiled, in a slanted and off-center kind of way. And he pointed a damn gun at me, and with that demented look on his face said, "Dawn my love, we could have made some really smart and beautiful babies, you and I. And now it is time to say goodbye."

I closed my eyes and remember thinking, "Lord, take care of my mother," and then an explosion jarred my eyes open, and most of Richard's face was gone. His bloody gun dropped to the floor as he fell back against the wall where part of his head had landed after he pulled the trigger. And then I passed out.

Thirty-Four

"DAWN, THIS IS Agent DuBois of the FBI. Can you hear me?"

And I've gotta tell you, the last thing I wanted to do was open my eyes as I came out of whatever my body had done to shut me down in such a peaceful feeling kinda way. But spending the rest of my life with my eyes closed didn't seem like a good idea, so I opened my eyes slowly and I spotted a hazy form a few feet from my face, but I'll be damned if I could focus on who it was.

"Dawn, this is Agent DuBois. You're all right; you're safe and on land. Take your time with opening your eyes and getting back here with us."

As he came into focus, I had to squint in the glare of the sunlight until he noticed and moved over to make it easier for me to see.

"What happened, um, where am…oh Jesus."

"You passed out in the cabin after Richard Phillips put his gun in his mouth and shot himself, from what Brian McMullen told us. You were probably in shock, since he also told us that Richard pointed the gun at you and said it was time to say goodbye."

And then I lost it, gang. I just burst into tears and began shaking and sobbing and I didn't give a damn. I like living on the edge, apparently, but this was going a little too far. And some woman I had never seen put her arms around me and I probably did a pretty good job of saturating whatever she was wearing. And she walked me into what I assume was a public restroom on the dock and I took my time going to the bathroom and splashing water on my face and blowing my nose, and man if I didn't look like a prize catch.

"Can I talk with Agent DuBois?"

"Absolutely, he is right outside."

We sat in what I guess was his car.

"Does my mother…"

"We are flying her here by helicopter. She won't be long, and she knows you are all right."

"How did you find…oh yeah, the necklace."

"We need to get you out of here because the press has arrived and I am sure you aren't thrilled at the idea of talking to them right now, after what you've been through."

"Actually, that would be fine. I'm up for it."

"Really? You have been through a lot, young lady."

"Hey, that's apparently how I roll. Let's do this together."

"All right, I'm with you."

And it was like coming home, in some kind of perverse way, since I had come to know three of the four reporters from the Fair Shore situation and then the bombing of the Consortium, including my friend, Joseph Bruschi."

"Hey Joseph, how are you?" And wouldn't you know it, Joseph started to cry. He tried to ask me a question and he lost it. Well, damn it that sure didn't help with the old fake composure attempt. So we hugged and I gave him a wad of tissues I had stuffed in my pocket and we all laughed when he made some wise-ass comment about how I could have at least given him clean ones, and then we were fine.

I explained what had happened. Questions about how Richard had been caught I turned over to my FBI guy, and I explained that Richard had been disturbed for a long time and how he was able to hide it because he was one of the smartest and most charismatic people around. At some point, the questions began to slow and I heard a yell and saw my mother running toward us. I ran to her and gave her the biggest-ass hug in the history of mother-and-daughterdom. We walked away from the crowd arm-in-arm and I reassured her that I was fine and that everything would now be all right.

And since I am alive to finish the story, I guess it turns out I was right this time.

Additional Thanks

There are two people who had a profound impact on the creation of this book. Orville Pierson, author of *Team Up!* and *Highly Effective Networking: Meet the Right People and Get a Great Job* and *The Unwritten Rules of the Highly Effective Job Search*, has shaped this narrative more than anyone else and has been with me through every draft. Thanks, brother. Claudia Gentner made a compelling argument for self-publishing and was the brains behind the book production for the self-published Readers Copy that was sent to close friends and members of the publishing industry for review. Her editing and comments on the last three drafts provided the final necessary focus. Besides being blessed with having these two as close friends, they also happen to be two of the most intelligent and creative people I have ever met.

Craig Baggott, my closest friend and an investigative journalist for *The Hartford Courant*, taught me courage and commitment. You died way too young, my friend.

Sarah Pierson Beaulieu provided insights I could not have gotten anywhere else and has been an inspiration through her work on the Enliven Project—www.theenlivenproject.com—and the speaking out she has done for almost fifteen years about her experience as a survivor of sexual assault and abuse.

Courtney E. Martin, a powerful writer and activist and author of *Perfect Girls, Starving Daughters: How the Quest for Perfection is Harming Young Women*, provided invaluable comments on the first draft.

Danny Goldberg's book, *Dispatches from the Culture Wars: How the Left Lost Teen Spirit*, motivated me throughout the writing of this book to stay focused on the importance of young people to the survival of our world.

Darren Mileto is an amazing writer and provided comments on the second-to-last draft that was a missing link in the narrative. John Sobecki, a friend for over thirty years and a very insightful writer and musician, has kept me moving ahead through our many conversations about music and life, and his comments on the narrative in progress.

Thanks also to Sue Lawley, a phenomenal poet and good friend and author of *Hieroglyphics of the Heart.* John Hoover, the author of more than a dozen books, including *How to Work for an Idiot: Survive & Thrive… without Killing Your Boss,* provided much-needed encouragement. Jean Baur, author of *Eliminated! Now What?* was helpful during early conversations. Doug Hill, author of the recently published *Not So Fast: Thinking Twice About Technology*, and who wrote the definitive book on Saturday Night Live called *Saturday Night: A Backstage History of Saturday Night Live,* is a trusted friend and a model of integrity in writing. My friends at Clearview Consulting were there for me at weird times in airports and hotels around the country. Jaye Smith provided positive energy and encouragement from the beginning. David Rottman's extremely thoughtful comments on the first draft steered me away from the cliff, while his book, *The Career As A Path to the Soul,* provided inspiration. Jay Colan, Pat Pursley, Josh Friedman, Beth Rizzotti, Jim Wescott, Joanne Killmeyer, Fran Parker, Kelsey Lawrence, Marcella Van Winden, Kathy Brooks, Dee Cramer, Bobbie Roessner, Tracey Duberman, Evan Schnittman, Ann Galloway, Sean Harvey, and my amazing Todd cousins all provided support and suggestions that helped move the book along. Meg Siegal provided energy and focus at a crucial time and is one of the most passionate and creative people I have ever met. She also happens to have helped save a lot of lives. Thanks also to Pamela Redmond Satran for creating the supportive Montclair Editors & Writers Group. Alyson Linefsky edited the final draft and provided not only brilliant editing but insightful comments about the final content of the book and strategic marketing suggestions about how to present the book to the public. She can be reached at Alyson@adlwriting services.com; adlwritingservices.com.

I also want to acknowledge some of the key organizations that are addressing both sexual assault and sexual abuse, and assisting both male and female survivors.

Culture of Respect (https://cultureofrespect.org/) – Culture of Respect is an independent, nonprofit organization that strengthens colleges and universities by providing them with a framework to assess and improve efforts to eliminate rape and sexual assault from their campuses.

Joyful Heart Foundation (www.joyfulheartfoundation.org) – The vision of the Joyful Heart Foundation is a community with no sexual assault, domestic violence and child abuse. Our mission is to heal, educate and empower survivors of sexual assault, domestic violence and child abuse, and to shed light into the darkness that surrounds these issues.

Male Survivor (http://www.malesurvivor.org/) - Male Survivor provides critical resources to male survivors of sexual trauma and all their partners in recovery by building communities of Hope, Healing, & Support.

Not Alone (www.notalone.gov) – Not Alone is a White House website focused on campus sexual violence.

One in Six (https://1in6.org/) - The mission of One in Six is to help men who have had unwanted or abusive sexual experiences in childhood live healthier, happier lives.

RAINN (http://rainn.org/) - The Rape, Abuse & Incest National Network is the nation's largest anti-sexual violence organization and was named one of "America's 100 Best Charities" by Worth magazine. RAINN also maintains a list of local centers: http://centers.rainn.org/

Stop It Now (www.stopitnow.org) – The focus of Stop It Now is child sexual abuse.

The Enliven Project (www.theenlivenproject.com) – The Enliven Project is a campaign to bring sexual violence out of the closet and lift survivors to their full potential. The Enliven Project is grounded in the idea change cannot take place unless we tell the truth about our lives, our organizations, and our social movements.

I want to be clear that I am NOT providing direct services or counseling support for sexual abuse survivors in this book, and if people are looking for help or resources they should contact the National Sexual Assault Hotline: 1.800.656.HOPE.

In addition I also want to acknowledge all the individuals and organizations who are dedicated to lessening the ability of the tobacco industry to continue to murder millions of people a year. The tobacco industry has done everything legal, and otherwise, to continue to be effective at getting young people under eighteen to begin smoking, the only way that tobacco companies can continue to be profitable. Their amoral behavior is personal for me since both my parents died of lung cancer. I will do everything I can to lessen their power and profitability so as to weaken the likelihood that they will be as effective as they are now at murdering my grandsons and members of their generation, who are their next target. If the work that Dawn Mortenson, Nathan Pomerantz, and their colleagues did in this work of fiction caught your attention, reinforced negative feelings you have about the tobacco industry, or unfortunately reminded you of loved ones who have died from cigarette smoking or second-hand smoke, please donate your time or money, or look for additional information about tobacco initiatives by going to one or more of the following organizations:

American Legacy Foundation – www.legacyforhealth.org – is a not-for-profit organization established in 1998, dedicated to preventing teen smoking and encouraging smokers to quit. The Legacy Foundation is responsible for "The Truth" anti-smoking campaign, which has been credited with preventing millions of young people from using tobacco – www.thetruth.com.

Action on Smoking and Health (ASH) – http://ash.org - has been a prime mover, since its inception in 1967, in domestic and global tobacco control and public health through advocacy, communication, the force of law, and their essential partnership with the Framework Convention Alliance for Tobacco Control. This is accomplished by taking action to educate the public and decision makers, track the tobacco industry, and work for sensible public policies at the local, national and global levels.

Framework Convention Alliance – www.fctc.org – The FCA works on three campaigns to support global tobacco control, using the World Health Organization Framework Convention on Tobacco Control (FCTC). Those campaigns are "Illicit Trade," "Shadow Reporting," and "FCTC: Action Now!"

American Cancer Society – www.cancer.org

American Lung Association – www.lung.org

World Health Organization Tobacco-Free Initiative – www.who.int/tobacco/en/

Campaign for Tobacco-Free Kids – www.tobaccofreekids.org – works to save lives by advocating for public policies that prevent kids from smoking, help smokers quit, and protect everyone from second- hand smoke.

Corporate Accountability International – www.stopcorporateabuse.org – works to end irresponsible and dangerous corporate actions in order to ensure a world where people and the environment can flourish.

Americans for Nonsmokers' Rights – www.no-smoke.org – The leading national lobbying organization dedicated to nonsmokers' rights, taking on the tobacco industry at all levels of government, protecting nonsmokers from exposure to second-hand smoke, and preventing tobacco addiction among youth.

Southeast Asia Tobacco Control Alliance – http://seatca.org

The Center for Tobacco Control Research and Education – www.tobacco.ucsf.edu

Africa Tobacco Control Regional Initiative – http://www.atcri.org

European Network for Smoking and Tobacco Prevention – www.ensp.org

Healthbridge – www.healthbridge.ca – Healthbridge is an international non-profit, non-governmental organization that works in partnership with local NGOs and governments in Africa, Asia, and Latin America to improve and initiate tobacco-control policy development and implementation.

Bloomberg Initiative – http://tobaccogrants.org – The Bloomberg Initiative (BI) Grants Program supports projects that develop and deliver high-impact, evidence-based tobacco control interventions.

Centers for Disease Control and Prevention – http://www.cdc.gov/tobacco/ - The US Centers for Disease Control and Prevention (CDC), through its Office on Smoking and Health (OSH), is the lead federal agency for comprehensive tobacco prevention/control.

Global Smokefree Partnership – www.globalsmokefreepartnership.org – A global partnership dedicated to promoting effective smoke-free air policies worldwide.

GLOBALink – www.ncdlinks.org/globalink/ - is the international network of the tobacco-control community. It allows users to share information and resources related to the tobacco industry and smoking.

Tobacco Atlas – available from the American Cancer Society – www.cancer.org – This reference book provides statistics about tobacco use and control, while also examining possible solutions and potential courses of the epidemic, and exposing the behavior of the tobacco companies.

Tobacco Control Supersite – http://tobacco.health.usyd.edu.au/ - This Australian-based site monitors how the global tobacco industry promotes its products in the age of advertising bans.

About the Author

Peter Prichard has spent the last thirty-eight years helping thousands of individuals, from high school students to adults of all ages, reach their goals. He has written dozens of articles and several book chapters on how to do that. He began his career by providing career guidance to college students, and he has been particularly interested in assisting young adults and those who want to drive positive change in their particular organizations, their community, and the world. As an acknowledgment of those efforts, he received the Youth Advocate Award from the town in New Jersey in which he lives. The teenage female heroine of this book is a composite of the hundreds of energetic and courageous young people and social activists he has met over the years.

CPSIA information can be obtained
at www.ICGtesting.com
Printed in the USA
FFOW02n0229291214
9885FF